Prize Stories
TEXAS INSTITUTE OF LETTERS

PRIZE STORIES

TEXAS
INSTITUTE
of
LETTERS

*Edited and with an
Introduction by*
MARSHALL TERRY

STILL POINT PRESS • DALLAS

Library of Congress Cataloging-in-Publication Data
Main entry under title:
Prize stories: Texas Institute of Letters.

   1. Short stories, American—Texas. 2. American
fiction—20th century. 3. Texas—Fiction. I. Terry,
Marshall, 1931–   . II. Texas Institute of Letters.
PS558.T4P35 1986   813'.01'089764   85-27953
ISBN 0-933841-04-3

Contents

Introduction

Publication of this collection of the award-winning stories of the Texas Institute of letters coincides with the celebration of the fiftieth anniversary of the Institute. The TIL was founded in 1936, Texas's centennial year, by Karle Wilson Baker, J. Frank Dobie, Walter Prescott Webb, Winifred Sanford, William H. Vann, and a dozen other writers and teachers for the purpose of "the promotion and recognition of literature in Texas." Its founding came at a time when the people of Texas were excited about almost everything else in their past and present except literature. The first meeting was held in the lecture room of the Hall of State at the Centennial Exposition in Dallas on the afternoon of November 9, 1936. Fittingly, the Institute chose this same location for its March 22, 1986, afternoon meeting featuring readings of outstanding Texas writing of the past by distinguished contemporary Texas writers in this Texas sesquicentennial and TIL half-century year.

Weathering the early years when interest in its activities in the state was slight, and the World War II years when it functioned on a reduced scale, the Texas Institute of Letters had established itself by the mid-fifties, with key leadership from Dobie, Arthur M. Sampley, Herbert Gambrell, and Lon Tinkle, as the focus of interest in writing in and about Texas and as a central encourager of Texas writers through the various literary prizes it awarded. By now, with a revived and enlarged membership reflecting the many literary endeavors and interests in Texas, the TIL serves as a yearly point of fellowship and reflection for its two hundred diverse members in and out of the state. The Institute awards some of America's most generous literary prizes, and since 1967 has awarded two fellowships a year primarily to young Texas writers to live and work on the former Dobie ranch, Paisano, outside Austin. (The story of the first thirty years of the Institute was told by the longtime TIL secretary William H. Vann, with a philosophical preface by Lon Tinkle, in *The Texas Institute of Letters*, Austin, Encino Press, 1966.)

The legendary SMU teacher and editor of the *Dallas Morning News* book page and the *Southwest Review*, John H. McGinnis, made the astounding suggestion at that first meeting of the Institute "that it might reward worthily a distinctive book each year, with something like a one-thousand-dollar prize." It seemed preposterous to imagine such a prize then, but the suggestion became reality ten years later through the generosity of Carr P. Collins. The Collins family generosity has continued until now the Collins Award is $5,000 for the best Texas work of nonfiction. Meanwhile, unmoneyed awards were given to the "best Texas book of the year" from 1939 through 1945, prior to the Collins award, including the controversial choice in 1939 of Dobie's *Apache Gold and Yaqui Silver* over Katherine Anne Porter's *Pale Horse, Pale Rider*.

The McMurry Bookshop in Dallas sponsored an award for the best first novel from 1948 through 1959, which was superseded by the Jesse H. Jones Award (now $2,500) for the best Texas work of fiction, donated by the Houston Endowment, Inc. The first poetry award was given by the TIL in 1945, the first children's book award in 1949, the first book design award in 1950. In 1960, the Friends of the Dallas Public Library established a $500 (now $1,000) prize for the Texas book making "the most significant contribution to Knowledge," and in 1963 William P. Hobby, Jr., of the *Houston Post* initiated the Stanley Walker Journalism Award, now split into deadline and periodical categories. That just about covered the literary territory, except for the extraordinarily vital form of the short story. Its award, in the amount of $500, came along in 1972, given first by an anonymous donor, then by Capitol Printing of Austin, and this year by the Library Associates of the William A. Blakley Library, University of Dallas.

This present volume collects all fourteen of the prize short stories selected since the award was begun, from 1972 through 1984, including both of the fine stories which tied for the award in 1978. As with all TIL awards, a jury of three writers makes the annual selection. The result of bringing the prize stories together is a remarkably strong and diverse collection, a grouping that celebrates in this anniversary year what Lon Tinkle spoke of in his 1977 talk to the TIL as the focus of the Institute's contemporary attention, not a provincial regionalism "but the artist in our midst."

I love the short story form for its ability to give us another time, another place, an existential definition of a person not ourselves, and so to enlarge us; its act of empathy that lets us, for its singular moment, understand a human individual or a type; its rich possibilities of rendering the various, the absurd and strange, the inevitability and the odd joys of life; its compression; its oblique revelation of large or small human truths; its play and struggle with its own chronology and voice. All these elements of language, craft, and content ripple through this collection of the TIL prize stories.

Some of the stories are made of historic and regional elements in the sense that they are set, like J. Y. Bryan's elegantly styled "Frontier Vigil," in a Western past, or, like Michael Blackman's "Golden Shadows Old West Museum" and Pat Carr's "Indian Burial," use icons of a cowboy or Indian past to inform present lives and hopes. Beverly Lowry's "So Far from the Road, So Long until Morning," Carolyn Osborn's "The Accidental Trip to Jamaica," and Laura Furman's "Eldorado" are achingly contemporary, as contemporary as terrorism, disorientation, or loneliness, while Thomas Zigal's "Curios" mixes emotions of nostalgia, regret, and anger at a past delimiting in its simplicity. Catherine Petroski's "Beautiful My Mane in the Wind" is a lyrical wonder, its power and mutability proven by the several forms, including a children's picture book, the story has taken during its life. Walt McDonald's "moment" in "The Track" and the allegorical behavior of Roland Sodowsky's *mbakara* in "Landlady" bring us into contemporary contexts of imperialism. Both stories are philosophical and political, as is my own, "The Antichrist," a *conte à clef* based on my experience with one of the most paradoxical characters I have encountered, a warm, brilliant teacher of the old language blinded and made absurd but dangerous by bigotry. Like Blackman's "Golden Shadows Old West Museum," David Hall's "The Smell in Bertha's House" and Allen Wier's "Cambell Oakley's Gospel Sun Shines on Roy Singing Grass" bring us directly into the experience of older people keeping their vitality and identity, that strange reality of aging and individuality I have pondered in my own fiction. The odd pair of friends Roy Singing Grass and old Prute, connected by Cambell Oakley's radio gospel music and weather reports out of Des Moines, are characters we will remember, as we will the haunting character of Doug Crowell's limited but terribly human drum-washer in "Work," as in his bewilderment he tries to understand his nonpersonhood.

Otherwise, there are a variety of forms and voices in these stories by women and men who themselves are writers as well as teachers, journalists, book salesmen, publishers, wives and husbands, poets or novelists, as well as crafters of short fiction. All the authors have, or have had, some Texas connection. Now they live and work in California, Arkansas, North Carolina, Pennsylvania, Colorado, and Alabama, as well as in various diverse parts of Texas from the llano estacado to the gleaming glass cubes of Dallas.

These stories brought together salute the Texas Institute of Letters for its fifty years of encouraging writing and writers. I want to thank Gould and Charlotte Whaley, publishers of Still Point Press, whose idea this was. This volume reflects the writer's commitment to telling stories that are true to the human situation and that attempt to transcend any state or region. That commitment, I believe, is the future of "Texas" letters.

MARSHALL TERRY

Southern Methodist University
November, 1985

Michael Blackman

The Golden Shadows Old West Museum

The lobby of Golden Shadows Rest & Care Home brought little excitement or comfort to Cowboy Bennett. The plastic chairs were painfully hard and the Holloway sisters demanded the old TV play only soap operas each afternoon. He was easy game for the nurses at pill time and somehow he was always running over the other residents' corns in his wheelchair.

But the lobby offered some refuge for Cowboy—at least it put distance between him and his roommate. Clyde Jenkins was 85, rapidly declining in mind and body, and was convinced a moat ought to be constructed around the home to ward off rattlesnakes and Mexicans. He frequently awoke in the night and upset Cowboy by screaming that one or the other was about to get him.

Golden Shadows, a T-shaped, one-story structure of tan brick with a tar-and-gravel roof, sat on a dusty West Texas hill about a mile south of Sandero between the VFW and the rodeo grounds. It was home for about 55 aged. Two giant picture windows of the lobby faced west, for the afternoon sunshine. In the hot dry months of summer Cowboy often rolled his wheelchair to one of the windows and counted dust devils.

Now, in the last days of autumn, long after the first frost, Cowboy would press closely to the window and search for cloudbanks building on the northwest horizon. When one was found, he immediately announced to all lobbymates:

"Well, looks like a norther's coming. Better get out your heavy garments."

Cowboy Bennett saw himself as a protector of Golden Shadows residents. He would not be living at the home except for the pickup accident three years ago. He drove a wheelchair now, had lost 30 pounds and he sometimes forgot exactly where he was, but he didn't consider these things major.

His daughter, Lisa, had urged him to move in from the ranch. She said with mother gone now he might fall down in a pasture and die before anyone would miss him. Ft. Worth was nearly 200 miles away and she just couldn't be checking on him all the time. But Cowboy preferred to chance ending up buzzard bait in some remote pasture. He finally gave in only after Mrs. Walters, the home supervisor, persisted that she needed someone like him to help look after the other residents—and after she promised he could move in his old cowboy gear. His room was decorated with a mounted pair of silver spurs, a rigging from his last rodeo, a bridle with rotting reins. All he lacked was a saddle.

"Know why they call me Cowboy?" He was sitting in his wheelchair in the lobby one afternoon, speaking to Grandma McAllister. She ignored him. The only others in the lobby were the Holloway sisters, holding hands and monopolizing the TV. "I say, do you want to know why they call me Cowboy?"

Grandma McAllister remained silent. In her lap she clutched a small black purse that, according to rest home rumor, contained her life savings. She in some ways was luckier than Cowboy. Most of her kids lived nearby, but she refused to live with any of them. After breaking her hip she lived alone for years, and had no trouble getting around in her wheelchair. Twice the town marshal had to pick her up for blocking traffic on the square when she wheeled out under the blinking yellow light. One day she journeyed almost a mile west of Sandero to the interstate entrance ramp.

That's when the kids gave her the ultimatum: us or the rest home.

"Well, I'll tell you anyway," Cowboy said. "There weren't no horse I couldn't break. When I was at the Flying W, ranchers came all the way from West Texas to get me to help out. They'd give me a corral full of wild broncs and I'd have them eating sugar outa my hand by noon. I used to ride in that big rodeo at Stamford, the Cowboy Reunion. They still remember me over there, lots of the old ones do."

Grandma McAllister reached down and pulled up one of her sagging nylons, paying no attention to Cowboy. He reminded her too much of her former husband, who ran off in the early '50s with a beautician he met at a rodeo dance. The only other men in her life were her five sons-in-law, four of them wife-beaters. The other had gout.

The Holloway sisters were meanwhile totally absorbed with "Our Daily Bread," an unfolding drama of a college girl who didn't want to come home for Christmas and tell her mother, infested with cancer, and her father, an alcoholic infidel, that she was pregnant by her colored boyfriend. The sisters were near tears.

"They brought an old bronc from somewhere up in the Rockies that'd never been ridden," Cowboy went on. "Name was Widow Maker. Mean as the dickens. You'd be getting down on him in the chute and he'd try to bite your fool leg off. See, he wanted to get you on the ground so he could stomp on your sideburns a little." Cowboy laughed softly and rolled his chair closer to Grandma.

He leaned forward. "Well, we exploded outa that chute, me and that crazy bronc, and he did the durndest to throw me off." Cowboy was all excitement. "I rode him. And I mean I didn't ride him a few seconds like today's cowboys do. I rode him around that arena nine-and-a-half minutes by the clock. You shoulda seen that saddle I won. I'd have it here but I lost it in a poker game to my brother-in-law. It's got All-Around Champion carved on it. Anyway the crowd went crazy when they saw I wasn't gonna get pitched off. I rode ole Widow Maker till he collapsed, and then I got off and--"

"Oh, Mr. Bennett. Mr. Bennett." A nurse had entered the lobby.

"And then after I got off--"

"Mr. Bennett, time to go. Have to get your chores done."

Grandma McAllister took a blue handkerchief edged with white lace from her purse. She blew her nose and wiped her forehead. Cowboy was disoriented; the story wasn't finished.

"Get all those toilets on the north wing and you'll be through for the day," the nurse said.

One of the Cowboy's responsibilities, along with changing the calendars and filling up the Coke box, was visiting the north wing rooms twice a day to see the toilets were flushed. It was a health department safeguard against poor memory—not the most pride-building chore but Mrs. Walters said it was very important.

He rolled his chair into a hallway.

"Wilbur Bennett." It was Grandma McAllister, her voice as cold and cutting as a blue norther from the plains. Cowboy stopped his chair and spun it around. "I'm on to your tricks," she said, not looking at him.

Cowboy Bennett gazed at her and then turned around and rolled off.

"They're at it again," said the nurse back at the desk. "He's telling her that story about riding old Widow Maker. Today she's not even talking to him."

The others laughed. One of the younger nurses said, "Old people sure are something, aren't they?" Another nurse said wouldn't it be funny if Cowboy and Grandma McAllister got eyes for each other and started sparking on the sly. They might even get married. Somebody speculated on the sex life of geriatrics, to which the young nurse said get your mind out of the gutter.

"Oh, I wouldn't put nothing past these folks," asserted one of them. "Just last year we couldn't find Mr. Bennett one day. He'd disappeared from his room. Know where he was? In bed with old lady Martin. She's dead now. Anyway, all he had on was his boots and long underwear with the hatch open. She just had on her gown. I jerked back those sheets, and you should've seen them. They were giggling like two little kids playing doctor." The nurse paused and shook her head. "You can't put anything past these old people. They're more like kids than kids are. Watch them at the Christmas party. Believe you me, there's no place where Santa Claus is more alive than in the old folks' heads."

The next day a letter came for Cowboy. It was from his daughter, Lisa.

> *Dear Papa,*
>
> *Just to let you know you'll be receiving a big box in the next few days. Don't you dare open until Christmas. Bruce has a bar association banquet and looks like we won't get to come for the holidays. Be sure to eat all your meals and do what the nurses say. I'll call you Christmas Day.*
>
> > *All my love,*
> > *Lisa*
>
> *P.S. The gift should make you the hit of the home! Merry Xmas!*

Christmas. Cowboy had almost forgotten. It was scarcely a week away. And a big box was coming. This puzzled him. He rolled his chair closer to the window for better light and reread the letter.

A big box, he said again to himself. Hit of the home. What the devil might it be? His stomach quivered. Always before Lisa had been predictable about gifts. Boots three years ago, boots last year, white shirts two years ago. And always she asked what he wanted. How would she know what to get? She hadn't called in two months and hadn't visited since last summer, when—he suspected—she had really come to see how her mother's grave was being cared for. That visit was a bad one.

Cowboy was rooming with J. Grady Edwards, "Sr.", retired president of Sandero First National, who used to glide through the halls in his electric wheelchair telling everybody the mashed potatoes were better than laxatives.

Cowboy and the old man were always fighting. Mr. Edwards had refused to let Lisa visit their room, so she and Cowboy were relegated to the lobby the entire visit, competing with television and the Holloway sisters. He was glad when J. Grady Edwards Sr. and his electric wheelchair moved into the new nursing home in Abilene.

Cowboy suddenly stiffened in his chair and gripped the arms tightly as he leaned back. His heart beat mightily, as if he were easing down once again onto a wild horse. It had hit him. Of course. Lisa was giving him an electric wheelchair for Christmas. With three speeds, no doubt. She had commented how nice they must be when she saw old man Edwards'. Cowboy flushed at how nice and tricky his daughter was.

"Say, Clyde," he called to his roommate, who was peeking out the other window toward one end of the parking lot. "Guess what I'm getting for Christmas."

"Shh," Clyde said with a finger to his lips. He had an old Army blanket wrapped around him from head to foot. "I think they're coming," he whispered. "My God, they are. They're taking my parking place!"

"Who's coming, Clyde?"

Clyde moaned softly. "They got my spot."

"Clyde, you know you ain't got no parking spot. You ain't been sneaking a little nip with Harley Wilson again, have you? Listen, I wanna tell you what I'm getting for Christmas."

"Those Meskins," Clyde mumbled. "Now they're coming inside. Oh Cowboy, what're we going to do?"

Cowboy looked into the parking lot. A battered '57 Chevy with reflector mud flaps and bumper stickers saying "God's Watching" and "Goat Ropers Need Love Too" had pulled into the lot. Catrina Valdez, a kitchen helper, was coming to work. "Don't worry yourself like that, Clyde. I once knew a bull rider who was a Meskin. Wiry little guy named Mendoza who could run faster and spit further than anybody I ever seen. He was real nice."

Clyde had his face pressed to the window to see where Catrina went. He looked over and said, "I read in the Reporter-News where they're causing trouble in the Abilene schools."

"Clyde, that was three years ago. They ain't even raised their hand to go to the bathroom since that bunch got thrown in the jug."

"They call themselves, CHEE-canos now," Clyde said, and shuddered. "They can really use them switchblades."

"You're right," Cowboy said, scratching himself. "They're coming across the parking lot. I'll have to take care of it. You get back in bed, Clyde. I'll take care of everything."

"I don't know what I'd do without you," Clyde said.

"You better keep that blanket on," said Cowboy, peering out the window. "Those clouds are really building in the north. We'll have a real spine-chiller blow through here tonight."

Clyde got back into bed and Cowboy started for the door.

"Just what are you getting for Christmas?" Clyde called. Cowboy smiled. "A three-speed electric wheelchair."

The Christmas party was the event of the year. Committees and subcommittees were formed. Everyone was given some duty, however slight. The Holloway sisters were in charge of entertainment. Sadie McDonald, a former cook at Truck City, headed the refreshments group. Nellie Hawkins, the old local elementary art teacher, directed the decorations committee. Anyone bed-ridden or unspecialized would be put in Nellie's group, for the first step in making tree decorations required merely cutting construction paper in strips.

Cowboy was named director of transportation for the

second time, which meant he had to make sure everyone got to the party. Fading memories required Cowboy to visit many rooms on the day of the party to remind residents. Even then many of them wouldn't show up until Cowboy personally came to lead them out of their rooms. Last year only old man Edwards missed. He locked himself in the toilet and wouldn't come out.

This year Cowboy was after a perfect record. He prevailed upon Mr. Walters to see Grandma McAllister was named assistant director of transportation.

The Volunteer Fire Department of Sandero gave the home a Christmas tree. It was a perfectly shaped blue spruce from New Mexico nearly seven feet tall. The decorations committee encircled the tree with four strands of colored lights. Construction paper rings backdropped with miniature Christmas scenes hung delicately from long-needled limbs, along with two dozen red balls surviving from last year. Atop the tree was a cherubic little angel boy with tin-foil wings and a golden halo. The little angel, which Nellie had made, held a hymnal and his mouth was open as if singing, his eyes painted reverently shut. A yellow light blinked from behind.

At the last moment, Clyde Jenkins and Harley Wilson pitched on a box of foil icicles without Nellie's permission. She was so mad she resigned as committee chairman.

"Hell-bells," said Harley, "icicles make it look real."

"No icicles ever looked like that—it's gaudy—all droopy and tangled," said Nellie.

Clyde said, "Long as I knew you and your mama, you two never could take a joke."

"Don't you dare bring my dead mama into this."

Peace came when some of the residents told Nellie her Christmas angel was the prettiest they had ever seen. They pleaded for her to take her job back. "I'll think about it," she said.

As the two men left the lobby Harley said, "Whoever saw an angel with no eyes?"

On the morning of the 23rd, a large box was delivered to the lobby of the Golden Shadows Rest & Care Home. It was Cowboy's, wrapped in brown paper and secured with twine. Immediately there arose among residents much curiosity and speculation. It was a stereo, a TV, a lifetime supply of cowboy boots, a half-dozen cases of Coors. Velma Roberts said it could only be a giant ceramic Praying Hands, but Harley Wilson said it was a galvanized pan and water pump for the live bait house.

Of course Cowboy knew, but he wasn't telling. And Clyde knew. And he only told Alta Mae Givens. By sundown the entire north and west wings knew Cowboy was getting a three-speed electric wheelchair. "All the way from Cowtown," it was said.

That evening Cowboy dressed up in his best white shirt with pearl button-snaps and went down to the lobby. A half-dozen residents were inspecting the sea of gifts beneath the tree, including Grandma McAllister. Cowboy rolled up beside her. "Ought to be a good party," he said.

Grandma grunted.

Cowboy thought maybe her hearing was failing and said, much louder. "They say this one will be the best yet. Those Holloway sisters got a actor coming over from the junior college to put on a drama. And I hear the home's kicking in presents this year. Nothing fancy but something."

Grandma felt the Christmas spirit growing within her. Her daughters were coming after her tomorrow after the party and she would see Santa Claus come for the grandkids. There would be a big turkey for dinner, which, unlike that of the rest home, wouldn't taste like it came out of a can. She looked at Cowboy and decided to be half decent. "Mr. Bennett," she finally said. "Why'd you get me on that committee of yours?"

The question, even her speaking, surprised Cowboy. He cleared his throat and nervously picked his nose. "I thought you'd be right for the job," he said. "It ain't everybody that's responsible these days. I mean, if you came by my room and said let's go to the party and I didn't want to go, I'd probably go anyways. You got the grit to influence people. I'd be afraid *not* to go." He looked down and grimaced. "I mean, I think anybody'd want to go to a party you was going to."

Grandma was chuckling to herself. Both of them knew she was a threat to his position. She could fill the Coke box if she cared to, and flush all the toilets, and nobody had to tell her when the clouds were coming and when to get out her heavy garments. Sometimes she thought she would like to challenge him to an arm-wrestling contest. They could do it in the dining room so everybody could see. But then she took no pleasure in such things as looking for cloudbanks building on the horizon. The home, she concluded, needed somebody like Cowboy, however distasteful he was at times. "Anyway," she said. "I just want to thank you. I cut so many decorations last year that I got arthritis in my thumb and it still ain't well."

"You're mighty welcome," he said.

They talked a long while that evening, mapping plans for who would get whom to the party. Grandma would go after the menfolk and Cowboy the women, the obstinate and the forgetful. They talked about how they got to the home and about their families. Grandma observed that she must have at least 30 family living in the area but, save two or three, they only came to visit on Easter, Thanksgiving or Christmas.

"That's the one bad thing about Christmas," she said. "You feel a little guilty about the things you should've done for people during the year. Everybody feels bad for old people at Christmas. I tell you, it must of hit the Seventh Day before the Good Lord could figure out his plan for the old ones."

Cowboy said yes, he knew what she meant. But he didn't really. He had only a vague notion of what she was saying. In fact, he forgot her words almost as soon as she said them. But the gist of what he felt compelled him to tell a story. It was about one of his foremen many years back who eventually got a ranch of his own. "His name was Homer, and he was 60 years old and never been married. People was always getting on him about his bachelorhood and he always just said he didn't want to rush anything. Well, one day he picks up and leaves and don't come back. Six months later he turns up with this 20-year-old Meskin wife. Them same people who was getting on him about not being married really hollered, especially the church groups. They were going to see he got kicked outa church, but they finally found out he didn't belong to no church anyway. They said it was the worst thang they ever saw, marrying someone that much younger. And her a Meskin. Well, they had seven kids and he was still digging his own post holes till his heart gave out a couple of years ago." He winked at Grandma. "And they say we old folks can't cut it."

She thought he was getting awfully fresh but let it pass.

Save the two of them the lobby was bare. It was getting late. The colored lights from the tree flickered eerily off the green walls and a gusty north wind howled about the windows. The cold front hit and another—already paralyzing the upper Panhandle with ice and snow—was due tomorrow. Grandma and Cowboy sat in silence for a while. Then she reached over and tugged his sleeve. "Good-night Cowboy." she said. "I'm so glad you didn't talk rodeos. I never could stand the smell. Or them dances."

Cowboy remained in the lobby. He wanted to take a last look at the box that contained his mechanical wizard. It was the only electric wheelchair in the home, probably in town. He savored the possibilities. He could help set up races, against time, from the dining room to the lobby. He could organize a caravan of wheelchairs on Sunday afternoons, all tied together like a train, to parade before visitors.

Then it occurred to him. What if the box contained no wheelchair? What if it were Praying Hands or a live bait house? He studied the box. It was laying flat, about three-feet by three and well over a foot high. Collapsed just right it would be perfect for a chair. He picked up one end. It felt light at first, no heavier than a case of beer or one of his old saddles. But he knew the newer chairs were streamlined and much lighter these days, and the batteries never came with them. So this would be about right. But he was still unconvinced. He finally loosened the twine, stretched it to one side, and tore back the tape holding down the brown paper and red gift paper underneath.

There was lettering on the end of the box: Contains (1) ea. 220542 Rocking Horse, Red Delux. *Godamighty*. Then he noticed the box was battered somewhat and had been opened before. What a scare! Lisa had gotten one of the kids a rocking horse and saved the box for future use. There was a hole near the flap at the end. Cowboy could see inside and he made the hole a little larger with his finger. He felt 70 years younger, and guilty. He couldn't feel much in the hole at first except the crinkled newspaper—then something smooth, soft and smooth, like fabric or simulated leather, the kind they often use on the backs and seats of wheelchairs. Quickly he rendered the paper and twine intact.

Just before turning in that night, he picked up his mounted spurs from the dresser and, trying to remember when he last used them, spun the little spiked stars, again and again.

The Golden Shadows Christmas party commenced promptly at five in the afternoon, almost the same time the first snow-carrying norther of the year hit town. The flakes were small and dry-looking and skittered around the porch. Darkness came prematurely and it was bitter cold outside.

To the credit of Cowboy and Grandma, attendance was 100 percent. The perfumed ladies came in their dresses of flowered print. They had rouged cheeks and permanents newly set by a fleet of beauticians who had descended on the home that morning. The men, with what hair there was slicked down by green Fitch, came in baggy dark suits and skinny ties.

The party might not have gotten off to such a rousing start except for the thoughtfulness of Harley Wilson, whose brother, Elmer, operated County Line Liquors. A fifth of

Smirnoff's vodka found its way to the punch bowl and, though it wasn't much, it was enough.

More than just the Holloway sisters developed wet eyes when the junior college actor read a condensed version of *A Christmas Carol.* Cowboy was so moved he volunteered to meet Mr. Dickens in a dark alley. He felt nobody could have written about Scrooge's being so mean to a little crippled boy without being that mean himself. There was a near fight between Sadie McDonald and old lady Mashburn over who'd get the bows from the Christmas wrappings. Sadie vowed she'd pinch old lady Mashburn's head off but they were separated before she got the chance. Two old maids started kissing all the men, an unprecedented passion at Golden Shadows, and one of only two major setbacks for the men that evening. The other was Harley Wilson. Harley, who had stationed himself at the punch bowl for refill duty, suddenly took ill and toppled into the Christmas tree. They had to rush him to the bathroom. The residents said it was the Asian flu, but the nurses suspected the punch. The tree survived.

Then came the opening of gifts. Mrs. Walters called names and shaking hands plunged into work. The men ripped at the packages while the women cautiously picked at them so as not to disturb wrapping or bow. The home gave the women knitting kits and the men bowties.

It was understood that Cowboy's box would be the last opened. As he lifted one end of the box with Grandma McAllister's help, the residents began to whisper. Realizing he was the center of attention, he suddenly looked up and said: "Y'all look here at Grandma. Don't she look purty? Smell that perfume? She smells 10 times better than the best sheep dip I ever smelt." Everybody laughed, including Grandma, but she didn't laugh very much.

"I ain't got no idea what this thang could be," Cowboy said pulling off the last of the paper. "Well, look here. Says here on the box I'm getting a rocking horse!" After the laughter died, he opened the card taped on the end of the box. The front of the box showed a man on horse-back in a snow-covered field, pulling a big evergreen from the woods with his rope. In the background was a little white frame building with belfry and holly in the windows, and there was a light glowing inside and smoke puffing from the chimney, and someone was standing in the doorway, waiting. The scene jarred Cowboy, but his memory focused no more clearly than a too-distant station on his old crystal set, barely here one moment, then faded away forever. There was a note inside:

> *Hope you like this little surprise, Papa. Mrs. Walters said it would be okay for you to have it. Uncle Ted was real nice about it. Merry, Merry Xmas. Sorry I can't be there. Don't forget, I'll call. Love Lisa.*

Then Cowboy, in the happiest moment he could remember, opened the box.

They were stunned at first, all of them. Finally Clyde Jenkins said, "Boy howdy, a horse saddle. We got us a regular cowboy museum now."

And then everybody crowded around with ooh's and ah's and ain't that nice and where're you going to put it?

"Gonna hang it from the ceiling and charge a nickel a peek?" Clyde asked.

Cowboy was shaking his head and grinning. His mouth was dry and he didn't know what to say. So it wasn't the three-speed wheelchair—but by George, they'd all have to believe him now, about him and old Widow Maker.

"Look," somebody said, "Got All-Around Champion-1927 carved on it."

Cowboy looked at Grandma for approval. "That's real nice, Cowboy. Real nice." Then she spun her chair around. "I gotta go see how Harley Wilson's doing. Poor thang."

The snow turned out to be a heavy one, wet and sticky, and it was to make this Christmas whiter than any in recent years. Cowboy sat up late in his room after the party and watched the gentle whiteness settle on the window sill and fields beyond. The home was quiet. Clyde and the old Army blanket were securely entangled and he was asleep. Cowboy felt awfully tired inside, and thought maybe the day had been too much. He was cold and began rubbing his arms, now bony and loose of flesh, no longer full of "sin and sinew" as his daughter used to say. He looked down to the shadowed heap on the floor, remains of the big box. Then he was startled.

"Why Mr. Bennett," a nurse said. "What are you doing still up? You shouldn't be staying up this late, not after a day like you had. Am I going to have to give you a pill?"

Cowboy didn't answer.

The nurse looked around the room. "I hear you're going to make this an Old West museum and charge admission. I think a nickel's too cheap. You could run them through here a quarter a head on Sunday afternoons." She couldn't tell if he were listening but continued anyway. "I don't guess I ever saw a real championship saddle before. You know, one that belonged to a champion cowboy from the old days."

Cowboy hesitated. "Never saw one?"

"Nope, never did."

"Never even been to a real rodeo, I'll bet," Cowboy said.

"Not exactly, but I did see a donkey baseball game down at the ballpark. People were getting throwed off all the time."

Oh Christ Godamighty, Cowboy thought.

"Those donkeys just scared the daylights out of me," the nurse said. "If one of them kicked you in the head it'd hurt as bad as a bronco, wouldn't it, Mr. Bennett?"

"Probably would," Cowboy said. "Course you know that they didn't used to worry about having arenas filled with sand, so you'd have a soft place to land."

"My, my," the nurse said. "You really had to be a man to want to rodeo in the old days."

Cowboy, feeling sprightly, said, "That's what a lotta folks say." They both were looking at the saddle in the corner, completely refurbished, eternal token to the conquest of old Widow Maker. Cowboy noticed the nurse smelled nice. A new hairdo, he supposed. He liked her. He could tell she was really interested in the rodeo.

"Here, take this," the nurse said, holding a pill and a little paper cup before him.

Cowboy looked at the pill and the cup, barely discernible in the faint light, and at the smooth arm extended. Suddenly he grabbed her wrist, knocking pill and cup to the floor, and quickly pressed his toothless mouth to her arm.

The nurse was frightened, thinking Cowboy was mad about the pill and trying to bite her. "Mr. Bennett! Mr. Bennett! Stop it! Stop it I say!" But Cowboy held on, as determined as he would have been with a wilder creature in another time. And he was not biting. It was, as the nurse would tell the others at the desk, the wettest old gummy kiss you ever saw.

J. Y. Bryan

Frontier Vigil

On the ascent to Hoping Hill, home of the Texas Allans, Dr. Springfield's saddle mule grunted and sighed, head down, ears slack and underlip loose from his teeth. The doctor himself felt about the same. In the last two nights he had not slept six hours, nor was he likely soon to improve the total.

The day was not bad, just indifferent. It was chilly without being cold. It reflected the gray decline of 1847, the lingering ugliness of the Mexican War as well, and constrictions of life for winter.

Weak rays of a sun about to set leaked through an attempted overcast. In this light the rather lordly dwelling before him, surrounded by wind-tattered trees, looked invaded by frailties which it usually seemed above. A cardinal on a downward bough ahead piercingly whistled, "Cheer, cheer, what cheer, cheer, cheer, cheer," but the yard otherwise showed the effects of Camilla Allan's illness. A norther which caught her riding home with a cold last week had frosted down the grass, buried much of it in leaves which no one had bothered to rake, and scattered wind-broken boughs across it. Anyone familiar with the place would know that what was missing here was Camilla's incessantly corrective supervision.

The snap of twigs under his mule brought the Allan bull terrier woofing around the house, followed by a run of children ranging from Burleigh Allan, the biggest and fastest, down to half-Indian, half-Negro products of the servant quarters. The children lost their vivacity as soon as they made out

who their visitor was, instead adopting the anxious, sub-
dued, vaguely alarmed respect associated with physicianly
calls.

Burleigh, a sturdy boy of ten, set an example for the rest
by pulling off his cap. "Hado sir. Feed your mule for you
maybe?"

"Thank you, son. Let him roll a bit first, uh?"

"Yessir. I'll rub him down afterwers."

"That's a boy! Hour or so from now I've got to ride over
to tend Mr. Timberlake awhile. Any fresh mount you can
saddle for me so Tom here can rest till I get back?"

"Oriole or Swallow be all right, sir?"

"Either's fine. How's mama this evening?"

"Poorly, sir." While the doctor disencumbered his saddle
of his medicine kit Burleigh held Tom's bridle, an unnecessary
service on a beast too tired to go anywhere without urging.
"Think she'll get better pretty soon maybe?"

"Well, we'll see. Your mother has always been a very
strong woman."

"Yessir."

His sister Dierdre, a year and a half younger, had been
absorbing every clue of expression in silence. Now, as the
doctor carried his kit toward the house, she dashed forward
to take his hand and walk beside him. Her run from behind
the house had blown her bonnet back to hang against her
shoulders from cords tied in a bow at her throat, but she did
not try to replace it; she gave rigid attention to the alternate
appearance of her boots under the gingham skirt flapping
around her ankles. Strikingly fine of feature (except for her
weedy, witchy hair), she represented a most interesting
reiteration of qualities prominent in her mother. Like her
mother she would someday attain a very graceful height; for,
small as he himself was, she at nine had already grown higher
than his shoulder. All the way to the veranda she held tight to
his hand, and not a word; she was keeping a grip on her faith
in him, he saw, also on some formless impulse to cry.

What could he say honestly reassuring to such a child as
this? Nothing. At the veranda he put his kit aside to give her a

momentary hug, noting professionally how slender and firm her body was, and how tensed by inchoate feeling. The instant he released her she kicked a fallen bough aside. With fists knotted as if she meant to punch somebody, she ran around the house, boots flying in flaps of windblown skirt, bonnet loosely bounding on her shoulders.

The front door opened for him as he approached it, and there was brown Roberta, grave-eyed, reserved, beautiful, sad. She spoke in whispers which told him much even though all she said was, "Evenun, doctor-sir. Please come in, sir."

Therefore, in climbing the stairs to the sickroom, he was weighed upon and wearied by the enormity of problems before him. Few, few were the people aware in wartime that the sum of difficult and draining battles fought out at home exceeds those where bugles blow. Here on the frontier the prince of cold weather killers was lobar pneumonia. Its tyranny extended to people who supposed they could with impunity ignore it—the strong, active young enlivened by illusions of permanent durability. Along rivers, bayous, and marshes near the Gulf malaria and yellow fever so dominated all thought during warm weather that frost was welcomed as a guarantor of better health, but back here on the high prairies these had no place to speak of except among travelers, and nowhere did so large a percentage of persons stricken with them succumb as to pneumonia. Once established, it was at least as effective as gunshot wounds in exposing the fragility of human life . . . also in revealing the ineptitudes of medical practice.

On the average one-third of all cases treated (or mistreated) in the usual ways proved fatal. He, with every sort of palliative his reading and practice had taught him, annually lost about one-fourth. Pneumonia, however, could take many forms, some more deadly than others. Of four cases which the last norther had left him to treat he would be doing well to bring two back to sound health. In fact, if more than two survived, it would not be his doing, at least not primarily so, but the result of factors just about as sequestered from his understanding as from anyone else's.

At the door of the sickroom he paused a moment to catch his breath and give his face the look of calm, confident knowledge which all patients always wanted to see in their physician. He tapped lightly on the door. A stir within brought forth Camilla's schoolteacher friend Maude Llewelyn, book in hand, her greeting a whisper.

"I'll be going now, doctor, but may I wait to . . . uh . . . to learn what . . . ?"

"Certainly." He dipped a hand toward a rocker whose motion indicated that she had been reading there under a window, helplessly watching her friend struggle to maintain a fingertip grip on the edge of life. "Be seated awhile. You may be able to help here."

Camilla lay flat under the bedclothes, a pillow angularly elevating her head, hair toruously strewn across it. Her respiration was audibly labored, rapid, shallow. Her eyes were closed, brows anguished. Flushed though she was, cyanosis had set in, making her lips blue, her ears also, a result of oxygen deficiency. Fingers of one hand weakly groped at the collar of her nightgown, and they too had blued. Checking her pulse in that wrist, he found it full and bounding but so very rapid that his own heart secretly, waywardly thumped. It did the same again when he felt how hot her forehead had become.

The cool of his hand on her brow brought her eyes ajar, but strabismically vague, astray from the line of focus. "Perry?"

"No dear girl. Too soon to expect him."

"Oh, doctor, hello. *So* glad you're back." Her tone incorporated no hint of complaint that he had not returned sooner. Certain people hereabout reproached him for sending his twin sons off to college in New Orleans again this fall, leaving him unable to take proper care of either his farm or his patients. But Camilla, even though close to delirium, transparently recognized that he had returned as quickly as conscientious regard for others would let him. "Silly of me to think it was Perry."

"Not feeling so good, I venture."

"I *hurt* so. My head . . . terrible headache. Chest and back are worse, too, chest especially. Each breath hurts so."

"Yes, pleuritis. We'll give you something directly."

"And I'm so hot . . . on fire . . . simply burning up."

"So I notice. We'll give you something for that too."

Her brief talking brought on a cough thickened by a discharge which she gathered into her handkerchief with ladylike nicety, but this did not prevent him from seeing that it was rust colored and flecked with blood. Some earlier had eluded her care during sleep and soiled a shoulder of her nightgown.

"Now, my girl, let's see your tongue."

It looked dry and brownish, another bad symptom. Before illness of such proportions he felt that what physicians knew about curing human ills was to what remained undiscovered as a pebble by the Nile to the pyramid of Cheops. It was imperative that he act, however, as if applying the little he did know could accomplish much; the attitude of frightened, helpless waiting which such extremities inspired in any home must be subordinated to conviction that everything a skilled practitioner could do was being done here, and promptly. The object, of course, was not to save his reputation but to save the patient and help the patient's family: often conviction of this sort seemed at least as valuable as any measure of his in promoting recovery.

He inserted a thermometer under Camilla's tongue. Fingering a chain across his waist, he drew his watch from a vest pocket, adjusted his glasses to see better, and timed her pulse. He counted 132 beats per minute—about twice its normal rate. Her bedroom, he noted meanwhile, even though the best he had seen in weeks, had a stale, purulent pneumonia odor which could not possibly be good for anybody.

"The windows, Maude," he said on his way to the door. "Better open one on each side."

"She won't catch more cold?"

"She needs air, oxygen—cool air too, feverish as she is." A flow of fresh air into a room could itself produce a lift of spirit, and resumptive whistling by that cardinal in the yard invited expectation of that result here. "Yes, open two at least halfway."

Out in the hall he found Roberta at the head of the stairs, waiting with foreknowledge that she would be called, and with a cup of coffee for him. "Coffee sir? All that ridun, you must be tard."

"Good girl!"

"Fix you some supper, sir?"

"Shortly. First, though, fetch us an extra pillow and some clean nightgowns that open to the waist."

"Don't none of hers open in front, sir."

"No matter. Just bring the kind that opens farthest. Left unbuttoned in back, it can be drawn down in front for the chest examination. Oh, and some fresh sheets, Roberta, also plenty of towels. If she passes through the crisis tonight she'll sweat heavily. Every stick on that bed will need changing two or three times."

"More handkerchiefs too, I reckon."

"Better than that, just bring some clean rags that you can burn after use."

"Last washun, sir, we had a sheet that tore."

"Good. Rip it into sections about two feet square and bring those, all of them. There'll be considerable need before morning."

To give the chief worriers a role replacing their helplessness with some feeling of effectuality and foreknowledge of what to expect—this was good medicine in any stricken household. He took only a few swallows of coffee at the moment, only enough to improve his breath and ease his weariness a bit, then returned to work.

The thermometer from under Camilla's tongue gave a reading of 103.4. Alarming, very! But a fever this high often seemed to work against the disease as well as the patient. If the patient could stand it long enough, it would prove that the disease could not. It then would impel rapid improvement. Indeed, this crisis in lobar pneumonia, often quite abrupt, seemed to take the form of a decision as to which could bear the fires of the contest best at their peak—the patient or the disease. Therefore, though not even an optimist could call a temperature so high favorable, it did suggest that Camilla would win or lose before morning. His role would be to use what few means he knew to help her stay alive till then. If she did, swift improvement might follow.

His immediate task was to restrain the fever, abate her pain, encourage expectoration to reduce toxins in her blood. The expectorant he relied on most was stramonium decocted from jimson weed. For an antipyretic he resorted to an extract of willow buds; rich in salicylic acid, it benignly fought pain while it combated fever. To strengthen the amalgam of these two drugs for cases where the pleura was inflamed, as it torturously was here, he added four drops of laudanum, blended all into some wine for palatability, and gave the draught to Camilla through a rubber drinking tube.

"Not so bad, eh, my dear?"

"No, doctor." As if they had spoken of Perry only a moment ago, she said, "He's coming, don't you think?"

"Yes, in time."

"Seems so long now, and I do think he's coming. He could make everything so different."

She in effect was obsessively continuing a conversation begun during his call two days back, when she was much more lucid, much less dangerously ill than now. Nothing else so preyed on her mind then or now as the lengthening absence of her husband, Capt. Perry Allan, who had taken a troop to the Mexican War a year and a half ago. Instead of returning when mustered out after the draining victory at Monterrey, he had proceeded to California, driven off by accusatory letters from her about his presumed freedoms with the doctor's stepdaughter Leticia, now the wife of Camilla's father in Washington. There was word afloat that he meant to come back for a settlement this winter, no telling precisely when. "I wonder, doctor," she had said in that talk about him two days ago, "what under heaven makes us such fools."

"Referring to what?"

"Well, first, to go back in time, a dozen years back to when Santa Anna was scourging Texas . . . when Perry was with the men out to stop him. . . . Back then he wrote me something peculiar. The great opponent of death, he said, is not life as most people imagine. No, he said that death is life's partner as night is day's, that life cannot exist without it. He . . ."

"True. They form a single process, a systole-diastole of development giving this old world its pulse."

"What *he* came around to was that the strongest, most tireless opponent of death is not life but love. Do you believe this?"

"Hm!" Just how could such an idea be squared with his own observation that extravagant love, when baffled or thwarted, predisposed its victims toward wasting health, suicide, murder or self-destructive drinking? He removed his glasses, breathed on the lenses, handkerchiefed them briskly, and put them back before his eyes. The aging of his vision had been to himself one more proof of decline, and yet these gold-rimmed bifocals seemed to reassure others regarding his professional competence. "Interesting turn of thought to say the least."

"He wrote further that where there's life there may, after all, be no real hope, contrary to what is so often said, but where genuine shared love exists, hope invariably does also. Haven't you found that true?"

"Fact is, my dear, I've not thought enough about it. Best to mull it over a day or two, eh?"

Disappointment that he did not at once agree momentarily clouded her brow. A smile followed. "There's one trait we've always liked in you, doctor: you do your best to be honest with us."

"Try to, yes."

"Well, regarding what makes us such fools. . . . People like Perry and me, with every conceivable reason to know better, why should we snap at each other and turn our backs on each other and close our doors against each other when we're so well equipped to understand that we should do the opposite?"

"Both of you set high standards for yourselves. Naturally,

they extend to anyone close to you. Possibly they're too high, though that fault's not so serious but what I wish to God that more people hereabout would share it."

"Only I carried it to such ruinous extremes. It's no wonder I'm sick. Makes me sick just to think of it."

"Then don't think of it. Just let this realization do all it can for you when he's here."

"Understand, it's not that he was ever brutal with me in any sense. Not once has he ever threatened me or called me vile names, as so many husbands do. No, he manages to remain something of a gentleman even when he's blaspheming. The foolish thing is how we'd snap and quarrel and stay apart."

"No need to think of any of that as so bad, Camilla." Had she been a patient he was less fond of, he would have changed the subject. This area having no priest or resident preacher, many people seemed to think he should be their confessor as well as physician. Their stricken tales were almost always prolix, using up unmerciful amounts of time, but he was of the opinion that, in cases like Camilla's, what they confessed did have a bearing upon their health. "Sometimes the best tonic for a marriage is to stay apart awhile."

"Such a difference, though, compared with how things used to be between us! Our first years together, doctor, were so very good. Our hopes, as Perry himself once put it—our hopes and joys were born new each day from the womb of dawn. Till sunset we worked like Trojans, and settled down for each evening together with grateful sighs.

"But seemed as though, after we had the best land tamed, after we'd taught the savages some respect and got a fine family started and made the lobos, panthers, wildcats, and coyotes a little gun-shy, we had to keep up the excitement by fighting each other, no matter that we knew better. We'd so enjoyed putting together a good life, and then we put energy into knocking it lopsided."

"Well, don't assume that the best is all past. What has been can be again."

"You really think so?"

"For people so young and full of vitality, yes."

He did like to think so, although he was by no means sure of it. There was no certainty, ever, about how any two people might interact, and less so when a third party of Leticia's little-recognized stature might come back on stage at any time.

Without actually changing the subject she asked, "Long as it's been since I risked having any more children . . . do you think now, after Perry gets back, it would be all right to have another?"

"There's always *some* risk, but I haven't thought the last three or four years that it would be as severe for you as for two-thirds of the women hereabout. You have a wonderful constitution, Camilla."

"Oh, sweet heaven, so much has been my fault, not his—just really my own." She followed a silence by asking, "Anything more from Leticia about when *she's* coming?"

"Nothing new, no."

"Rather remarkable, don't you think—both coming back at about the same time."

He did not miss the sudden bitterness in her stress on *remarkable*. "I'm not at all sure she will be. When she wrote she was just weighing the thought."

"Oh." After reflection about it she had concluded that prior confession by saying, "Anyhow, I hope to heaven he does come soon, no matter what."

And now today, while her pulse was being timed, she murmured, "I so wish I could talk to him. It's not all his fault, doctor. Not by any means." After recovering spent breath, she stressed, "I'd so like to confess that."

"Next thing, dear girl, we must listen to your chest. Maude and Roberta will change your nightgown while I have a bite to eat. Then we'll see how things sound in there."

After the change he had Maude, from the far side of the bed, maneuver the sheet bit by bit around the symmetries of Camilla's breasts as a concession to usages supposedly indispensable among ladies regardless of how many babies he had helped them deliver. Meanwhile, he applied a Laennec ausculator to her chest. Resembling a trumpet, it was made of wood with a bell-shaped mouth. On the opposite end was a small rounded opening to which he could apply either ear. In addition to causing female patients less embarrassment than placing the ear directly against the chest, as most rural physicians did, it was far more efficient in capturing instructive sounds.

Today it picked up noisy rales in the upper lobes of Camilla's lungs. Behind these he could hear rasps of pleural friction, also the labored, hasty accents of her heart. The diversity of sounds in this part of her chest, amplified by his ausculator, resembled a storm blowing through a forest where dwarf woodsmen rhythmically, resolutely swung their axes to complete their work despite it. The basal lobes, however, were largely mute, and percussive tapping confirmed the presence there of extensive congestion. As the cyanosis in her lips and fingers attested, the areas absorbing oxygen were already dangerously reduced. By his count, she was drawing breath thirty-six times a minute, every breath at the cost of stabbing pain, and yet the air this gave her was not enough.

One of the hazards in pneumonia was that its inflammatory influence sometimes spread to the heart. The clicks in her auricular valves were as yet free of fuzzing which would signal this invasion; and its repetitive lub-dub, lub-dub, lub-dub, though racing, remained strong. Occasional flutters in its pace were attributable, at least in part, to the sedatives he had given her. The quieting they enforced was showing also in a diminution of pain reflected on her brow.

As one measure more before she slept, he decided to rub her chest and back with oil of wintergreen, a demulcent stimulator of circulation which might afford some benefit even if it could not penetrate to the inflamed pleura. Most patients, in any case, felt tonicked by concerned expense of energy on their behalf, especially when it entailed a rhythmical laying on of hands.

This plainly was true of Camilla. Her breaths incorporated grateful little moans as the rubbing progressed. Further, the wintergreen spread through the room a pleasantly scented (and therefore more hopeful) atmosphere.

His method of applying it could hardly be more caring.

Advice from him had been directly responsible for bringing her to this part of Texas a dozen years ago, and Perry also. Through all the interval since then he had seen admirable influences flow from and around her. He had so affectionately put his best thought into promoting whatever he supposed would do some good in her household that she had come to seem a daughter to him and her youngsters more like his own grandchildren than the little boy of Leticia's known to him only by letter and daguerreotype.

But compared with not so many months ago, what a change today! Camilla then had seemed to be just entering the full bloom of womanhood. The difference now was about equal to that in a garden blighted by early frost. She was thin, dismayingly thin, and the look of finely, subtly compacted strength was gone. Nevertheless, her skin retained the satin which always had contributed to her exquisite effect, and the form, the articulation, the harmony of bone and joint underneath were of a kind to promote fresh admiration for potentialities inherent in the human race. He *had* to save this excellent young woman, if that could by any means be done. Her presence among the living served notice that human life, after all, is worth at least some of the veneration it gets.

By the time he finished the rubdown her torment in breathing had partially succumbed to the relaxants he had given her. He elevated her head and shoulders a bit with a second pillow to promote easier action of the heart, and perhaps easier breathing.

"Feel a little better, honey?"

She attempted a blue-lipped smile. "Uh, thank you."

"Get some sleep now, do. I must ride over to Jake Timberlake's, sick as he is. That won't take but a couple hours. I'll come back directly from there, then stay right by you till morning. Meanwhile, the more phlegm you get out of that chest the better. The more you sleep the better too."

He released Maude Llewelyn to go home: she had a husband and livestock of her own to tend. He instructed Roberta in what to do during his absence. He asked her also to get the children to bed early. A few grandfatherly words to each of them himself, and he left for Timberlakes'.

Darkness was long established around Hoping Hill when he returned. Roberta again greeted him at the door, bringing a candle by which to light him up the stairs.

"Any change, Roberta?"

"While ago she cough powerful lot, and a mess come out most every time she cough."

"Good thing, really."

"We use up three them rags entirely. Past hour or so she been quieter. Seem like maybe she's better."

His instant impression on entering the sickroom was that she was deceived by her wishes, that Camilla's thick, faintly stertorous breathing was a bit more labored than before. A lamp now burned at low wick next to a pitcher of water on the bedside table, revealing that the cyanosis in Camilla's lips had spread, turning her cheeks bluish. Because of superstition about night air, he guessed, someone had closed the windows. It was not Roberta, after all, to whom he had mentioned the need for more oxygen, for a chance to make the most of every inhalation. His first move was to re-open them.

Camilla lay in a semidelirious doze, eyes restlessly astir behind closed lids. Light from the lamp angling across her throat showed a carotid artery pulsating in erratic haste, and tortures associated with attempts to seize more air again constricted her brow. Her temperature now stood at 103.8—not much higher than before, yet a sharp disappointment: he had expected the drugs he gave her to effect some decrease. Indeed they might have, but complications at Timberlakes' had kept him so long that the effect had worn off.

His watch gave the time as 10:22. This meant he had been gone more than four hours. Further, she had taken her medicine at least half an hour before he left; it was past time for more. To hasten her discharge of mucus and open her bronchi for reception of more air, he decided to give her a larger dosage of expectorant. Her weakened condition would require that this be accompanied by a decrease of laudanum, if not of the willow extract. The good which moderate amounts of all three might do did not assure that more might be better. Like so many medicines, they entailed risk; all were in differing degrees poisonous, and fatal in excess. He had learned to stay within the limits he could expect to behave benevolently.

He measured half again the normal dosage of stramonium into one-fourth less of laudanum and willow extract. These he mixed into some wine as before. Giving the glass to Roberta to hold close, he bent a drinking tube to Camilla's lips while lifting her head, his hand professionally registering the shapely size and weight of cranium hidden beneath the silken luxuriation of her hair.

"Here, Camilla. Some more medicine now."

Her eyes unsteadily opened.

"Can you drink this, honey?"

She did so. It brought on a bubbly cough and more blood-laced phlegm. Her gasping afterward was exceedingly rapid. When it eased she murmured, "I'm very sick, doctor."

"Well, don't despair. Courage, my dear! Despair tends to produce its own justification. So does courage."

"Yes. I believe that myself." More rapid gasps, and she added, "But it's only by the mercy of God, if He'll grant it, that I'll live to see another day."

Dr. Springfield reflected that to the extent God's mercy did manifest itself here tonight it would assume the form of having long ago given her a strong heart and durable spirit. This he kept to himself. A deist disinclined to tamper with anyone else's beliefs, he neither discouraged nor promoted religious views in his patients. "Anyhow, this medicine will help you feel better."

"I'm glad." Restlessly gasping, she asked, "Think he's really coming?"

"No doubt he is, only not right soon. Better be quiet now. Let the medicine take effect."

"All right."

Her retreat from consciousness was as prompt as reduction of light when, one at a time, window shades are drawn. Careful not to wake her, he had Roberta help him straighten her bedding, bring her fresh drinking water, dispose of soiled cloths, and supply him with a fresh cup of coffee. About fifteen minutes had passed when another cough wakened Camilla. A heavy discharge flowed into the rag he held to her mouth.

On recovering her breath, she asked, "Moon up yet?"

"Rose before I got back. It's getting old—had one bent side."

"Exactly how I saw it just now, dreaming." A phrase at a time between breaths, she went on, "He came over a ridge, riding at a trot, moon on his left, three riders behind him, all at a trot. Why at night if he—unless hurrying to get here right away?"

"Travelers off west sometimes ride at night to avoid—" On the verge of saying *to avoid savages* he checked himself. "To avoid the heat of day or reach good water."

"Moon rising on his left—that would mean he was riding south. I'm sure, though, he was coming this way."

"Yes. All those trails zigzag considerably."

"He wasn't on Marquis . . . some darker horse. I called but he couldn't hear me." After several gasps, she murmured, "What could it mean?"

"No one can be certain what such dreams mean."

It probably did mean, he reflected, that the medicine was taking effect. Many times in human experience stramonium and its relatives had been used to induce prophetic dreams.

In an attempt at realism, she asked, "Sure he won't come till winter?"

"Well . . ." Temptation to hold out a carrot of falsehood clamored within him. He thought it likely that the sort of love and hope in which he put so much trust were at least as sustaining to her as any drug he gave her; but she herself, when most lucid, realized that Perry was unlikely to appear any time soon. "Seems a reasonable conclusion, don't you think?"

"Yes." Her brows strained to impose clarity upon her mind while she labored for more breath. "I honestly . . .

thinking what a little while we all have to live, I do so want to be charitable, doctor."

Another cough interrupted her. She had managed only a prologue to what troubled her, he saw, and should be allowed to say the rest. He awaited it in silence.

How patients bore an eye-to-eye confrontation with death was of unending interest to him. Many, seeing it among shadows near their bed, shrank into themselves, wretchedly self-pitying, terrified and trivial. Others, to the end, could not believe that it was there for them. Still others took refuge in illimitably, unintentionally conceited expectations of life eternal.

But not a few who survived a brush with death gained hugely from the encounter. The only experiences known to him which could rival it for instruction were the onset of love and discovery of the beautiful as a directive force in life— both marvelously, luckily given him by the woman whom, against all advice, he took to wife.

Again and again he had seen awareness of death's mute vigil spur a larger awareness of life. Characteristically the wider vision which followed lent grace to all the patient's days thereafter. It already was apparent that, if Camilla lived, this would happen to her.

"I hope you won't take it amiss, but. . . ." Again several rapid snatches of breath before she concluded, "Still, it does prey on my mind so, Letricia's coming just when he does."

He fully comprehended why. A year ago, on receiving from his step-daughter Leticia a daguerreotype of herself and baby boy, he had been as charmed by it and proud of it as if she were authentically of his own blood and Leighton the indubitable son of her husband, his longtime friend Cedric Burleigh. Not until he witnessed Camilla's shocked, incensed, bitterly stifled reaction to it did a restudy of it alert him to Leighton's resemblance to Perry.

Common though it was for his practice to reveal sharp differences between demeanor and deportment among seemingly blameless people, he too was shocked. Not that he was one to think accepted patterns of behavior invariably right or breaches intolerably wrong. His love for Leticia's mother seemed to him to this day responsible for everything best in his life, certainly better for himself than for her or Leticia. His friends in New Orleans, though, had let him know that they considered it stupid for a prominent physician to marry an actress with a tainted reputation, an illegitimate girl-child, and weak lungs. They so slighted her and Leticia that one reason for his emigrating to Texas was to spirit both beyond reach of such hurt.

Still, no prior experience had hinted to him that Leticia and Perry, upright as they always seemed, might fail to keep their obviously strong attraction to each other clothed in prohibitions which others approved. Many days were to pass before his indignation cooled enough to let him comprehend that, taking into account all the circumstances, such a result of Perry's Washington visit was virtually foreordained. Yes, but neither understanding as much nor recognizing how anguished over it the principals themselves must often be need incapacitate him from doing something about it when he could.

"It's premature to fret over it, Camilla." He stroked a hand across her brow, surprised afresh at how hot it felt. "She was just raising a question about the suitability. Personally, I expect to be in New Orleans at Christmastime, so I've written her not to come till spring."

"Oh, really?"

No, not really. Here, though, a lie did seem the right medicine, and he could give it the taste of fact. His response to Leticia, little more than begun when devastations of last week's norther left him no time for anything else, had in truth rejoiced over the propect of seeing her and Leighton a few months hence. Being now convinced of the error in her coming at that time, he resolved, if only Camilla could slip through the impending crisis, to tear up that beginning in favor of a letter disapproving of their visit until March or April, indeed prohibiting it until then.

"You see, I have to get my glasses changed, also lay in a new stock of medicines and buy all sorts of gear and implements and supplies. It's my thought to spend a couple weeks in December shopping in New Orleans, then have Christmas there with the twins. Besides, she'll find travel far pleasanter in spring, whether by sea or land."

"That's true."

"She'll wait till then, my word on that. Best thing now would be to rest quietly. See how soon you can get back to sleep, hear?"

She managed a faintly comic imitation of childhood obedience. "Yes-sir."

When she again appeared asleep, he whispered to Roberta, "The crisis won't come, I expect, till midnight or after. So you go rest too. If we need you, I'll call."

"I'n stay awake, sir."

"I know you can, but don't." Seeing her about to protest further, he raised a hand. "No, we can't have you taking sick too." Roberta, brown though she was, had been to Camilla like a valued cousin—had grown up with her and shared a never-mentioned fraction of her ancestry. In this household she truly was, to all the children, an "auntie." Without her nothing here would go quite right. "Everybody else needs you, and needs you in good health. So get some sleep and stay well."

"Only thing is . . ."

"No more, Roberta. Go to sleep."

Camilla, whom he had thought deep among disordered dreams, spoke with eyes shut. "Pray for me, Berta."

"Deed so, mam. Been prayn, hard, and will some more."

"Pray for . . ." A cough interrupted her, and she herself applied the cloth to receive its result. "Pray for him also."

Whom she meant there was no need to ask. "Him too, yessum. Him too."

Left alone Dr. Springfield again checked Camilla's pulse. It remained swift, swift, swift, and unsteady as well. This was one of the risks with stramonium, this erratic heartbeat, but there was strength in it still, and some risk to help her lungs clear had to be accepted. The only thing to do for the present was await the consequences.

He turned the bedside lamp a bit higher to help him remain awake, then drew a rocker near and assigned himself the task of noting in his record book every significant detail regarding her condition and treatment. In the quieted house her respiration laboriously, hastily rasped despite the sedation he had given her. Off in the dark beyond the windows he heard bullfrogs gutterally conversing down along Otter Creek. A mockingbird in the dooryard grove went through an autumnal fraction of its moonlight serenade, and far away somewhere the keening of a lobo wolf pierced the breadths of darkness.

"Don't you dare!" Camilla rapped out suddenly. "I won't stand for that. *No!*"

Back on the edge of delirium, and it seemed to him a sign of how indelibly old quarrels could stain a mind even as it groped toxically to retain some hold on life. Slumped in the rocker, pencil in hand, he reflected with a sigh that his record of facts, facts, facts was sterile, that everything most significant and overwhelming about such a case as this eluded his pages.

During his three-mile ride to Timberlakes', haunted by the image of this splendid young mother hanging by a shredded cord over the drop to oblivion, an idea had besought his attention: qualities most responsible for the superiority of such a person, it insisted, might all along have been exerting an influence toward her destruction. The same had been true, very clearly, of his own loving, lovely, generous wife, now so long dead. He also had observed others in whom a conflict of excellences assumed destructive expression, and often enough to cast doubt upon the classical postulate that tragedy flows from flaws of character.

Such flaws might be one source of tragedy, yes. What could be learned, though, from a search the opposite way to determine how common it was for the strongest qualities which animate and drive the able to impel them toward a bitter denouement difficult to avoid? Now that he reflected again about it he saw every human life, however flawed or superior, following a zigzag course toward its own destruction, therefore toward tragedy, with differences arising chiefly from the quality of life attained along the way. Sometime when not so infernally tired he would bring each of these premises before the full tribunal of his experience and see how convincing a case could be made for them.

To herself Camilla murmured, "I know! Now I know." A series of snatching, fragile respirations and she whispered, "Too late, too late, too late. . . ."

Among trees fringing the yard a screech owl grieved. Somewhere a yearling lowed, no longer a calf nor yet quite mature, and again the wail of a lobo rode its witch's broom through the moonlight.

Not one syllable in all the language of darkness acknowledged this young woman's right to stay alive—no, nor anyone else's either. A night like this rebuked all optimism.

Of the room's three windows one remained shut. While taking in the sounds from beyond it he chanced to see, reflected in its glass, a small, gray, deeply weathered man with glinting spectacles and a clipped gray mustache. He was reluctant to accept the image as his own. He seldom thought of himself as old and ineffectual, seldom felt that way either, but the fact was plain enough here. This was one of those times when he wished he had chosen some calling less certain to expose how makeshift man's best efforts to preserve life or enlarge it could be.

Back in Louisiana his reputation for skill at both traced solely to comparison with the run of general practitioners, too many of them ill-trained or fraudulent or blockheaded or presumptuous. Their malpractice, no less than his few successes, produced heavy demand for him among well-to-do families. Living modestly, he too became well off. By that time he had wearied of treating favored people with overfed bodies and scorbutic minds; therefore he sold his lucrative city practice to a younger man at a bargain and brought his lovely consumptive wife to the sundrenched prairies of Texas.

Their benefit to her was soon apparent. So was the profound stimulation of a pregnancy which brought them twin sons, Alonso and Rafael. Eventually she too came down with lobar pneumonia rather like Camilla's. The most rending and humbling hour in his career occurred when every measure known to him failed to bring her through such a night as this.

Since that time he had labored along life's rutted road rather like a man with one leg. Only because he had his equally loving stepchild Leticia to accompany him and help him bring Alonso and Rafael toward manhood did he resist an impulse to dip into his pharmacopoeia for unalterable release from the struggle.

Now here before him on this bed was another exceptional patient in her thirties, as his wife had been, and what was he able to do for her? Crushingly little. He could only soothe her a bit until the drama of pneumonia's crisis began.

His watch told him that it was 10:51. Between midnight and dawn the decisive grapples between life and death in such a case as this were likely to occur. Thus it had been with his wife, and thus he expected it to be here.

To nap an hour or so himself, he reflected, might fit him better for that battle. But no, this was no time for self-indulgence. If her heart wearied of the fight or if she smothered in her phlegm while he slept, he would have the hounds of conscience snapping at his heels all the way to his own grave.

Merely by way of resting his eyes a bit he lowered the lamp's wick, pushed his glasses up onto his forehead, slumped more comfortably into the rocker, and propped a hand up where he could tilt his head against it and keep his watch ticking by his ear as a reminder to stay awake. Beyond these, beyond the open windows, beyond the nearer trees, he could still hear Otter Creek bullfrogs bellow in debate. Again an owl's lament shuddered through the grove, and from high above the house came the yelping honks of geese in flight by moonlight. His thought followed their strange night journey southward. He wondered vaguely about their destination— and drifted into sleep as their signals faded toward the Gulf.

What finally woke him was a strangulated coughing alternately open and smothered. Camilla lay twisted to one side, back his way. She had thrown aside her top sheet, and yet her nightgown was wetly sweated to her body. So painful were her coughs that her knees had drawn up almost to her chest. She had snatched a towel to her face to capture the discharge from her lungs.

Neglectful of his watch, which had slipped down to dangle on its chain as he napped, he sent one hand groping for her pulse while the other felt her brow. Wrist and brow alike were wetly sweated, but he thought a bit less fevered than before. The bounding of her pulse indicated that her heart, though beating to desperation under the strain of this seizure, still remained strong.

He hastily circled the bed to place in her hands a fresh cloth for capturing the phlegm. He also removed her pillows to lower her head and induce freer cleansing of her lungs.

The abrupt creaks of flooring under his boots brought Roberta hastily upstairs. With hair in a housecap skewed by napping in all her clothes, she glided through the door. "She bad, doctor-sir? Something bad happnun?"

"Only what's got to happen. Hand me that drinking tube and glass of water, eh?"

"Yessir."

"Then towel her off good. She's wet as a sponge."

He recaptured his dangling watch. The time, he noted, was 12:13. The concord between his earlier prognosis and the facts before him planted in him a little mustard seed of confidence. He mixed almost the same draught of drugs as before, this time including extra drops of febrifuge.

Once Camilla's coughing subsided he said, "That's it, my girl: get your breath back, and then more medicine."

"Oh," she gasped, "this cough does hurt so!"

"Thing is, that stuff must come out of there. It poisons you. This medicine will help loosen it up and get at that pain also."

"Thank you."

"Now a big drink of water, eh?"

"Yes . . . very thirsty."

"But take your time. Drink a little, breathe a spell, drink some more, breathe a while longer: that's the way." While she did so, he said, "Roberta, spread a couple dry towels along yonder side of the bed where we can roll her onto them."

"Yes," Camilla panted, "perspiring this way, I'd soon have the bed soaked."

"More important, we want the other side of your chest to drain out too. The side kept highest drains best."

"Seems to, yes."

"Wisest course, honey, would be to get that wet nightgown off and have only a sheet over you. Mind if Roberta takes it off? After that she can towel you dry under the sheet, and gentle rubbing will do you good."

"All right."

"I'll step out couple minutes until you've changed."

After returning, he had her lie on alternate sides about half an hour at a time, always without pillows, so that gravity could encourage the outflow from her lungs between spells of sleep. Her sweating remained copious and persistent, and Roberta was no less persistent about toweling her under the sheet.

By 2:00 a.m. her temperature had dropped to 101.6. In the first gray of dawn it stood at 99.8. While he was reading the thermometer, she fell asleep again, only to be wakened by further coughing as sunlight began gilding the easterly side of trees in the yard. What her coughs brought forth this time, though still heavy, was not streaked with blood as before: it was acquiring a yellowish cast.

"Tell you something, my girl," he said in happy, weary, immeasurable relief, "you're not only seeing another day; you'll see many more."

"Thank heaven," she whispered. "And you . . . bless you, doctor."

A cardinal on a hackberry tree near the front windows was whistling as if life were indeed everlasting, and the matins of a mockingbird endorsed his cheerful tidings. Noisy though both were, Camilla swiftly went back to sleep.

Pat Carr

Indian Burial

Nobody knew about her spot and she sure as hell wasn't going to tell them.

She hitched up a shoulder to scratch the small of her back and took out a cigarette. She held the steering wheel with one hand, tamped the cigarette to let the bits of tobacco flake loose out on the dashboard.

That prissy Lena with her flowery pack, some silly woman filter to show off dainty and let some man light it for her. What the hell kind of smoke is that? She touched the red circles of the lighter to her Camel.

Men're so damned stupid. Weak and stupid, the lot of them.

She ought to know. Married four times with five kids, twins with that namby pamby Willis, and who'd think he'd even have one kid let alone two at once. Four husbands and not one of them worth the powder to blow him to hell. Twenty-three lovers besides, or was it twenty-four, she always had to stop and count if she wanted it exact and "lovers" certainly wasn't the word anyway, not a one of them worth a damn.

In all those years if she'd just found one, even one, that'd given her anything. Anything at all besides some accident that'd come bursting out nine months later leaving her with another squalling brat just when she was getting the others so they could take care of themselves.

But she had to hand it to Matt. He'd had sense enough to take off on his own without waiting to have her throw him out, locking the door and chucking his shoes out a window the way she'd done with all the others when she was sick of them drinking up her restaurant money.

She ground out the half-smoked cigarette, feeling the damp tip where her lips had been. No matter how hard she tried, she never could keep from wetting the paper, and then the clammy end in her mouth always ruined the smoke.

Maybe she ought to get one of those holders with a plastic mouthpice after all. Matt suggested her getting one once but she'd just sneered at him, having better things than that kind of damn nonsense to spend her money on. She'd kind of hoped he'd get one anyway, let her know it was a gift, let her know he was boss, but he didn't. And a couple of years later he was gone, taking Sammy with him.

She'd never understood that. Sammy wasn't even his own kid but belonged to that lazy Manuel who was her husband the shortest of all and who she was never sure why she married in the first place except that she was angling for his brother Raul and he'd got in the way. And Sammy was certainly no damned bargain with all that dark skin and her blue eyes, but wishy washy like, staring off into space, floating like loose marbles in his head if she ever shouted loud enough to get his attention. Always fiddling with a pencil or a crayon or some damn thing, one time even drawing up a whole pad she needed for taking down orders. That was the one time she'd seen Matt mad, violent mad, pushing her off from Sammy, jerking away the belt she was beating him with, yelling at her not to touch the kid. He even tossed a couple of dollars on the floor to pay for "the fucking paper." She remembered it exactly, his angry voice using a word she always made clear no one was to use in her presence.

"Oh what the hell." No use spoiling the day.

It wasn't often any more she got away from the restaurant what with not being able to afford much help and trying to stay open as much as possible. It was funny how with the country getting prosperous again that the food and motel business had gone off so. Of course Flagstaff wasn't what it once was with big chain motels moving in and all. She didn't ask questions when somebody checked in for a couple of hours at the full night's rate, but you still had to change the sheets after, wearing them out with washing.

Well, no use thinking about that either.

Here she'd got the afternoon away and that was what she ought to be thinking about. Getting to the spot no one knew about, digging out in the sun, letting the heat warm her clear through, maybe making that big find she could sell to the museum in Tucson. Matt was good for that at least, getting her onto the digging for Indian treasure. No use thinking about the other crap.

A dense flight of orange butterflies rose ahead, hundreds of them filling the sky, the highway ahead of her, catching in the air currents as the car overtook them, smashing out of control on the windshield, leaving yellow blotches of insect entrails over the glass.

"Goddamn nuisances." It was hard enough to see with the damned glare on the hood and the blacktop with all that mess.

She peered through the yellow-white scum. The car kept hitting into them even as they tried floating, flying out of the way, hundreds more of them.

And the dirt road was along there somewhere. She had to slow down.

There it was.

She turned sharply off the highway onto the road that was hardly more than a wagon path, and great banks of dust rose immediately on each side of the car.

She was forced to slow down even more, guiding the car in ragged tracks hard and stiff as concrete.

Past the first crop of foothills in a little valley sort of place was where it was, where she'd found all the arrowheads that last time.

She kept her eyes half on the rise of the hills, half on the ruts, looking hard through the dirtied windshield, and she was suddenly jolted to see a man beside the road.

She got closer and saw it was an old Indian, hair lank and dirty-looking below a round-brimmed gray hat, shoulders stooped in a greasy jacket too big for him.

As she drove slowly past she saw him dig in the little brown dime store sack he carried, extract a red candy ball and put it carefully in his puckered mouth.

"Old fool." She glanced back at him from the rear-view mirror. Standing out there in the middle of nowhere sucking ten cent hard candy. "Probably not a tooth in his head."

But then as she got to the row of foothills she forgot about him. It was right along there, and she had a feeling about her luck that afternoon.

She drove through and got to a spot she thought she recognized, the sagebrush looking right. She stopped, stared at it until she was almost sure, and turned off the motor.

No use pulling off the ruts and risking getting stuck in that soft looking dirt when nobody'd be coming by anyway.

She jammed a sweat stained hat down on her head and got out the shovel and trowel.

Matt'd been good for something anyway. More than the rest of them.

She walked out from the car to where she was sure she'd found the points that last time. A rain had eroded down the side of what looked like a mound and she stooped to look at the gouge in the dry earth.

Sure enough. There were two pot sherds sticking straight out of the water cut. Red clay pieces about the size of quarters but there they were all right. It was the place.

She put down the trowel and started digging in the side of the little hillock. Slow, careful, methodical, watching sharp-eyed each shovelful as it was pulled out of the earth and dumped to the side. Whenever she saw a sherd or a chip of flint or a shred of bone, she stopped, picked it out, and put it aside. At least half a dozen different bowls or pieces of them were in the mound.

Sweat collected under the hat brim, on her upper lip, ran down her backbone and down the crease between her breasts. She always felt like taking off the heavy drill shirt and digging in her bra, but she never did. Matt'd've liked that. All they ever thought about was sex.

To hell with them.

The pile of dirt grew as her shovel dug, lifted, emptied. Then it happened.

The way Matt described it might when he'd got her interested in hunting for Indian burials in the first place.

The shovel struck rock where there should've been only dry loam. She tossed the shovel down and started with the trowel, scraping off the dirt to expose flat stones laid carefully over something the Indians wanted to protect.

She worked steadily, carefully, laying bare the stones that fitted together like a flagstone walk.

She'd cleared a space about four feet long when the stones ran out.

It was too damned small. She couldn't remember if they were supposed to have flexed burials or not.

Maybe it wasn't a burial after all.

She dug some more, but that was all of it. Only four feet. The end stones went down, encasing, enclosing whatever it was in a stone box.

That's the way it always happened. Just when she had something good going, it all went to hell.

She got down on her knees and started lifting the rocks off the top, afraid she might drag away some and the rest'd fall in and crush the treasure, if there was one. But as she worked she could see the hole had already filled with dirt and she could lift the stones off without worrying.

She started with the trowel again, the sweat running down from her hat to her eyebrows, and she wiped it off with her sleeve. Her tongue felt swollen, dry as the earth as she heaped it out.

She didn't stop to examine any more, just watched as the dirt was lifted out by the trowel.

"Damn."

It was a burial after all.

Not of somebody flexed, but of a kid.

From the size of the skull and the teeth she could see coming out of the dirt, it'd probably been about two years old.

She leaned back on her heels.

Little bone hands lay at the sides of the rib cage filled with dirt. Beside the head was a buff colored bowl and some rough beads curved like they'd been strung on a thread long since rotted away.

She dug carefully again until at last she had it all exposed, the little skeleton, the bowl, the flat stones of the grave floor.

Her hands rested on her knees and she looked down at them. Dirt stuck to them in random patches and the enlarged blue veins at the backs protruded in great ugly ridges. Her hands were old, old like the rest of her, dry and crackled.

She could feel the back of her boots against her thighs.

Out there all alone it wasn't enough, wasn't anything. That old fool Indian in the middle of nowhere sucking hard red candy.

A movement caught her eye and she looked up from the grave.

The mass migration of orange butterflies had reached where she was. They filled the air above her in a thick orange cloud, fluttering like burnt-orange ashes, sifting, glittering stained glass wings hazing against the sun.

"God damn you," she said softly. "God damn you to hell."

Doug Crowell

Work

I make my living washing drums, and there's always drums to wash. Every day the dirty drums come in on trucks, and every day I wash them. It's a good job. Some guys don't like it. Harold and R. J. and fat Charles all used to be on the drum-washer, but they got moved off it fast as they could. Me, I like it, being on the drum-washer, and I plan to stay as long as I have any say so about it. It's a good job, washing drums. And there's always dirty drums to wash. I don't really *wash* them, of course. It's all automatic. If I had to really get down and scrub them I likely wouldn't like it either, but it's all automatic, and I just get them ready to go is all. Drums come in on the trucks, I get them ready, push the buttons, and off they go. Clean drums. The job's all right. I mostly like it.

The two things I don't like about it are that there's no women around, and that the bosses don't seem to understand what it is I'm telling them. There is one woman at the plant, who works in the factory office, who's the secretary, but she's sort of old and dumpy and so the guys don't talk about her the way they would a younger, better-looking woman. I like her. We always get along, though I'm not in the office that much. She likes me too and that's easy to see, and so the guys kid me about that. She's a widow. The way they kid me means they like me, but still it gets old sometimes, gets pretty tiresome. They kid in the usual way, but that's all right, and I'm not going to let it keep me from being friendly to her. I like her. She walked by the lunchroom door one day just when someone was saying something. I know she heard it too, and so I was a little red-faced next time I had to go into the office, but she didn't seem to notice. I suppose she's used to it, though, working in a factory office instead of some other kind. I wonder sometimes what it was like for her when she was younger though, back when she was married.

The guys kid more about the women they can't have anyway, the married ones or the ones who come once in a while from the head office in Atlanta, to walk around the plant for a day or two. Those women make two, three times what we do, some of them. They do make that much, and I know some of the guys think about that sometimes. As soon as they walk in the plant we all know they're there and we all wonder what they look like underneath, those women who make that money. We know we could never have them, and so we kid about them a lot, the women who make that kind of money.

It's hard sometimes to get girls when you're only a drum-washer. I go pretty often down to the Cascade, to drink some beers and listen to the music. I know a couple of the bartenders pretty well, and usually a waitress or two, but they turn over pretty fast. The pay's not much. Two girls have been waitressing there ever since I've been going regular, and that's over a year. I wonder how they make it sometimes, or if they get money other ways. Maybe they get tips better than most. There are usually six bartenders there, even more on the busy nights. Maybe a dozen girls out doing tables. The Cascade's a big place, a big old-fashioned dance hall. Sometimes I do all right, sometimes I don't. Even when I do it's usually with a girl sort of like me, sourmouthed about one thing or another, and so the night never gets down to being too much fun. We mostly seem to just get drunker and drunker, and more and more sourmouthed, and nearly always I end up having to get out of their bed about the middle of the night and go back home to my own, all alone. That's not the way I want things to be, it sure isn't. I bet it's not the way they want things to be either, but neither of us seems to be able to do anything else.

The kind of girls I imagine could make me smile and laugh and have a good time are always the girls I can't get. Who don't want me. Every month the work in the office piles up for a day or two, and they hire a girl or two from the temporary help place. Mostly they're young and pretty, but they're not the kind of girls who would want me. The guys always kid me about them though, and they wish on those days that they got to go into the office as much as I do. I go in to the main office now and then, because the drum-wash is close to the shipping office, and the guys up there are always getting me to carry down invoices and papers for the bosses to sign. It's not only because I'm close, but also because the drum-wash is about the only job that can be done pretty much at my speed and not at the speed of some machine or other. I come in earlier to work than all the other guys except for Herbie, who unloads trucks, and so I've always got two batches of drums washed by the time the other guys start working. We never run more than two batches before lunch and hardly ever more than one, so I can pretty much wash drums at my own speed once the other guys come in, and I'll still have more drums than we need for the day's run. The guys kid me about that sometimes, how I'm the man of leisure around the plant. So I end up doing a lot of odd jobs. I work hard those first two hours, but I can slack up after that, and I'd rather have it that way than have to go the same speed all day long like the guys on the machines do. So I get the hard part of my work done before the other guys get there, and then doing odd jobs now and then helps the day go by.

It's bad, though, in some ways. I know all the guys in the plant, but I don't know any of them very well because I don't really work *with* any of them. If you're on the drum-wash, you're pretty much off in the corner by yourself. Still, it's a good job. I get off at two-thirty instead of four-thirty like everyone else. I used to come back to the plant at four-thirty and go down with the guys to the Corner for a beer, but then I quit doing that. It's not the same when you don't get off at the same time. No one said anything, it was just diffrent somehow, them just getting off work and me already out for two hours. So I quit going to the Corner, except now and then on Fridays. I like getting out early though, I like being out already while most people are still working. I don't go home right away, but I don't do anything with my time either. For a while once I went downtown every day, to a cafeteria down there. I thought that maybe downtown would be different. It was in some ways.

Once I realized that someone had been watching me, someone I had not been seeing. One of the girls who worked there, cleaning tables, pushing the tea-cart around. One day she refilled my coffee cup and smiled at me and said hello. She'd been watching me, and I hadn't even known it. It was a funny feeling. Every day we talked a little, and finally I asked her out. She didn't seem sourmouthed like most girls with jobs like hers. I thought we might have a good time. Still, something seemed funny to me, so I didn't tell any of the guys I had a new girl lined up for Friday. When I went to pick her up, she lived with her parents, which she hadn't mentioned. I'd thought she was too old for that. Her father looked at me in a funny way, asked me about myself then seemed not to believe anything I said. Things seemed strange to me, but I thought it was only me, because I had not expected her to be living with her parents. We finally left, and I was glad to leave, glad to get away from her father's eyes. I just didn't know. We didn't go to the Cascade, but went to a quiet place instead, because we hadn't talked much. Not at all really, just her saying this or that and me smiling back, agreeing, when she came by with the tea-cart, or was cleaning off a table near me. And then I had asked her out. So there was no way I could know. It had never occurred to me. She seemed all right, but as we had a couple of drinks, it struck me she wasn't very smart. And it wasn't just that, it was something more. When the waiter came with our second drinks and looked funny at me out of one eye, I realized what it was he already knew, that I didn't yet know. Everything became clear. The girl was not only not smart, she was a retarded girl. She wasn't really bad, just a little bit, but that was enough. I wondered what the waiter thought. I had never known because it had never occurred to me. I guess I hadn't paid that much attention to her in the cafeteria. She was retarded, even if it was only a little bit. Everything was clear, the way her father had looked at me, why she wasn't sourmouthed.

There was nothing in her eyes, just nothing there. Otherwise, she looked and talked normal. She did. She had a job and was friendly to me, and I never noticed, not until the waiter looked at me the way he had. I didn't know what to do. We hadn't been gone an hour yet, I didn't want to take her home, but I didn't want to go anywhere with her. We left the bar, I bought beer, and we went to a drive-in movie, where no one could see us. I didn't know what to do. It crossed my mind to drive off when she went to the bathroom, but I couldn't do that. We drank the beer, and then I took her home. She wanted me to fool around with her, and once I started feeling her breasts. But I couldn't do it. I wondered how many guys went out with her, knowing. She seemed eager. It made me sad. She was normal looking except for her eyes, and unless she talked too long she only sounded not too smart, not retarded. She let me know that I could make her easy, but I couldn't. I felt funny. Her kisses were as blank as her eyes. I thought of Crazy Joe, a guy at work. He would have fucked her and left her and told us all about it at lunch on Monday. But I didn't tell anyone. We drank the beer, and I took her home. Her father was up and stared at me. I felt creepy. But when I was driving away I laughed out loud, and it was okay then. I even wondered what it might have been like. There was nothing in her eyes, nothing. I never went back to where she worked. I thought of her cleaning up tables, smiling and saying hello to guys sitting alone. She could smile because she just didn't know, didn't know anything. No wonder she hadn't been sourmouthed.

Girls think I don't know anything either, sometimes. I know they do. I try not to think about it. It's frustrating, thinking that, knowing that the bosses don't listen to me either. They won't say why they won't listen, and when I'm feeling bad it makes me wonder. It's like they know something I don't know, and never will. It makes me feel sometimes like I don't know anything. I make a suggestion about how the drum-wash, or some other job, could be done better, or faster, or easier. But they won't listen, they just smile and nod, and then things go on like always. Sometimes I do think they know something I don't, but good for me I don't feel that way too often, because it makes me feel bad. Makes me want to go get drunk. Makes me mad. The girls at the Cascade smile like that sometimes too. Sometimes I wonder why and sometimes I get mad and say, fuck you bitch, and sometimes I try to smile that smile back at them, but it never feels right. They do know something I don't, or seem to, or think they do. There's nothing wrong with me. What's the matter with washing drums?

Once I was sitting down the table from two girls who were pretty nice looking; they were laughing and talking and seemed up for a good time. I was trying to decide to go down the table to talk to them when some other guy beat me to it. So I listened. The three of them talked, and those girls seemed okay. I wanted to join in, I almost did. Especially when one girl went off to dance with that guy and left the other by herself. She looked at me but didn't smile. I pretended I hadn't seen. The other two came back in half an hour, and when the guy got up to go buy drinks, one girl asked, What does he do? and the other girl said, He works in a factory, he puts fans together. They laughed then, like that was funny. When he came back with the drinks they all kept on laughing, but the girls were laughing at him now. He didn't know it either, but he'd find out I knew, at night's end if not before. They wouldn't go home with him. I got up then and moved to another table. I hated those girls, and I almost hated myself.

Those are the kind of girls Crazy Joe says you gotta get 'em on their knees, like you're gonna screw 'em from behind, then fuck 'em through the back door. That'll teach 'em, he says. Crazy Joe was going to go to Canada once, way up north, and live by hunting with arrows. He took archery for six months to get ready, then came to work drunk one day with a two-hundred-dollar bow in his hand. He smashed that bow to pieces on the walls of the loading dock, crying all the time. His wife had left him. The bosses almost fired him but let him come back after he sobered up. Crazy Joe's okay, he's just a little off sometimes. Three days later he was back, talking about some sixteen-year-old hitchhiker he picked up somewhere. Jim says those are the kind of women you've got to forget about. They don't do anybody any good. I like Jim, we get along all right. The first week I was working we were talking down on the docks. I was waiting for more drums to come in. He was telling me about his son. I asked how old he was and Jim said seven, and I asked when his birthday was and Jim said January 1. Hell, I said, that's *my* birthday. Okay, Jim said, his is the 2nd then. Ever since we've gotten along just fine. I get along with everybody though, more or less, except for Doyce, and I get along with him too, in an odd sort of way. The first week I came to work, Doyce caught me on Friday afternoon and told me to come in to work the next afternoon. When I drove up on Saturday there was Doyce and a few of the other guys drinking beer in the parking lot, waiting for me to show up so they could laugh. I didn't mind much, I thought it was pretty funny myself, but there was just the wrong kind of edge to Doyce's voice. We had to fight, though neither of us wanted to. We both bled a little, Doyce bled a little more than me, and ever since there's been something a little off between us. There haven't been any problems, but we don't get along real well. We both get along real well with Jim, but neither of us cares much of anything about the other. The beer we drank in the parking lot that afternoon was the only beer we ever drank together. We don't kid each other much either. Hardly at all.

Sometimes I wonder if I want too much, if I'm asking too much. I don't have a lot to offer in some ways, but I'm a good guy. I could do right by a girl. I want a girl who's not sour-mouthed, but it seems sometimes that the only girls I can get are the tight-lipped ones. We're all in the same boat. I try not to be that way myself, but sometimes I can't help it. I work hard and don't get much of anywhere, and probably won't.

What can I do? The girls that I want want better than me. The girls I can get scare me sometimes, they're so hard. What can I do? Once I was at the Cascade, sitting at a back table alone, and one of the waitresses I liked came and sat at the table behind me, on her break. Another waitress joined her. They were talking about all the lonely girls, all the lonely guys who were at the place that night. If only the guys would realize, I heard the one I liked say, that all they have to do is just go up and say hello. It's not that easy, I thought, it doesn't work like that, and you, you work here, you should know better. You should. I wanted to tell her that, I wanted to turn around and say it. She should know better. If I had turned around and said hello to her, she would have stopped me cold, I knew, because I had seen her be approached before. She wanted better. But would she have seen the point I wanted to make? No. It's not that easy, and she, she worked there, she should know better. She should.

Mostly when I come to the Cascade I come alone. Sometimes I bring a girl but not too often. I like the fact that I'm always alone, ready for anything to happen. I feel better that way. The Cascade *means* being alone, to me. Sometimes I wonder why I like the place the way I do. Watching the people, talking to the bartenders, looking at girls. It's hard to say the way I like it, the Cascade. Even when the girls say no, it's just part of the place, for me. It's the Cascade.

One time at work one of the women from the head office forgot some papers she had brought along. It was a Friday. I was caught up on the drums, so the foreman asked me to take the company car and drive her back to her motel. Usually three or four come at a time, but this time this woman had come by herself. I recognized her, she had been there before a few times. She seemed nice. On the drive over she asked me about the plant, about my job, about the people I worked with. I answered her. She picked up the papers from her room. On the drive back she asked me more about me, what I liked, what I did, where I went in town. Things like that. I mentioned the Cascade to her, said a little about it, about the music mainly. When I told her I mostly went alone, she seemed surprised. Then she asked if I might take her there. She said she would like to see the place. I didn't know what to think, whether she was kidding me or not, playing with me or not. She made a lot more money than me, but she had been friendly, so I said sure. I picked the woman up that night at her motel room, not sure how I should act. She made more money than I did by a long shot. She was smarter than I was. She was dressed too much for the Cascade. But she had a bottle in her room, and she asked me in for a drink, and she was friendly, and I started to think I might have a good time after all. She wasn't sourmouthed at all. She smiled at me. She talked to me. I didn't want her to ask about me, so I asked about her. She told me about herself. We had another drink. She had gone to school three different places, and had lived in three others. She'd been to Mexico once, and to Canada. One time she had even lived in Greece, seeing ruins and living on an island. I hadn't been anywhere. I had only seen postcards or pictures of all those places. She made three times what I did. But all the way through she was friendly to me. I even started talking to her, different from the way I usually talked to women.

On the way to the Cascade and then when we got there, she mostly asked about me. Or about the Cascade, why I went there, what I liked about it. She liked it too. She was surprised at the size, inside. It didn't look so big from outside. She didn't know much about the kind of music they played there but she said she liked it better than she would have thought. We danced a lot. We drank a lot of beers. In between dancing, I started telling her things, things I knew but hadn't ever thought much about. She seemed interested and kept on asking me more about things. I told her about my bartender friend, T. Paul, who played music and hoped some day to get in with one of the bands who played the Cascade. There were some big-name bands who played there. T. Paul nearly always got to play a few songs with the band, and they would usually let him have a little solo too. T. Paul was known. But T. Paul played flute. There wasn't much room for a full-time flute player in the bands who played the Cascade. T. Paul knew that, but I never asked him what he thought about it. He kept on working the bar and playing whenever they'd let him get up there with them. He could make that flute fit into any kind of music. T. Paul could play, he could play his flute.

I told her about the waitress I knew who made quilts and sold some of them at shows. She had even won a prize one time, or an award. I pointed out things going on in the Cascade. Nothing much, but she seemed interested. I would point out a guy going up to a girl and tell her what was going to happen, how the girl would act, stuff like that. I was always right. I pointed out people who were always at the Cascade. I told her stories about the night they did this, or that. I had her laughing. She said I must know a lot about people, but I told her I didn't know anything, that all I did was watch. Just watch. And somehow, thinking about myself watching, it made me feel funny. She noticed, and asked me what the matter was. I said nothing, tried to snap out of it. But she knew that something had happened to me. I knew it too, but there was no way for me to say what it was. She said we should go, I said sure. I didn't feel bad, I just felt funny. I was thinking about myself always watching.

I never even thought about how I was going to say good-bye to her. I was thinking about myself too much. When we got back to her room she asked me if I wanted to come in for another drink, and I said all right. I wasn't thinking about anything. The ice in the plastic bucket had melted. While she went out to get more, I stood in the middle of her motel room and looked around me. Some of her clothes lay neatly across one of the two beds in the room. Her suitcase cost a lot of money. It sat on one of the chairs in the room with the top open and lying up against the back of the chair. I had never seen a packed woman's suitcase before. The things inside looked soft to me. On the desk were the papers from her work, the ones we had driven back for. She came in then, with a bucket full of ice and a smile for me. She shut the door and fastened the chain. I wasn't thinking of anything though, nothing at all.

She poured two drinks, and sat down on the bed her clothes were on. I sat in a chair across from her. I felt my lower lip quiver then. I hadn't known it was going to. She looked at me and said if there was something I wanted to talk about, she would be glad to listen. I believed her, and wanted to talk, but I didn't know what I wanted to say. It was then I began to break. Because she had said such a simple, kind thing. I started telling her things I hadn't known to say until I said them. She seemed to understand. I was about half crying. I told her how it seemed I couldn't have even the simple things I wanted. I told her how I hated the way I felt sometimes, of not being able to do anything, or to have anything, of being always on the outside. I told her how the bosses never listened. I tried to tell her why I fought Doyce. I told her about the women at the Cascade. I was crying out loud. I couldn't stop. I tried to tell her everything, but I knew she wouldn't know the half of it. She might be friendly, be kind, but she just wouldn't know. She couldn't know. She came and put her arms around me though. She took me to her bed. I was crying out loud. I wasn't thinking about anything. I was just crying, trying to talk in between the deep breaths I had to take. I started telling her about something that had happened to me once, at the Cascade. I don't know why it came back to me then, I talked, trying to think about what I was saying. She kept saying yes, yes, and put her hands on me. I tried to tell her, and she began to take my clothes off.

I had gone to the Cascade one night, and when I got there I saw a girl who was really attractive. Before I realized what I was letting happen to me, I was telling myself that I had to have her. She was beautiful. I had never seen the girl before. She was with friends, a couple, but she was by herself. She was too good for me, I could tell. There was something about her though that I really wanted. When I see a girl like her I usually forget about it, but this girl attracted me so strongly that while her friends were dancing, I went to talk to her. She let me buy her a drink, but she didn't listen to me. When her friends came back it was like I wasn't even there. She ignored me. It's happened to me before, but it never bothers me much. This time it did, I don't know why. When I got up from her table and left, I felt that everyone in the Cascade was watching me. I went to the far end of the place and sat by myself at one of the small round tables in the back. All around me were couples talking, but I sat alone and brooded. I tried to laugh but couldn't. I tried to think but couldn't. I sat and drank beer all night. I got mad. I never moved from that table, not once. I didn't notice anything all night. A little after midnight the girl's friend came and sat at my table. When I looked up and saw her there I hated her. She told me her friend was real drunk and wanted to leave, but she and her boyfriend didn't want to leave yet. She asked me to give her friend a ride home. I hated her more. I hated her, but I said that I would. I was drunk too. The girl and I left the Cascade. She fell down twice on the way to the car. I put my arm around her to help. She was drunker than I was, and I had been drinking to brood. When she got into my car she passed out, fell right asleep. She lived a long way off. I took the long way to get there, taking streets instead of the freeway. I found myself touching her whenever I stopped for a red light. She never knew it. The closer we got to her house the bolder I got. I felt her thighs. I felt her breasts. I rubbed her crotch. I put my hand inside her knit top, rubbed her belly, her breasts. She was beginning to come out of her drunk. She touched me back, but I knew she wasn't fully awake. I would stay stopped through half a dozen light changes, touching her, rubbing her. I never kissed her. When we got to the address her friend had given me, she said it wasn't her house but her friend's. They lived in a rich part of town. She said she was too drunk yet to drive home. I said I'd take her there. She said she couldn't go home without her car, her father would not like it. She said she'd stay with me until she could drive. We sat in my car, on the street in front of a very rich house. I wanted her. No matter the way she had treated me earlier, I wanted her. I hated her too, because I wanted her like that. As she came out of her drunk, she touched me, rubbed me. She was smiling, but I knew what it meant. She was playing with me, I knew that, but I let her do it, because I wanted her so much. I was nothing to her, not anything. I felt ashamed of myself, for letting her do it. I could never touch her. She would let me do anything I wanted to her, and it wouldn't matter, because I was nothing to her. Nothing. She wasn't even seeing me, and I knew that, yet I wanted her, still. I touched her body. I took her knit top off and bent to kiss her breasts, and all she did was smile that smile. I hated her, and I hated myself, but still I took her pants off. Her smile kept on saying, you can't touch me, you could never touch me, you're nothing. And I wanted her so much that I did it, fucked her, and I hated myself after. I hated her too, and her friend who had given her to a stranger to take her home. They were careless people. And they could be as careless as they wanted, because I was nothing to them. And they knew that even I knew that. But I had wanted her, and I had fucked her, and I had hated myself after.

I told my story to the woman from Atlanta, and when I finished I was on my back in her bed. She was on top of me and moving, and I put my arms over my face, and I was yelling at her, what's the matter with me, is there anyting the matter, what is it that's the matter, what's wrong with me, and she was moving above me and saying as she moved, nothing, not anything, there's nothing the matter, nothing wrong with you, not at all, nothing.

The next day she flew back to Atlanta, and the next time she came to the plant with the others, it was as though she had never known me before, as though I had not shown her me, myself. I washed drums, and she walked by.

Laura Furman

Eldorado

The boy at the gas station was the first to notice the condition of the car. I go to that gas station because they check the oil and water whether I remember to ask them to or not, and this time the boy told me, "You're leaking oil all over the engine."

"The car's showing its age," I told him. "Put in more oil. Maybe it'll hold better this time."

That was in October. By December I had to face it. The car was taking oil every time I bought gasoline, and worse, if I tried going on the freeway—not just stop and start, but going somewhere—the engine missed. At forty-five, instead of rising into the next gear, it hesitated, then gave a burp. It could get to fifty but it didn't like it.

Christmas morning my daughter Melissa called and we had a nice talk about old times and a party she was going to that night. It was raining and dark, not the kind of day that makes you feel like doing anything. Still, it was Christmas, so I went to church, not because I'm so very religious, but it's what I'm used to doing. I keep things going in a certain way in my life. The condominium I bought when I sold the house is convenient in the way I like. I bought it when Melissa left home and I didn't need all that space to myself. Everything fits into it—the white couch and matching love seat, the flowered drapes that remind me of a bush outside my bedroom window back home. The drapes had to be hemmed and the furniture is just that much too large for the room, but you notice that only if you look closely and I'm not about to buy new furniture.

It's my first place on my own. In my parents' house I shared a room with my sister, and when my husband was alive and Melissa at home, you could call that sharing too. My daughter seems young to be on her own, yet I was only a year older when I married her father and took off, not just across the breadth of Houston but all the way here from Maryland. I don't regret that move, for a minute. If I regretted it, I'd be regretting my whole life, and then where would I be? Like so many of the ladies I see in the store, I'd be wandering, wanting something but not sure what, and when asked if I could use some help or suggestions, I could only answer that I don't know, just looking.

I'm in ladies' sportswear at Battelstein's. On my store badge I put my initials—T. C. Jefferson. I don't mind customers calling me Mrs. Jefferson, but I don't want to be called by my first name when all I've done is help match a skirt with a blouse some odd shade of blue. It's part of my liking things to look right, my being in the fashion business. When I first went to work, when Donald was alive, it was a kind of hobby. My friends call me Terry. My husband always used my full name, Teresa. He said it made him feel like he was married to a foreign woman. And I never called him Don or Donny or Donny Joe. I called him Donald from the first time we met.

When the collection plate came around I gave five dollars, five times what I usually give. I thought of when I was a little girl and the minister at home talked about the homeless and lonely, and sharing Christmas and our good fortune.

During the final hymn, I closed my eyes and tried to get a picture of myself later that Christmas Day. I saw my kitchen, and I was there, high heels kicked off, making myself a cup of soup. That's all. And to complete the picture, there was the Eldorado sitting outside my window, not shiny as it was when Donald bought it, but still the car he always wanted. He could have bought a Sedan de Ville but he said two doors were enough for the two of us. Melissa was ten then and acting as if she was already grown. He wanted it dark green, though it was a custom color and held up delivery by six weeks. If he could have seen the way dark green ages, he might have changed his mind. I can't complain about the Eldorado. I finished paying for it fourteen months after Donald died, and it was still running seven years later.

The service ended and the congregation shuffled out, and people were shaking the minister's hand. When it came to my turn, the minister covered my one hand with both of his, just the way the minister where we used to live did after Donald's funeral, and I wondered if he could look at me and see me as I saw myself, putting on my cup of soup, sore feet and all.

The Cadillac hesitated a few blocks from home, then the engine stopped. When it rains, the streets in Houston get oil-slick from the high shell content in the pavement, or so Donald always said. It's only because the Eldorado was such a good heavy car that it didn't skid all over the place. The engine started after a few minutes, and when I got home I parked the car as I always did. I lost a hubcap a few years ago so I parked with the side to the street that still showed two hubcaps. That's the side where Melissa drove too close to a wall. I don't know why she couldn't have stopped halfway, but she's always been like that. There was a deep scratch that ran from one end of the car to the other. The passenger side was perfect outside, though the carpet on that side was stained with something I could never get out. The air conditioning had been broken for years, the radio only got two stations, and there was all that oil leaking and the hesitating. Maybe it was a screw loose and maybe it was the end of the world, but I was ready to part with the Eldorado.

Inside the house, I kicked off my heels and made myself my cup of soup. I settled at the kitchen counter where I could look out the window and see the car and the woods next door where the next block of condominiums will go. The billboard across from me showed condominiums just like this bunch—your choice of French, English, or Spanish style. Usually I keep the curtains closed, but I opened them to look at the car while I had my soup, waiting for some sign that I shouldn't sell it. I'd get a small car, I thought, an economy model, and then I'd take trips in it if I found someone to go with me. Maybe I'd go to New Orleans for Mardi Gras, something I've always talked about but never done.

The next day I composed an ad for the *Greensheet* and gave it to them over the phone. I knew Donald would say the exact right way to sell a car is to get the list price and deduct for damage, but I just guessed what the market would bear. I came up with an ad that said it all: *'68 Eldorado, 93,000 Miles. Runs. $500.00.* That seemed a little spare for ninety-three thousand miles of life experience with a car, but at twenty cents a word I wasn't going to tell the whole story.

I didn't get any calls right away. The paper came out Thursday and of course I work until nine that night. I was back home early enough Thursday and Friday nights for calls, but none came. I thought maybe I hadn't seemed enthusiastic enough about the car in my ad, maybe the bare truth is less than anyone will fork over five hundred dollars for. But Saturday morning as I was leaving for work, I got a call. It was a young girl, or sounded like one, and she had a list of questions: Was it a single-owner car? How were the tires? How was the body? I told her the bad news and the good, then she asked if I'd be home in the afternoon. I told her I'd be back by six but had to leave by seven. Melissa was meeting me for dinner at a new Japanese place out on Westheimer. That was at eight but it takes forever to get anywhere now, the city's so spread out. The girl said they'd be there on time and took my address.

They drove up in an old white convertible about the same age as the Eldorado. The girl was dark-haired and on the short side, but a pleasant-looking person. He was taller with lighter hair. They were dressed alike, denim jackets, denim pants. They walked around my car and she pointed to the scratch. He crouched down to look underneath and she looked at the condominiums and the woods and the billboard. Then both of them walked up the path to my door and rang the bell.

"Hello," I said. "I'm Mrs. Jefferson."

"T. C.," said the girl.

"I beg your pardon?"

"I see on your badge," she said. "Your initials, T. C. My name's Jane and this is Jim."

"Come in," I said. "I just this minute got home from work. Didn't even take off my badge." Donald always warned me about letting strangers in the house, but I said, "Come in." I motioned for them to take a seat and they settled side by side on the white couch. I took the love seat opposite and said, "Well, if you have any questions. You can see there's some things wrong and I can warn you—it's leaking oil. All over. And the air conditioning doesn't work either." Jim made a gesture with his hand as if to say, "Air conditioning, what does that matter?" and I continued, "You can see the scratch down the side. What a shame. That car was a gift from my husband, who's dead now, a gift to both of us, really. He loved that car. The most comfortable car in America, Donald used to say."

"How long has it been leaking oil?" Jim asked.

"A few months," I answered. I could see he didn't care if Donald was alive or dead, not in an unfriendly way, just businesslike. But I saw a flicker in Jane's eyes and she looked around the room as if I'd handed her a key to me.

"And you don't know why it's leaking oil," he said.

"No. I'm thinking of buying a new car. Would you care to drive it?"

"Actually," he said, "We're waiting for our friend Bobby. We just got to Houston, you see, and I don't know anything about cars really. He's worked on Cadillacs."

I looked at my watch. "Well, I'll have to be going in half an hour. I'm meeting my daughter at a new Japanese place. Way out on Westheimer, and you can't tell about traffic." I offered them coffee, but they both declined it. To put them at ease, I asked them about themselves. "What will you do in Houston? Do you have jobs?"

"I just finished engineering school," Jim said, "and Jane's not sure what she's doing."

"That's a coincidence," I said, "because Donald was a structural engineer. That's why we came to Houston ourselves. Even years ago it was the place to come. You'll make your way here if you work hard. So many people come here. A thousand a week, the paper says, and I guess that includes children."

Jane smiled. "It's just us," she said. "We don't have any children."

"Whereabouts are you looking to live? If you're thinking of a condominium, you might as well have a look at this one. They're going up all over town." From the looks of them and from their interest in my Eldorado, I didn't suppose they had much cash, but it never hurts to be helpful.

"Sure," Jane said. "I always like looking at other people's houses."

I showed them downstairs first, not that there's much more than you can see from the couch. There's the small bedroom I always keep in case Melissa spends a night at home. They seemed to like it, and Jim said it was a nice big window for a room that size. The window lets in too much light, so I keep the curtain closed to protect the carpet and bedspread. Donald was particular about protecting furniture.

Upstairs, the first thing you see is my bed and I don't know what triggered me off, but I said, "It's my first place. I got this place for myself really. Though I keep that downstairs room for Melissa." I saw them looking at the king-size bed and the drapery I have over the cushioned bedboard. "It's the first time I've been alone," I said. "I love it. I don't think I'll ever remarry. I meet men but none of them are worth it. They want more than I have to give. I had my marriage. I respect Melissa for leaving home. I wasn't much older than she is when I left home and came all the way to the bottom of Texas with Donald. It's only healthy she's gone, young as she is."

I showed them the balcony outside the bedroom. "It's not big," I said, "but it's pleasant to sit here if it's not too hot, and this high wall protects you from the neighbors. I could sunbathe nude if I were that kind of person."

"I used to like Sunday mornings," Jane said. "When I

lived alone. It's all a question of how you like yourself, isn't it, whether you can be alone."

"It sounds right," I said, "just like living with another person you like."

"It's a good-size condominium," Jim said. "Maybe sometime we'll be able to afford one."

I took them downstairs again, but since their friend still hadn't arrived, Jane asked if they could come back in the morning. "Bobby's jogging," she said, "and he probably lost track of the time." I told them I'd be back from church by noon and they'd be welcome to bring him then.

"I like the looks of the Eldorado," Jim said. "Don't sell it to anyone but us," and he smiled for the first time.

There was a traffic jam where Westheimer meets Hillcroft, don't ask me why. I try not to get tense and angry in traffic jams the way Donald used to, so I thought about Jim and Jane doing the same thing Donald and I did years ago. There was nothing wrong with our life, nothing I can say I wish had gone one way when it went another, short of Donald dying when he did. I thought of things to say to both of them—"Don't waste your money on furniture right away," "Don't expect too much when he comes home from work. It takes it out of a man to work every day, day in, day out." I never said these things to Melissa either, and by the time traffic started moving again I was feeling sad about all the things I had to say that I probably wouldn't ever say to anyone, and if I did they would sound dumb anyway.

I say to customers in the store, "If you're not born beautiful, you have to make yourself beautiful," and most of the time they just smile and ask me if I think it looks all right, the blouse or skirt or ensemble, but some of them look startled and I realize I've said the wrong thing. They hoped they were beautiful, you see, and doubted it at the same time. So my saying that hit them just the wrong way, and I knew Jane and Jim and Melissa would think I was speaking to the wrong people, that their lives would never be like mine. The customers still buy, most of them, but that's not the point.

I got to the restaurant before Melissa and chose a table where I could see the door. It must have been a Hawaiian restaurant before it became Japanese, because it had that kind of dark carving you see at Trader Vic's over at the Shamrock. At both places they serve drinks you just know will come in plastic pineapples or coconuts. Donald and I went to Trader Vic's once and didn't think much of it.

When I'd waited twenty minutes for Melissa, I went ahead and ordered a Scotch. When Melissa didn't come after an hour and the Scotch was long gone, I could tell the waitress wanted the table. There was a line of couples out on Saturday-night dates waiting to eat, and there I was, alone, with my empty glass. I'd come all that way, I thought. I could have ordered some oysters tempura on my own, but I'd lost my appetite. I drove home and made some soup, watched the news on TV, and fell asleep. I could have watched the late movie, but it was a horror film and they always give me nightmares.

Melissa called just after eight the next morning. I knew she was really sorry, otherwise why would she be up so early on a Sunday morning? At the last minute she'd been asked out on a date and she'd tried to call me to cancel, but first my phone was busy and then there wasn't any answer. I hadn't been on the phone all afternoon—I'd been at work—but I didn't want to start an argument with her. I did remind her she could have called the restaurant, but she said they were in a movie that started at seventy-thirty. We made another date for Monday night. For Melissa to come to my house for dinner. I was looking forward to seeing Jane and Jim again. I'd thought of some real-estate people they could see about a place to live, though Jim's last remark about money made me think they couldn't afford to buy right away.

Sunday was dark and sultry, just on the edge of rain. When I got back from church there was an old red Volkswagen parked in front of my place and a young man was sitting in it. He watched me as I parked and walked up to my door, then he called out my name. He came up to me and said he was Bobby, Jim and Jane's friend, come to check out the car. I handed him the keys and told him he was welcome to drive it. "I'm starved after church," I said, "so you're on your own. That's why people go to church, you know, to work up an appetite for Sunday lunch." Bobby smiled and took the keys from me. I went inside and as I was changing from my church suit I remembered Donald always reciting that old saw about church and Sunday lunch. There were times when I knew he was going to say it, and then he did, and I thought I would lose my mind anticipating a lifetime of Sundays and that joke. But that was just part of thinking he'd be around forever. You don't marry a man expecting him to keel over from a heart attack at the age of forty-two. When Donald died I couldn't sleep for crying. The pills the doctor gave me put me out only for an hour or two. I'd wake in the morning before the light and feel so desperate. The only thing that calmed me down was to go out to the Eldorado and sit there, just as I was, in my nightgown. I didn't care who saw me sitting there behind the wheel, it was such a comfort to me. No one saw me. No one else was up at that hour. I did that for five mornings, then I felt strong enough to stop.

I decided on chicken pot pie for lunch. The oven was preheating when Bobby shut the hood, got into the car, and drove away. I waited for some feeling of regret at seeing the car go, even for a test run, but there was none. I opened the Sunday paper to the car ads, and was balancing my life between a Ford Granada and a Dodge Aspen when the Eldorado pulled up again. Bobby parked it with the wrong side showing, then came to the door. I wondered where Jim and Jane were. They'd have the energy to fix the car, and milk a few more years out of it, just running from one end of town to the other. The pie was almost ready when I let Bobby in. He accepted my offer of coffee and sat at the kitchen counter.

"It really needs work," he said. "I don't know that much about cars, but I wouldn't be surprised if it needs a valve job."

"Still, it's cheap at the price," I said. "They'll get good value if they treat it right. I know I haven't, but it isn't too late." So he wouldn't think I was giving a hard sell, I said, "By the way, before I forget, I have the names of some real-estate dealers for Jane and Jim. Are they coming soon?" Bobby looked puzzled, so I explained, "They were interested in a condominium like this one."

"I don't know about that," Bobby said. "I thought they were looking for a car that doesn't need work to get them to L.A. next week. I mean, your Eldorado has a lot of potential, but it needs a lot of work. A Cadillac's never really cheap. Parts alone."

"But they looked at this condominium," I said. "They told me it was just the one they'd want." Bobby didn't argue with me. He seemed like a nice quiet person who says what he has to say and that's the end of it. "I must have misunderstood," I said. "I guess the car is fated to live and die in Houston, just like me."

When Bobby left, I took the chicken pot pie from the oven. It had passed the point of hot and gone on to dry. I wondered why Jim and Jane had lied to me about moving to Houston and settling here. Maybe they'd lied about everything—even about being married, and him being an engineer. Why did I show them my place and tell them about Donald and me? I went to the window and looked at the Eldorado. There it sat, big and useless. If it hadn't been a Sunday, I'd have driven it to the nearest used-car lot and gotten rid of it there and then.

I telephoned Melissa, just to talk to someone who knew me, but she wasn't home—why should she have been on a Sunday afternoon? The rain that had threatened all morning started down, and since the windshield wipers on the Eldorado didn't always work, I couldn't go anywhere even if I'd had somewhere to go. I went upstairs and lay down in bed, and I tried to take comfort from the clean sheet, from knowing the blanket was the right shade of blue for my eyes. Just when it seemed I would have to get up and figure out something to do with myself, I fell asleep. I slept away the afternoon in a deep kind of trance, and woke at six with a different feeling. I didn't feel ashamed of myself, nor did I feel I'd been tricked, for I figured the thing out in my sleep. Jim and Jane hadn't really lied to me, any more than I lied to Melissa when I said to her, "You go. Cut the apron strings. I'm fine by myself." It's a luxury we have, to tell people what we'd like to be the truth of our lives, and it's the feeling behind the lies that makes them acceptable to both parties.

The next evening when Melissa was over for supper, the phone rang. A man came along an hour later and bought the Eldorado in fifteen minutes. I told him the truth about the car, but he waved it all aside. He wanted a car for his son to fix up, he said, so his boy could learn the value of making things work.

David Hall

The Smell in Bertha's House

When Bertha Stocker heard the wolf whistle ringing up from behind her, she didn't even have to turn her head to see who it was but pictured the tall gaunt old man grinning from the porch of the Colonial Estates rest home. She stiffened and walked on, wondering what John would have said if he were still alive.

Bertha shuddered, her heavy make-up burning like a mustard plaster. Fifteen years ago, or maybe twenty, she needed very little of the muddy coating that smothered her face now. Even that short time ago, her eyes had been like cat-eye marbles—or so John had said—and her skin had been like milk. Ah, but so long ago. Now, she knew, her face was lined by miles and miles of wrinkles, like the network of trenches that John said ran all over France during the war. She sometimes felt that way—like a war-torn country, and the deep wrinkles, like abandoned trenches, were only the last lifeless stage of defeat. She lifted her head and stared at the sidewalk a block ahead of her, half shutting out the vulgar whistle, half turning her head to catch it.

Behind her the old man leaned out over the porch railing. Laying a hand on his brow, he watched her quicken her steps on the other side of the street. He smiled, the lips peeling back from yellow teeth.

"Bertha!" he called in a cracked voice. "You're gonna drown if it rains! Better get your nose down!" He chuckled, his sunken eyes glittering for a moment. "I'll be down to see you soon, you sweet thing! You can't run away from me forever!" The man, who was simply called Playboy—for reasons long since forgotten by all but a vanishing few, smiled as he watched the proud old lady counting her steps. "I'll be down to see you soon, honey!" he yelled. "Put the tea kettle on and set me a place!" After a while, Playboy stopped squinting and sat back in his wicker rocker and fingered the bright red suspenders that held up his baggy pants. He sat and smiled and rocked and let his dreamy gaze fall upon Bell Arbor Boulevard.

Once the street had been the pride of the town, had hosted dozens of fine mansions and had seen hundreds of pampered children grow up and move away, taking the money with them. Colonial Estates itself had been among the finest. Now it housed the elderly, some of whom had once ridden in splendor over the old boulevard and had once puttered idly in the big gardens that stretched out from the mansions, where black gardeners had once pruned and clipped magically and rich life had sprung up from the rich earth. But the old people who still lived on Bell Arbor knew they were the last. Every day brought more and more contractors to look over the old houses, and each day's mail brought new offers for the crumbling mansions, each one lower and more insulting than the previous. Soon Bell Arbor would be blacktopped, and flimsy apartments would rise over the glory of the past, over the trails and tracks of the rich and the grand. And the Reynoldses, the Tanningtons, and Stockers—all would be forgotten. They had only to lift a corner of their dusty blinds to see the future in one hellish place—Colonial Estates. The old house sent chills down stiff and crooked spines all along Bell Arbor. An unsuspecting passerby, hearing the muffled tinkling of neglected chandeliers and seeing the old people jerking about like wound-up dolls in the windows and on the wide porch, might be reminded of a giant's grotesque music box, the tinkling sound keeping in motion a host of rusty mechanical figures.

One glance was enough on this day to remind Bertha Stocker that she was alone in the world and that, should her meager savings run out before her meager life, she, too, would pass her last days in such a house of the dead and dying. In the doddering steps of the inmates, Bertha saw her own impending and sorrowful trip through mindless senility to a pauper's grave. She couldn't bear to look into the faces she saw on the big porch, faces she once had smiled at across a crowded dance floor at the elegant country club. And in the old house itself, Bertha often saw herself, too—sterilized against germs and cheaply painted, doused nightly with a dozen useless and foul-smelling tonics, filled with bottle after bottle of pills and capsules, finally rouged and powdered at dawn to sit and stare blankly at Bell Arbor and curse the smell that clung to the very walls of her creaking house like mildew. Human mildew, she often thought.

Once inside her own yard, the whistle still ringing ominously in her ears, Bertha stooped to pick up the afternoon paper. She felt a few dull thuds in her chest and a series of dull pains in her back, and it saddened her. Exercise, he had insisted upon. Just like he had insisted on the paper, to the point of buying a lifetime subscription, and which Bertha now collected daily from the lawn and deposited in a trash can by the back door. In the eleven years since her husband's death, Bertha had begun to realize that a lot of what she had thought of as "ours" really was "his."

Sometimes it almost overwhelmed her to think how much of her life she had given up to him. It wasn't that she resented the efficient way he had run both their lives—it was just that now her own was so empty. Theirs had been the kind of marriage that called for the weaker, the more passive, to die first. And there had never been even the shadow of a doubt that John would outlive her by many prosperous years. Then one day he had dropped dead at a city council meeting and Bertha was left with a teenage daughter and a tottering old house, a surprisingly large stack of unpaid bills, and a life that seemed to stretch before her like a desert.

The newspaper was a constant reminder. Bertha could not once stoop to pick up the thing from the overgrown grass without remembering how her husband had hungrily devoured each and every page and had insisted on reading at least half of them to her as she sat and read her ladies magazine or mended his sock. These days she often thought of herself as a child whose beloved teacher and parent and guardian had suddenly moved away and left her lost and afraid. He taught, she mused to herself this day, but he never let me learn.

On the porch Bertha paused to give her knees a rest. She was not a big woman, but lately her joints had begun to ache.

"You don't get enough exercise," Dr. Charlie Mason had told her at her last checkup, the same checkup at which he had told her he wanted to run an electrocardiogram on her heart soon.

"My heart's much too weak for that sort of thing," she had told him. Charlie had been a friend in the days when they had all been young and happy.

"At least you've kept your sense of humor, Bertha," he had said, shaking his head.

"It doesn't make very good company, Charlie." Dr. Mason was the only person Bertha ever confided in anymore. He was sixty-four but looked ten years younger. And twenty younger than me, she always reminded herself. It was hard to imagine Charlie retiring in less than a year. Such a handsome man. And such a married one. The fact that Charlie had remarried after his wife had died four years before—and to a woman thirty years younger—was sadly pointed out to Bertha every time she saw the gaudy gold ring on his left hand, with its popeyed diamonds that stared like blind eyes at her. She felt sure the silly young wife had picked it out. Charlie would have better taste.

"You let your life be too much ruled by John, Bertha. It's hard to believe you didn't know him any better than you—"

"Should I have had affairs, Charlie? Lined up a few things for my old age?"

"You needn't try to shock me, Bertha," he had told her patiently—too patiently, she had thought—"I told you even then, when I saw John start running around like he did, I told you that you needed to develop a few healthy masculine friendships to give yourself some hope of support in case—"

"In case John left me."

"I hate to see you this way, Bertha . . ."

"Ah, Charlie, John was wild, but he was a good man. He was always so good with the baby. And then when she grew up a little, he was the perfect father."

The doctor had looked at her hard, his old anger and outrage barely contained in the level voice. "That's only half the job, Bertha."

Bertha had felt suddenly very tired. "All right, Charlie, let's not drag out old corpses. I'm not as stupid as you think."

"I never said you were stupid," the doctor had muttered. The conversation, Bertha had known from experience, was over at that point. While she finished dressing, she had listened to him growling about sonsofbitches who do this and that, while in her own mind Charlie's ring and the sound of Playboy's whistle continued to blend to a degree that astonished her more and more as time went on. John, John, she had thought, why did you leave me this way?

When Bertha reached the front door on this day, she suddenly remembered the smell. Each time she stood with her hand on the knob this way, she tried to recall it clearly, but something about it resisted the effort. It was indistinct, a great hovering mass that would envelop her when she walked inside and almost leave her ill. She had never noticed it until her grandson had pointed it out. And now it wouldn't go away.

Bertha's daughter rarely brought the boy to see his grandmother, and Bertha saw through all the feeble excuses Sharon contrived—the house and the lonely old lady were simply too depressing for a sensitive boy of eight. And besides, Sharon was having her own problems. She was divorced, and the husband never came to see his only son, never sent any money, never gave either of them any indication he even existed anymore. Sharon always went to great lengths to cover up the obvious, though; and while Bertha was not actually heartbroken, was almost past such selfish emotion, it saddened her to think that her daughter had grown so bitter and small.

"Fifty miles is a long drive in that old car," she had said

the last time she came, several months before. "Everything is starting to go wrong with it now, and I'm afraid I really don't know anything about cars. I just don't want to be stranded a long way from home, that's all."

"I understand, " Bertha had said as they sat in the big dark living room, under the pale glow of lamplight, each trying to think of something to say to the other, while the ghost of John Stocker made the room echo like an empty theater.

"You really should get that light fixed, Mother," Sharon had said at last, just when the silence threatened to turn them both to statues. "You can barely see your hand in front of your face."

Bertha had glanced up at the huge blackened globe on the faded, rain-splotched ceiling. "It's been out almost four years now," she said. And this is the first time you've noticed? Quickly she reprimanded herself. Dear God, how small we are getting. "Your father was the only one who could get up the nerve to climb up there and change it. The ceiling is almost fifteen feet high, you know."

Sharon had shivered. "Yes, I know. You should have mentioned it to Bill when we were here last time." Sharon still talked of her ex-husband as if he were only away on a trip. And do I do any different? Bertha had to remind herself. John, John, sometimes I wish it could all be over.

They had sat in silence a while, Sharon looking around occasionally as if she were afraid her son had vanished into a dark hole somewhere in the old house. After an eternity in the vacuum of the big room, mother and daughter had heard the child approaching through the front hallway. Slouching under the heavy strain of childish boredom, Roger had made his way to the couch and flopped down.

"I wanta go home."

Sharon had whispered something to the frowning boy. Bertha assumed it was assurance they would leave in a very short while. But the frown had deepened. Suddenly, Roger sat up and stared around at the huge crumbling walls.

"You know what this place smells like?" When no one answered, Bertha sitting politely to hear the boy out, Sharon shaking her head vigorously as if she knew what was coming, he continued. "It smells like an old folks home." He spat the words out disgustedly. Then he got up and slouched out the door to the front yard.

It took Sharon several seconds to get to her feet. "Roger, you come back here and apologize to your grandmother!" She ran to the door. "Come in here, young man! Right this minute!"

Bertha couldn't help thinking that her daughter had chanced, however embarrassingly, upon a lucky excuse to make her escape. She wasn't surprised when Sharon turned to her, genuinely red and stammering.

"Mother, I'm sorry. We're going to have to leave. I don't know what made him say a thing like that." Her lip had quivered. "It's been so hard not having a—"

Bertha had put her arm around her daughter's shoulders and kissed her cheek. "He's only a child, honey. And I know it's been hard. He's a good boy. He just needs time to adjust. It's only been a year. Don't worry about it."

Bertha stood now on the porch thinking of the smell. Growing old in Fenley was not the same, she suspected, as growing old in Sun City and all those other places rich people congregate in the magazines and on TV. Fenley, she had heard all her life when it didn't matter and had been only a funny thing to say, was a good place to do two things in: be born and die. Anything between was lost time. And now she was beginning to realize it was not even a good place to die. With little money, old people tended to vegetate. The daily walk to the A&P that had become a ritual with Bertha was also an ordeal—passing all the lonely old houses where so many parties had lit up so many summer evenings decades ago. And yet the walk was the only thing that saved Bertha's day from complete and utter nothingness. And only lately had she begun to realize what it was about the walk that gave life to the day—the brassy whistle that assaulted her as she passed Colonial Estates. At first, when she had begun to see this, it had shocked her, and she had quit taking the walk. After several days, though, the deathly quiet of the house and the awful smell buried in its walls had driven her nearly to despair. She had resumed the walks, making it a point of honor and pride to walk on the far side of the street and not to turn her head too far when the whistle came. And it always came.

Bertha drew in her breath and opened the door. The sprays and incense candles had done little good. A waste of her Social Security check. Even holding her breath, Bertha was aware of the odor, as if it had substance. Long hours she had spent trying to track it down. Perhaps the cellar. Or the attic. She had scoured the whole house. And then came the deodorizers. Nothing worked. Bertha had sniffed her way through the house over and over, but it was in no particular room. It only came on her, damp and evil-smelling, when she opened the door again after having stepped out for fresh air. And yet she couldn't sit in the house. She felt the noxious cloud all around her when she did, even when she had sat for a while and could no longer smell it. I don't want to become accustomed to it, she told herself. Dear God, not that.

"It's a terrible smell, Charlie," she had said not long ago to the doctor. "I've almost stopped going outside altogether because it's so bad when I come back in."

"It's your imagination," Charlie had said.

"Charlie," she had said, raising her hand, "imagination is for the young. The house stinks and we both know why." She had smiled and patted his arm. "Yours is a new house, and you have a young wife and people coming to see you all the time. Sit alone for a while and let the house grow old around you. It's age, Charlie, nothing but old age. But what a terrible thing it is." She paused and leaned closer. "What worries me is that maybe it's in me, too, that people can smell it when I go to the store. I don't want to ruin anyone's supper."

"That's damned ridiculous, Bertha. And it's not funny at all. You're lonely, that's all."

"That's all?" Bertha had said, chuckling sadly. "Thank goodness it's nothing serious."

The doctor had looked at her for a long time. "Bertha, don't you have any friends left from the old days?"

Bertha thought a moment. "Playboy whistles at me."

The doctor put away the golf club he'd been inspecting and frowned. "That's not what I meant and you know it."

Bertha smiled. "Oh, I don't know, Charlie. He used to be considered quite the gay blade. In fact, you and John and Playboy made a memorable trio, as I recall."

The doctor had shifted uncomfortably and reached under his desk to get his golf shoes. "Yes, well, his mind is going now."

"His mind and his money," Bertha had said quietly.

Bertha walked through the massive living room, still holding her breath, her mail in her hand. She went on through the parlor and into the kitchen, where the light was strong enough to read by.

"Hello!" she called as she entered the kitchen. Why she did it, how the habit started, she couldn't remember. The word echoed briefly, then died away into the recesses of the house. His mind is going, she thought. Isn't that what they always say?

The first letter was from the gas company. A bill. Nineteen dollars and forty-four cents. When John was alive, the bill was never more than ten dollars, even in the dead of winter. And now it was barely October. Sharon's husband had told her once that she must have a leak but that had been the end of that. He had left Sharon and his son a week later. Bertha didn't think it was a leak, anyway. She knew Mrs. Jonas next door got the same exorbitant bills. In fact, Mrs. Jonas' bills were often twenty dollars and more. Mrs. Jonas, an invalid living in a single room of her enormous house. The worse off you are, Bertha had come to think, the more they take you for. She was fairly certain that if she were to slip one day on the steps and break her hip, her gas bill would jump accordingly. The city, it seemed, knew exactly who was likely to cause trouble and who was not. John wouldn't have stood it for a minute.

Bertha put aside the bill and opened the next envelope. It was a letter from her daughter. A note, actually. Sharon never wrote more than a paragraph. She always started, "Just a note to let you know . . .''

Dear Mother,

Just a note to let you know we won't be coming to see you this weekend as we'd planned. The car is on the blink and Roger and I don't know a sparkplug from a drainplug (ha ha).

Ha ha to you too, dear, Bertha thought. Oh, what am I becoming?

How are you? Well, I must run. Eddie is coming to dinner tonight. A lot to do.

Love, Sharon

Eddie. Bertha had never heard of him. Her eyes turned to the living room, where, in the dim shadows, the picture of her husband sat, barely visible, on the yellowing mantel. Through the dark parlor, she could see him smugly sitting on his perch, passively surveying the ruins. You wouldn't have liked this Eddie, would you, John? He's probably young and smart-alecky . . . just like you were back then. Bertha recalled how vehemently her husband, coming into his middle years, had distrusted and despised young men. But wasn't that natural? Ah, we could have had such a fine old age. He would have settled down as time went on. She smiled as she squinted through the shadows at the handsome, brooding man in the gray sharkskin suit and the bold dark moustache sitting high atop her mantelpiece. She felt a dull throbbing start again in her chest. It rose from somewhere deep inside every time she went for a walk. At first, she had ignored it, but lately it had begun to take her breath away. She had mentioned it to Mrs. Jonas not long ago when she had gone about her daily good deed of taking the old lady her mail.

"You're on the road to an attack, Bertha." Mrs. Jonas had lifted her head an inch from the pillow to be sure she was heard. "That's just how mine started. All of them."

Bertha had looked for a long time at the tiny shrunken

creature, sitting for a while even after the old lady had fallen asleep. Then she had gone back home. She hadn't been back for a week now and felt guilty because she knew how dearly Mrs. Jonas, stranded sick and alone thousands of miles from her nearest kin, loved her mail. Bertha felt certain that one day soon they would come in an ambulance and take Mrs. Jonas' body away, lifting it from the worn carpet in the front hall where she had been making her slow and painful way to the mailbox on the porch. I'll go over there tomorrow, Bertha told herself. Right after the checkup. And the electrocardiogram. Right after Charlie finishes shaking his head over my heart and thinking about his young wife and his golf game. I'll go. Until the examination is over I can't bear to look at the poor thing. It's too much like watching someone die in a mirror.

Bertha was breathing easier now, the pain having subsided. She thought of her appointment with Charlie Mason. She wondered if her appointments weren't sometimes made more out of a need to see another person than a need to see a doctor. There really wasn't anything the electrocardiogram could tell her that she wanted to hear . . . no matter what the results. In old age, she had come to believe, loneliness is a more powerful force than concern for one's health. She thought of all the waiting rooms around the world filled with old people. It is not that they—that I—are hypochondriacs but that paid friends are better than no friends at all. The pain was starting again, small this time but definitely there. Is it in my head? she always asked herself. And she always knew the answer. Like the smell, the pain was real. She knew, too, that she would not keep the appointment.

The last letter was from Mr. Harris of the construction company. Bertha dropped it in the trash without opening it. She stood up and gazed out the little chest-high window with its sickly yellow curtains to the flat plot of raw earth across the street. A grader was at work where Mrs. Bloomer's house had stood only a week ago. The letter would contain another offer for the house into which John Stocker, tall and charming and ambitious, had carried her forty years before, and this time it would be a little lower. Wasn't property supposed to appreciate with time? Bertha thought of all the silly TV shows she had seen—before the TV had gone blank a year ago—where the old ladies, feisty to the end, barricaded themselves in their delapidated houses and shot at the bulldozers with ancient muskets or shotguns. Bertha knew that when the time came at last to put her out, there would be no heroics, no valiant stand. She was too tired. Bertha knew she would be just one more piece of dead lumber to tunnel under.

Ah John, my husband. She stared at the dark picture two rooms away. What kind of old man would you have made? How would these eleven years have been different? She shook her head and looked at the picture a little resentfully, envying the man his eternal good looks and health. He had been such an attractive man. And the times—hadn't they had the times? Hadn't they been the darlings of Bell Arbor? Or had it been just John who was the darling? John, John, she thought sadly, I am such a wreck.

Bertha turned back to the window for a moment. She had trouble keeping her mind on things these days. She pictured Mrs. Jonas babbling sometimes as if the room were filled with lively friends, often going on and on even after Bertha had left. She closed her eyes and listened to the throbbing of her heart.

"Time to make tea," she said loudly to ward off the pain. It helped a little. Maybe it really is in my head, she thought. But Bertha knew that her ritual was nothing more than a last-ditch attempt at mind over matter, that she was like the dying man who jerks and writhes to keep away the vultures, knowing all the while they are patient and infinitely hungry. She began making the tea.

The phone rang just as the tea was coming to a boil.

Bertha made her way slowly to the parlor. Who? No one had called for weeks. Mrs. Jonas had no phone. They had come and taken it out. Sharon wouldn't call unless something terrible had happened. Then suddenly Bertha remembered the other caller. Her chest ached as she recalled the low, breathy voice and the frightful things he'd said. Do you see,

John, what is happening to me? She picked up the receiver on the fourth ring. Maybe it was just a wrong number. Maybe they would hang up. Phones. Just one more little torture. Bertha held the receiver nervously to her ear, trying to prepare herself for the gruesome low laugh, the raspy breathing, preparing to hang up and stand by the table, fighting the blaze of pain that would consume her chest.

"Hello, Mrs. Stocker?" said the woman after Bertha had spoken. "This is Jane Mecker, Dr. Mason's receptionist . . ."

Bertha's knees went weak with relief. "If you're calling about my appointment. . . ." If you're calling about my appointment—what? What could she say? That she didn't want to know?

"Well," the voice interrupted, "I am calling about your appointment, but I'm afraid I have some bad news. Dr. Mason has had a heart attack. We're naturally cancelling all his appointments."

Bertha listened to the woman for another minute or so, aware only of a voice, scattered words, a sense that the last stop had been pulled out and a great flood was washing over her. She sat down and looked at the receiver, hearing the distant buzzing that meant no one was there. Did I imagine the phone call? She hung up and put a hand over her heart, where the pain was flashing like a busy signal. The parlor where she sat seemed to grow smaller, the faded green carpet reaching up to grab at her ankles, the ancient fading red wallpaper peeling away from the wall, reaching down to cover her, the acres of swollen white carnations embedded in the paper looming closer and closer, as if the walls themselves were toppling onto her. She shut her eyes and saw the doctor as the woman had described him, trying to imagine him lying on the manicured green, his putter flung far away, the tiny cleats of his golf shoes tearing and digging at the velvet grass, lying blue and gasping while his gaping friends tried to loosen his trousers, while his stupid young wife sat miles away inside her new house, gazing raptly at soap operas.

Tears came to her eyes for the first time since John had died, and she opened them to erase the monstrous scene of her last friend and support jerking his life away on the grass of the elegant country club golf course.

Slowly, Bertha became aware of the tea kettle whistling from the kitchen. After a long time, she rose and walked, as if in a trance, to the hutch against the wall and took out two cups and set them meticulously on the mahogany coffee table in the parlor. Very carefully she set the steaming tea kettle between them. Instead of sitting down, Bertha walked around the table, straightening the cups and placing and re-placing the little silver spoons and the containers of sugar and cream and lemon. Then she stood back and, without a trace of expression on her face, looked at the arrangement.

When everything seemed in order she walked to the big picture window. A block up the street, on the other side, Bertha could see Colonial Estates. Squinting in the late after-noon light that struggled in through the dingy glass, she tried to make out the figures on the wide front porch. At last she saw him, saw the red suspenders. He was leaning out over the porch railing, as he always was at this time of the day, his white hair slicked back immaculately, a slightly wild look in his eyes at this distance, craning his head around to see her house.

In a small voice, barely audible even to herself, Bertha murmured through the window, "Tea is ready." After a while, she saw the tall, slender figure drop back into a wicker rocker. Still, she kept her eyes pinched against the light. She sensed a pounding in her chest and felt the eyes of the picture in the next room at her back, outraged and damning. I am sorry, she said to the picture without turning around, without ut-tering a sound. Tears gathered in her eyes again and Bertha made no motion to wipe them away, letting them fall in-stead over the rouge caked on her cheeks. I am truly sorry, she said silently, sensing no forgiveness in the strong unseen face. But this, my husband, is something you would never understand. Bertha felt a scream rising in her throat and choked it back. You didn't leave me anything, John. Dear God, you didn't even leave me myself.

When her eyes were again clear, Bertha saw that the figures all were gone from the porch down the street. Called in, no doubt, for supper. Or a nap. As she sat drinking her tea, she dabbed at the smeared makeup on her cheeks. We get so foolish, she thought, so sad and so foolish, like children on a rainy day. Bertha sipped her tea slowly and kept her eyes on the steaming cup, away from the window with its dusty fog of dying light, away from the picture with its ageless piercing eyes.

Beverly Lowry

So Far from the Road, So Long until Morning

She has stood at this window she cannot imagine how many nights, in the darkness counting cars. Up on FM 190 a huge RV goes by. *One.* She is going to *five* this time. After three more he will come home. After the fourth car passes the Grand Prix will turn in. The night will start to wind down and Roselle can go to bed. *Two's* headlights make a double ribbon through the night. *Three* crawls by and close on its tail, *four.* You wouldn't think there would be such heavy traffic this time of night. Roselle holds her breath. The night is so dark in the country. With no streetlights and nothing left blinking, the air turns to solid blackness, like something soft and slippery which if you gave it half a chance would wrap around your face and smother you in a second. Only the headlights break the night apart and, off in the distance, the glow of the lights of the job corps center where kids go who have no other hope. *Five* is coming. Roselle keeps her eyes glued to the road. It's coming fast. It's not them. There are yellow foglights. A towtruck. He has broken her heart in more ways than she would have thought possible. *Come Home*, she says to the window. *Please.*

The floor is cold. Roselle stands with the sole of one foot across the arch of the other. The realtor said a wood floor with parquet tiles was special but they don't have rugs and she is used to wall-to-wall and why would somebody build a new house with old and hard-to-keep stuff in it anyway. A new trend, the realtor said. It didn't make sense, building a new house to look old. And not just old. Old's one thing if you're talking about English Tudor, but this one was tacky, a tarpaper shack but fancy. American farmhouse, the realtor called it. American Poor, Roselle said to herself.

She can hear Londale snore all the way from here. She slipped out of bed inch by inch so he wouldn't know, then took her time getting down the stairs in a quiet creep. The dogs are sniffing at the door and wagging their tails, wondering why Roselle is downstairs at this time of night again, at the front window still as a post. The front door has an oval pane of glass in it, beveled at the edge, with a scrolling flower design in the middle made of frosted glass you can't see through. Like a door to a church. Or maybe an Old West bar.

A big truck goes by, loud, taking charge of the night. Sometimes she can hear the trucks changing gears from their bedroom. Diesels take the back farm-to-market roads to skip the troopers. She talked to a driver once whose truck had broken down. He was carrying bananas. He needed to move on quickly, he said; he was traveling 3,000 pounds overweight. When they said overweight, Roselle never dreamed they meant so many. A lowslung sedan swerves from one side of the road to the other. Probably a lowrider, drunk. Lowriders are everywhere around here, so are drunks.

Sometime she feels like Elizabeth Taylor in *Giant* when Liz first got to the ranch and stood on the porch looking out, thinking Oh My God. There are 15 acres of land between their front porch and FM 190. The 15 acres are planted in maize and so naturally the land is flat with no trees. And with the house set back so far it gives a person a funny feeling to stand there, lonely as anything. The maize is not theirs but neither is the house. She and Londale have a one-year lease. Somebody else plants the maize.

Not really like Elizabeth Taylor. A flea-scaled version of *Giant*, 15 acres instead of who-knows how many.

Maybe she was using too low a number. Maybe six will do it. Not the sixth car, six and then the Grand Prix. Their driveway goes by the maize field up to the road. When the Grand Prix comes she will see a car slow down, the lefthand blinker come on, the lights swing around toward the house. Roselle waits for *one*. Somehow it feels like counting cars helps the right one to get there. That doesn't make sense but still. It gives her something to do to help keep her hopes up and make the night pass.

A big car speeds past. *One.* Toward the cemetery. The ones going back don't count. The cemetery and then Martindale. Prairie Lea, Luling, Flatonia. Shulenberg, Columbus. Eventually, Houston.

They had thought the move would be good for the boy. That wasn't the only reason they moved but it was one. He had been getting in a lot of trouble in the city. He had been talking about getting out for a long time, having a dog, going hunting, riding a horse. And since Londale had grown up in the country he knew things to teach the boy. The boy could be a help in his new business, Londale said. He would teach him to drive. Which he did. The boy learned nothing. Great ideas, no payoff. Londale looks ready to explode. There is a vein on his temple that stands out like a baby snake crawling into his hair. He chews Rolaids like candy. If his new business doesn't pan out, then no telling.

Two. Three. They always bunch up that way. And there is always the hope she is wrong, that one of the counting cars will be the Grand Prix and she will not have to wait until *six* goes by.

The maize is headed out. It used to be a golden yellow corn color. It has turned now to a smoky burnt brown. It's nice either color. Roselle has watched it change. Londale said the maize would be gone soon, which is hard to feature. The maize has been there since they have.

Four. A small car, bug or something like a bug. *Five* is another diesel, lit up like Christmas with colored lights turning up and down the grille and over the cab and across the trailer. From seeing the Burt Reynolds movies the boy wants to be a diesel truck driver. Or he did, before Londale got the trucks. Which might queer the deal of that ambition in a New York minute.

Tonight they blew. Dinner was on the table, only bites gone. A good meal, chicken, potatoes, salad. Not fried chicken. From working for Kentucky Fried all those years

Londale says the last thing on earth he wants is another piece of fried chicken. For dessert Roselle fixed oatmeal cookies, half with raisins, half without. They started a safe conversation, filling their plates, talking about football. They all three follow the pros, especially the Oilers. Londale and the boy make bets. They started to eat, more football. And then she felt the conversation change, a dark cloud start to boil up underneath what they were saying. She knew it was happening and that it was going to get worse but there was nothing to do once it started but let it steamroller on.

Londale got off on Earl Campbell and whether he would have a good year or not and how it would be if the Oilers traded him. The boy said Earl was overrated and Londale blew. How in the world, Londale said, such a smartass know-it-all if he knew so much, could be managing to fail Driver's Education when he already knew how to drive a car, was beyond him. That was it. They both blew. Only bites gone. And then they were gone, stormed off to their rooms leaving Roselle at the table with the food. Roselle went ahead and ate, even though her throat was closing up. But she'd cooked it and they hadn't. It was easier for them. After a while the boy came back, asked which cookies didn't have raisins, took a handful and some milk and went back to his room. Londale went to bed without eating.

One boy, a man, her. Even though she is the boy's own mother and she and Londale have been married only six months, still and all in a lot of ways Londale and the boy understand one another better than she does either one of them. She thinks she is the outsider, making cookies, making peace, even though Londale says he is, and the boy does too. Maybe they are all three outsiders. Outsiders from each other thinking they're a family.

"I feel like a third thumb," Londale said the other night. Sometimes he says, "The boy wants you, Roselle. He wants me dead and gone and you to himself."

Londale has only a few things to say about the boy and he says those things all the time, repeating and repeating himself until Roselle can tell which one he is about to say by a certain look he gets.

Six. The next car is bound to be the one. When Mondo and Angel bring her boy home, she will sneak back to bed, take off her robe and crawl back into bed the same way she got out, inch by careful inch. Not a sound in the house. Only Londale's snores. And her own quick breath.

The next car is a pickup. The lights from the job corps center look like oil refinery lights. They make the sky over there turn orange, like a constant sunset. Sometimes the job corps center kids run away. She sees them on the highway wearing bandannas and carrying stereo machines, hitching rides. Roselle has no telephone number to call. All her boy's friends are Mexican. Mondo's parents don't speak English. And Angel doesn't have a phone. She doesn't even know Angel's last name. Sierra? Rivera? Gomez?

The house looks like a hat. It is an exactly square house built flat down on the flat ground on a concrete slab, just all the way down there. The slab extends from the house on all sides making a flat and useless excuse for a porch with posts at the corners to hold the roof up over it. There is a second story crammed down close to the first floor with only two windows so that from the road you can't tell it's there. The roof of the house is pitched steep and high to accommodate the second story, so the house is like an ordinary share-cropper's shack only fancy, with a pointy roof, made out of, of all things, tin. Roselle never thought she'd see the day when she lived in a house with a tin roof.

"It looks like a hat," Roselle told the realtor when he told her that about American Farmhouse. "Like a farmer's hat thrown down on the ground."

A man designed the house himself, after the house he grew up in, for memory's sake, thinking of his mother. The man and his wife had the house built, moved in, stayed less than a month then separated, left Texas altogether. They couldn't agree on a settlement and so they decided in the meantime to lease. Roselle and Londale came to see it the very day it went up for lease. Londale liked the idea of being out from town. The lease was good and there was plenty of room for his new trucks and so they took it.

They are not in the real country, only five miles from town. But when you have lived in the city all your life, being without neighbors and curbs and garbage pickup is country enough. This black, black, pitch black night.

Everything in the house is brand new and everything is fancy. Chandeliers, a wet bar, a fireplace with glass doors. But every room is a tiny square box with one regular-sized door and so once you're inside, you feel stuck. If anybody else comes in, it's crowded. And there are funny leftover spaces which have been turned into halls and useless closets. Probably space the husband had left over which he didn't know what to do with and on paper it just looked like maybe a half inch here or there. The wooden cabinets in the kitchen are impossible to keep. And with all that white for a background. The realtor said white was very popular, as if popular was the main thing. Roselle always thought a kitchen was supposed to be yellow.

Outside the house is nothing, no shrubs or flowers or trees, no sidewalk, no garage, no nothing. Just the hatshaped house out on that flat piece of ground. When the maize is gone the house will look like a deserted orphan for sure.

When a car comes down the driveway, headlights flash across the bedroom ceiling. Roselle lies flat on her back in the bed with her arms by her side, waiting again. When the lights flash the car is nearly to the house. There are all kinds of signs she has learned to watch for, tokens of hope to hang onto. She wishes Angel and Mondo were not Mexican. Londale says she is looking for anything to blame to get her boy off the hook, the fact for instance that his friends are Mexican, but Roselle doesn't think that is so. She is not prejudiced; in Houston she worked with black people all the time, also some of the Vietnamese and Arabs who were flatly taking that city over as far as low-to-middling paying jobs were concerned. She would take black people over the rest of them any day. Black and white people are just about the same in most ways. Mexicans are different, like Arabs, giving you that look, going off in their own language when it suits them. Angel and Mondo doing their rat-a-tat. Like she didn't know.

She watches the ceiling for headlights. She lives a lot of her life in this kind of expectation, one foot and then the other, waiting for the next thing to happen. After the flash of light she will hear tires in the gravel, the loud radio playing rock and roll, the car door, some quick goodbyes, the front door. The boy will go to the bathroom, stay a long time, then to his room. And that will be that for one more night, Roselle can sleep, the night will be over.

It happens, happens. Over and over the same thing. She keeps letting herself be fooled, thinking things are different, better, it won't happen again. She keeps finding ways to think things are getting better. But they aren't. Nothing's getting better, it's only going on. And what Roselle is afraid of is how it will all turn out. When you watch a movie you have a certain feeling somewhere along about the middle, how it's going to end. She hates to think how she would be feeling if she was watching this one.

Roselle would like to sit up, check the clock, decide how worried she should be by what time it is. But if she moves she may wake up Londale. And Londale might get up and go after the boy, riding around town looking for the Grand Prix. And there will be all that stormy uproar. The last time she looked it was after one.

Londale sleeps deep, does not dream. Roselle's is fitful and she dreams all the time. Not only dreams, remembers. The boy dies in her dreams, over and over. Real deaths. She has to go to the morgue and identify his body, there are other dead bodies all over, laid out on tables. Somebody pulls back a sheet and there he is, dead as dead. She wakes up with her heart feeling like an empty hole in her chest.

The house creaks. Londale says in the winter the north

wind is going to blow free and clear across the maize fields and freeze the house to a chunk of ice. He says their feet will be like icicles all winter long.

She and Londale sleep close, him in his underpants, Roselle in hers. Roselle doesn't mind, although at first it made her feel funny. She had always worn nightgowns. Londale asked. He likes to have a breast to hold onto while he sleeps. Roselle moves her head up the tiniest bit off the pillow. Her neck muscles quiver. The clock is a digital radio alarm with green numbers. Londale sleeps with the numbers in his face, Roselle can't imagine how. Two thirty-two. She hates digitals, knowing the time down to the exact minute and the way it passes not in a circle but a row. The boy is supposed to have been in by 12. It's a Thursday, a school night, he is failing every subject. Sometimes Roselle changes time around. Sometimes she lies in the bed and thinks hard enough that it's a different time from what it is, that she starts to believe in herself and when the boy comes in, he is not late at all.

She eases her head back down, keeping Londale's shoulders between her and the clock numbers. If she only knew what to be afraid of. Night. Cars. Mexicans. Drugs. Broken bones, a smashed face, the criminal life. So many things. And the nights last so long, lying in the pitch black country dark waiting for time to go on by. Will nights ever be for sleeping again?

The Mexicans are smaller than her boy by a lot, Mondo especially. Most of them are fully developed by the ninth grade but small, like miniature grownups. Angel is the quiet one. Angel may even be smart but no one will know, with those nervous eyes. No one will ever trust Angel. It's Mondo who has the Grand Prix. Not him actually, his parents. It's the family car, which Mondo seems to get anytime he wants. Mondo is handsome and slick with a rolling city walk and a snappy manner. His hair is cut in bangs across his forehead, long enough in back to swing when he walks. He has a way of combing it out of his eyes with his fingers, very charming. One night, one scary night when she couldn't help herself,

Roselle went to Angel's house to ask if anyone knew where the boys had gone. The house was dark except for a television set turned up loud. A woman in a housedress came to the door. Roselle introduced herself and asked her question. "That Angel," the woman said, and then she shook her head. "No," she said. And then no again. Roselle felt like a fool.

The stars are out in a big way. The moon is a thin sharp sliver. Roselle stands on the concrete slab outside the front door barefoot, holding her robe together, feeling the night wind blow. Fall is moving on, the wind has a chilly center. She thought she heard a car earlier and then nothing. No one came. She imagines the Mexicans giving her boy pills of some kind then when he has passed out, dumping him on the road. She has read the warning signs of dope, she watches, but who can tell drunk from drugged, normal eyes from dilated, or how much sweets he eats? His friends all work at the franchises, they give him free food. How can she keep up with what he eats?

In Houston she did not notice such things as stars and the moon and what kind of birds come in which season. She lived a city life then, which went on on its own. She listens to Londale. She has learned new expressions some of which please her to say. But none of it means much, does it, if you think your boy may be drugged and left for dead on the road.

The wind blows across the maize field. The dogs lie close. Roselle pulls her robe together. Fall is moving on in to itself, the Oilers are losing, the Cowboys are not. She bought some bulbs at the Bulb Mart, tulips, daffodils, a book on planting. She should plant the bulbs in drifts, the book says. The tulip bulbs are in the refrigerator. She hasn't touched the daffodils and they should already be in the ground. Londale turned the earth by the porch, she bought a sack of bone meal like the book said and there it all sits. She is not sure anyway exactly what a drift is. The maize is gone, harvested in the night after dark, in less than an hour. It must have been after ten o'clock. Roselle looked up from something in the kitchen and here came a big piece of machinery with one headlight toward the house. At first she thought it was a helicopter landing, until she came and looked. The dogs went crazy. Roselle and Londale went to watch, even the boy came. The combine had a big cab, air-conditioned Londale said, with windows the length of it. You could see inside the cab. A child stood by the driver, watching out the front window, holding on to a bar to keep his balance, a boy of maybe three or four. Londale said farmers work anytime to get the job done. When he started making speeches about work, the boy went inside.

It's words like *combine* Roselle has picked up from Londale.

She misses the maize. The field looks butchered, like a man with a new crewcut. Londale said you have to get used to seasons in the country, that things change more out here but they always come back, in time.

A car slows. The Grand Prix. It turns in. Roselle runs back into the house, like a child playing Hide-and-Go-Seek, that tight clamp around her throat, bowels loosened, wondering if she'll be caught, the next It.

He is not Londale's son of course but as her new husband Londale said he wanted full responsibility, that since he didn't have kids himself he would look forward to it. That was then.

The boy's real father was nuts. Not crazy, nuts. He used to wander off, disappear, get out of the car and not come back. Roselle lost him in J. C. Penney's once, in the middle of a sentence. When he didn't finish his thought she looked up and he was as gone as Christmas. It wasn't like he abandoned them. He never had them. It all drifted from his mind, everything, every fact and person. He went AWOL twice in the Army, they finally let him out. That was just how he was. One day he went to work and never came back.

It embarrassed Roselle the way her first husband acted. She wasn't the one doing the disappearing but it was part of her life and she couldn't stand for people to know. And so after a while she started staying home all the time with the boy. And their life wasn't too bad then, when he was little. He was such a sweet child.

She wanted to tell people that, the school counselor who had her come in to tell her what bad things her boy had been doing, the truant officer who came after him when he skipped, the policeman who brought him home for public intoxication, the man at the 7-Eleven who said he stole gum and cigarettes. She wanted them to know how he used to be. She looked at pictures of him as a child sometimes, just to remind herself that he hadn't always been this way. She would open the album and there he would be, his blonde hair pasted to his forehead, his face red from running, that look on his face of pure delight. Play was hard work and her boy did a lot of it then. There was one picture she particularly liked, of the boy hanging by one arm from a magnolia limb, pretending to be a monkey. He had this look of all-fired fun on his face, his knees were bunched up and he had his hand curled up under his armpit, like a monkey in a zoo cage, scratching.

Roselle could not pinpoint when he changed, but she thought it was around the fifth grade. Why was another story. She didn't even come close to pinpointing why.

The boy was 13 when she met Londale. She and a girlfriend had gone dancing and there he was. Londale wasn't much of a dancer but he could talk. He spun Roselle's head around quicker than she could say boo and her having made up her mind never to get married again. Londale told her that very night he was going to marry her.

She had raised the boy by waiting tables and working as a menu hostess until she got the day job managing a Baskin Robbins after he started school. With benefits and all, Baskin Robbins was not a bad job. They had those ice cream cartons all over the house. The boy built with them, made forts and school projects. Londale was in the food business too, working for Kentucky Fried, which he hated. Londale wanted to do something outdoors, he said, something with his hands, honest work. He was district manager for Kentucky and was moving up but he hated it. Londale helped Roselle get the money from the Army by declaring her first husband legally dead. They bought Londale's trucks and moved, a garbage truck, dumptruck, backhoe, gooseneck trailer. His new business was hiring out in the trucks, delivering dirt, doing jobs. Roselle keeps the books. The trucks are all painted a brilliant aquamarine color, his trademark. But it takes a long time to get people in a small town to trust you and Londale is worried, she can tell. He needs time.

Roselle loves to dance. Her first husband was an excellent dancer, the best thing about him in fact. Funny how the kids don't dance. Rock and roll is their absolutely main topic of conversation but they only listen to the music and do not dance.

Roselle is in bed taking an afternoon break with a cup of coffee and a magazine article she's been saving about midlife depression in men. She tries to keep up. She hears the boy's footsteps on the stairs.

"I want to read you something," he says and he lies across the bed. Roselle puts her magazine away. Londale will be home soon from Lockhart, where he has a job delivering sandy loam.

The article is from the new issue of *Sports Illustrated*. It's about the Cowboys. Like everybody who is an Oiler fan, the boy and Londale hate the Dallas Cowboys.

Everybody, the article says, either loves the Cowboys or hates them. Tex Schramm says it's fine with him to be hated and Tom Landry says he has other things to think about. The players say they don't play for fans anyway. Roselle has heard this before and when she thinks about it, it makes her feel stupid for watching if the players don't care if anyone cheers or boos.

The boy hates the Cowboys most of the time. All his friends and everyone in town, everyone in this part of the state, are Cowboy fans. And sometimes when Londale knocks down the Cowboys, the boy makes a switch, sides with his friends just to rile Londale. He might say, "You can't argue with success," somethng like that.

Her boy is tall like his real father with long messy hair. Girls tell him he looks like a rock star when his curls bounce so he keeps them. He wears a red baseball cap, the bill bent to accent his curls and give him a perfect offhand look. His eyes are a hazel color that in the light switches shades, turning almost green in direct sunlight. He needs to shave. He has that fuzz on his chin and across his lip. Also there are two blackheads on his nose that drive Roselle crazy. He's had them for a year, he says he's tried to squeeze them and they won't go but Roselle knows better. She would like to do it for him but doesn't. And so there they are. Like seeds.

His arms are long and bony, his nails bit to the quick. Watching him turn a page, Roselle wonders where his hands have been, what they have touched, who has held them. Girls call, Angela, Martha, Gabrielle. In Houston the names were different. Tiffany, Jennifer, Nicole. They all hang up fast. His life is a total mystery to Roselle. She has no idea how much he knows or what he does when he is away from the house.

He is reading what Tony Dorsett thinks when tires crunch on the gravel. The white dog barks then hushes. No reason to get jumpy, everything is fine. She has sent out the statements, no reason she shouldn't be lying in the bed taking a break. The boy reads on. The truck door shuts. Londale speaks to the dogs. The front door opens. The boy turns the page and keeps on reading as if nothing else is going on. "Anybody home?" Londale says that every day of the world. The front door closes, a hollow sound. "We're up here," Roselle shouts. The boy goes on reading. He repeats the sentence she interrupted. He does not look up but reads louder. Londale comes up the stairs whistling. The boy reads. Londale is there. Roselle looks from one of them to the other. Londale makes a big remark about his day and throws his cap across the room. He has dirt all in the creases of his face. Roselle feels caught, the room is too small. The cap sails by.

The boy is in the middle of a Tom Landry quote. He slaps the magazine shut and goes downstairs.

Londale stands there as if to say, "See?"

When the telephone rings Roselle grabs it before the first ring is finished. She has been waiting in the kitchen close by. She knew it would ring.

"Mom," the boy says, "it's me." It is three-thirty in the morning. The next thing is about to happen. "I'm in jail." His voice is slurred. He sounds teary. The upstairs phone picks up.

"Jail?" Londale says. "What did you do?"

"Mom?"

"I'm here."

"I'm just going to kill myself, Mom, that's all. You just don't know."

Londale makes a grunting noise that sounds like a dare. What does he want, for the boy to prove he is not bluffing by doing what he says?

They were drinking, the boy says, but he had not had as much as the others and so he was driving. In Texas anyone caught DWI is automatically taken straight to jail. Roselle tells the boy they will be right over, where is the jail? The boy starts to say over by the American Legion at the same time Londale is saying never mind, he knows. The upstairs telephone clicks.

The boy lowers his voice to a whisper. "They put me in handcuffs, Mom. The backseat of the police car doesn't have handles. I was behind that wire screen. The cell has a bed and a pot and that's all. I'm hungry."

Roselle tells him they will be right there and asks if the officer who picked him up is there. The boy says yes and gets off. Upstairs, Londale is making loud noises, getting dressed, stamping around. The officer is a woman. The town has just hired two women police officers. The policewoman says there is no way for the boy to get out of jail unless a judge okays it and at this time of the morning she wouldn't advise calling one, but of course Roselle is free to do as she wishes. She says the judges' names are Cynthia Mendez and George Ruby.

"Who else was in the car?" Roselle asks.

"No one," the officer says in a flat tone. She sounds so hopeless, like there is nothing to do about any of this. "The boy was alone. The Grand Prix was weaving and so I pulled him over and administered a breath test, which he failed."

Mondo and Angel got out in time. The boy was left to take the business.

"Where is the car?"

"Towed. Saucedo's has it. You can get it after nine."

"It's not mine."

The boy's voice rings in her ears. Handcuffed me, Mom, I'm hungry. Like a 4-year-old boy tattling on a friend.

Londale comes downstairs buckling his belt. The buckle is a huge flat sterling silver oval with a lump of turquoise set off to one side. Londale bought the belt in Tucson. Roselle gets off the phone and reaches for her purse, but Londale says jail is no place for her and he gives Roselle a lawyer's name to call. How does he know these things, where the jail is, who to call? In the night, when things are so hopeless?

"I'll try to spring him," Londale says, zipping his down vest. "Scumbag," he says. "Little shit."

He is wearing bluejeans and house slippers. Londale has gained weight, the jacket is hard to zip. He smells minty and dusky at the same time, a combination of Rolaids and night breath. Londale also looks pathetic, his curls tight down on his forehead, his eyes red and sleepy. He looks mad enough to chew nails but mixed up too, as haywire as Roselle. Roselle hopes he doesn't get an ulcer from all this, if he doesn't already have one.

"Tell him I'm at the jail," Londale says, meaning the lawyer.

Roselle calls, apologizing for waking the lawyer. The lawyer is abrupt but not angry, wide awake at once, as if this happens all the time. He says the boy should not have taken the breath test but that getting him out of jail will be no problem, he will call Cynthia Mendez.

Roselle waits, her hand on the telephone in case it rings so that if it does she will be quick to answer it, in case. In case what? She doesn't know. Every possibility tears at her heart. She had never thought of a heart before as something that actually broke the way they say in songs but lately she has felt it a lot, the actual physical heart of her split apart in five directions at once.

Outside, the north wind blows across the empty maize field. The wind sings inside the hatshaped tin roof and under the front door. Winter is coming. Only the mesquite trees still have their leaves. The white walls and cabinet tops of the kitchen hurt her eyes with the light glaring against them. Waiting is the worst thing, especially in the night. Especially when the night is so dark and so much is going on out in it and she is so alone.

Roselle counts to a hundred by ones, then fives, then tens. She will do it again and by the end of the last hundred, the telephone will ring. She wonders where this will end, what the boy is feeling and what will happen next. And why did Londale buckle up his belt that way as if for a reason? She is afraid he might be planning to use it on the boy. If this was a movie she would have known for a long time a terrible end was bound to happen. Just like with James Dean, his life and all his movies. You just could tell.

She should have gone. He is her boy. Londale doesn't know how he used to be. As a baby he had big cheeks she always wanted to chew on. Big cheeks and no hair. She breastfed him a whole year. And now he is in jail, in a cell, like a common criminal.

Roselle feels like a jangling telephone wire herself, sitting in the white kitchen counting, wondering what will happen next and how the story will turn out and most of all when in this pitch black night her boy will be home.

She decides to go to five hundred by tens.

They're home. Londale has stalked on off back up the stairs to the bedroom. Roselle and the boy sit in the white kitchen. From the outside the kitchen is so lit up it looks like a chicken coop.

"Well?" Roselle says.

"Well, what."

He makes his hands in a basket then brings his fingers apart, lacing them and unlacing them. She has no idea how to be a mother.

"You have nothing to say?"

The boy turns to Roselle then and she feels her heart turn to jelly. Thinking of him hurt, of policemen taking him away in their car, of him in a jail cell, she feels a shiver go down through her, from her throat through her chest and on down. Like a razor blade slicing her flesh apart. It doesn't hurt. It only does its damage and then, is gone.

He starts to upbraid her, as if she'd done it to him. He tells her how she doesn't know what it's like and what a mistake it was to bring him to this town, he was better off in the city, had better friends there, could have had a better shot at things. His voice rises. Roselle gets up from her kitchen stool and goes to him. Before he knows it she has clamped her hand over his mouth. He pulls away. Strong, he's strong, just from size, not from working at it.

"He'll hear," Roselle hisses at her boy in a loud whisper.

"Don't you understand. He'll hear." Her fists are doubled. She'd like to pick up something and throw it. The boy laughs.

He comes over to her and takes her by the shoulder, holds her hard. Anything can happen, anything. She is afraid of him, and of Londale, loves the boy, hates the policeman, wants the boy home safe so she will know, wants him to be happy but more than happy, safe. Wants her heart back in one piece.

She lowers her shoulders from his grasp. He releases her, gives her a phoney tough-guy look, then goes on out. Her boy.

Anything is possible but nothing happens. Only the same old song. Once the credits roll and the movie starts, there's nothing for it but to go on.

Walter McDonald

The Track

By noon Bien Dien sweltered, the humid air heavy like deep depression. The clouds had not built far enough to block out the sun, which beat down almost too bright to see. For the first time since the rocket blast last night, the base was quiet, as if totally shut down. I could not hear a jet or bombs or gunfire anywhere. The whole war seemed to have been called off.

I felt my back baking already as Lebowitz guided me, jogging the three blocks to the track, a dirt oval bulldozed around a field laid out for football but covered now in dead yellow grass, a collapsing rusting goalpost at each end. Lebowitz said that in the old days, with a half million Americans in Vietnam, the base was famous as Bien Dien-by-the Sea, its beaches a favorite R and R center. But after most of the troops were withdrawn, there weren't enough left for proper patrols, and the VC began mining the beaches. Now they were off limits, and jogging was the best hot way to relax.

A road paralleled the track and cut north to the flight line a few blocks away, hidden by hangars and quonset huts. Along the other side of the field were wooden bleachers built between the forty-yard lines, a platform at the fifty like a parade reviewing stand. Behind the bleachers a sagging cyclone fence ran the length of the field and on beyond were rows and rows of tin and wooden shacks where Vietnamese airmen lived with their families. And at the far end of the field, beyond a great wall smothered with vines, there was a huge French mansion with a red roof and trees everywhere around it, like part of the jungle.

There were a dozen or more men in trunks already on the track, some of them jogging fast, some shuffling along with their heads down, their arms hanging. Lebowitz drew the towel from his neck and wiped his face and threw the towel on the field. His thin face was drawn, almost emaciated, and his eyes were deep set in dark hollow sockets, his stiff hair pepper white.

"Six times around for a mile," he said, not breaking stride.

"How many miles do you go?" I asked, my bones already heavy in the heat.

"Four, five, I'll let you know."

He ran light on his feet, a thin man with long muscles. He kept his fists straight out in front of him, knuckles up. He was taller than me by several inches, his long stride hitting three for my four. His high voice chattered like a separate thing that could not be winded.

"See that guy rounding the endzone? That's Fleming. He runs every day. The only guy here who can outlast me."

"Yeah," I said, still trying to fall in with his pace. "I see him."

Fresh from the States, I was used to handball and an indoor track, and running here in this humidity was like treading deep water with boots on.

I watched Fleming round the turn and enter the straightaway, running fast with determined desperate lunges past a group of slower joggers and along the row of Vietnamese shacks. Two or three children broke from the bushes and ran toward the track, whirling and darting away out of sight as Fleming ran past. When the children broke toward the group following him, one of the men lunged at them and the children scattered.

We approached the turn and the old wall of the French estate towered before us, lush with vines, shaded by the great limbs of trees beyond the wall.

"The Frenchman's place," Lebowitz said, tossing his thumb at the wall. "It's their private club, now."

I had read about Bien Dien before leaving Saigon. I knew it was one of the American bases built in the sixties, bulldozed not merely out of jungle but out of an old French colonial plantation on the bay by the name of Bien Dien. At the peak of United States involvement, eighteen thousand Americans crowded the base, along with a handful of French still running their plantation and a few hundred Vietnamese. Now, only four hundred Americans remained, and thousands of Vietnamese, and still the handful of French, who lived apart and never troubled themselves with Americans except invitations to the base commander and his staff at Christmas and the fourth of July and Bastille Day.

I heard a board thudding just beyond the wall and then a splash cut trimly into water.

"Swimming pool," Lebowitz said, his face parallel to the wall, his fists pumping. "Those cats still think they're in the Promised Land."

We turned down the backstretch and came even with the shacks. There was an awful smell, like rotten cabbages and wine.

"You numbah ten!" a child's voice screamed, the worst insult possible. "You 'mericans numbah ten!"

Lebowitz never turned his head toward that supreme insult, just kept jogging the same steady pace. And when the child screamed at us again, Lebowitz called back friendly, "You numbah one! You numbah one, boychild!"

He answered my silence as we jogged on. "Want to trade places with them?"

"No way," I said.

"You're right," he said. "If we can't be friends with the kids, there's no way."

Shackler and Malatesta arrived from the officers' hooches, and we fell in behind them as they entered the track, jogging heavily. Shackler lunged along, leaning forward like a heavyweight, but Malatesta brought his knees high and trotted with his shoulders thrust back as if he were marching.

"They hit the village again?" Lebowitz called.

"Naw," Shackler replied, not looking back. "Must be getting ready to hit the base."

Rumors. At breakfast someone had said three NVA divisions had crossed the demilitarized zone and were last detected twenty kilometers north of the base. Estimates of casualties from last night's mortar attack ran as high as dozens of Americans and hundreds of Vietnameses killed and god knows how many wounded. Someone said the VC had overrun half of Plei Nhon and massacred scores of villagers during the night.

I waited for someone else to speak, but all ran quietly, all alone. Now and then we would fall into step and there would be the thump thump thump of our running. Then the steps would syncopate and break rhythm and in the heavy depressing heat I would find myself having to concentrate to maintain stride.

Fleming caught us in the second lap and passed without looking, his breath heaving, the tendons in his neck stretched tight. He was a good-looking kid with blond hair and flushed cheeks and he looked too young to be out of high school. He raced on, as if trying to outdistance fear.

Each time we passed the great wall I would listen and once I thought I heard sensual laughter, and another time I heard music, slow and light and peaceful, like Paris in springtime.

A muscular, middle-aged man ran past us, deeply tanned, an old sergeant or a colonel, his stiff white hair glistening with sweat. Around his waist was a wide leather back support, gleaming black, a .38 holstered on one side and a knife scabbard stitched to the other.

"Watch him," Lebowitz said. "He won't go near the shacks."

Sure enough, the man ran swiftly along the inside of the track, next to the football field.

"Hates kids?" I asked.

"Naw," he said, grinning. "Just afraid someone's gonna nail him before it's over. He's not the only one."

After three laps Shackler and Malatesta dropped out, panting heavily, but Lebowitz jogged on, staring ahead. I glanced at them walking slowly back towards the quarters, their arms limp. I felt more like that than running, but something in my legs kept going and after a few paces I caught up with Lebowitz again.

"It all counts towards DEROS," he said grimly. Date of Earliest Return from Overseas: months, impossible months from now.

We must have jogged around that track for an hour. One by one the others dropped out and returned to the quarters for showers and back to duty. After awhile there were only Lebowitz and I and, lapping us every two or three rounds, Fleming, haunting the day with his fear.

Lebowitz paced me like a record spinning around and around, lap after lap. I caught my mind wandering off the track, dozing, drugged with fatigue and the heat. I no longer heard the children jeering at us, only now and then a woman's high strange scolding from inside the shacks or a crying baby. I listened for the swimming pool to splash again or for music, but there were not even birds singing in the Frenchman's jungle beyond the wall. After awhile even Lebowitz hushed and there was only the thump of our toes jogging on dirt.

My lungs numbed in the heat and my legs came to feel like things apart, able to go on and on. My eyes burned with sweat, and I squinted so tight I could hardly see anymore, and because they stung it was impossible to think. I was adjusting, though, lost in rhythm, like a mechanical animal caught on the rim of existence, going round and round, getting closer to DEROS. It felt good and I was slipping deep in dreams when I heard a noise with my name on it.

"Moose. It's time, Moose," Lebowitz called.

I jolted to a halt off the track and dropped my arms. My hands were numb. I heard jets roaring from the flight line. Drenched in sweat, tasting salt and iodine, I shuddered. It was overcast, the sky boiling with clouds, and in the distance there was thunder, or bombs, and I had the feeling there was still a long, long way to go.

Carolyn Osborn

The Accidental Trip to Jamaica

It was an accident, our going to Jamaica, and you had to prove you'd been there by crawling around on the bottom of the too-blue sea to snitch a piece of coral I carried home. When I got back my students asked me, "Where have you been?" They demanded to know because I'm not Mrs. Somebody-or-Other but somebody they know. That's the way they are these days, knowing. I did not tell them. Not many school teachers go to Jamaica in January or any other month, and they would not have understood. I put the coral next to a papier-mâché dinosaur made by my middle child. It's a striped blue and green dinosaur as blue and green as the water at Ocho Rios. I thought it fit, made a pair of things. The shape of the dinosaur and the coral finger are the same. They are both disasters, one belonging to a prehistoric past, one belonging to a month ago. Yet the dinosaur still inhabits the earth—SEE GIANT DINOSAUR TRACKS FIVE MILES OFF THIS HIGHWAY—and the coral is the unmoving finger which wrote FOLLY.

Why did we go? Why didn't we stay here? The weather was just as peculiar at home. It snowed twice that week for the first time in seven years. I wonder and you float. You always float, not in my dreams, in my wakefulness.

AUSTIN DENTIST DROWNS IN JAMAICA

Is it real? Yes, as real as birds in trees or gritty bits of sand in shoes.

> *There's blood in the sad-dul.*
> *There's blood on the ground.*
> *And a great big pud-dul of blood all around.*

Cowboys don't go to Jamaica. They go home on the range. But we went, you in your white linen cowboy suit and me looking like a well-kept go-go girl though the go-go girls have all gone. A woman has to have some sense of history to be a well-kept anachronism. You always wanted to be a cowboy and I always wanted to be anything but a school teacher. We met dressed in our disguises, our everyday clothes worn over our everyday lives.

Two secrets are clawing each other inside my head: 1) you are dead; 2) we went to Jamaica together. I have told the most cunning lies. Mother lives in Florida, which accounts for my tan. She believes I was in New York seeing plays every noon and being pursued by murderous addicts every night. My husband believes I went to New York, then to Florida. They do not talk to each other often, but if they ever do Mother is so forgetful now that I can convince her I was in Florida in January and she forgot.

Why did we go to Jamaica?

We were going to Sun Valley. Skiing. At least you were.

We had to buy all new tropical clothes. Mine are still hidden in a locker at the Dallas airport. The Goodwill Store or the Sisters of Charity or whoever gets clothes left in airport lockers is going to get a mess of batik, two bikinis, and lots of black nylon panties and bras, your fetish, not mine.

You are floating on a whim.

That's what took us there. My whim. I had never been to Jamaica. I had never been to Sun Valley either. You said why not and I said I don't go places like that. You said I was an over-sheltered academic intellectual. We nearly parted then. I said don't speak to me of shelter. I worked my way through undergraduate school as a waitress.

There is an ancient rule written in the back of every woman's head: Don't go anywhere with a strange man.

I erased the rule.

You had some rules of your own. You tucked them in and pulled the covers over their heads.

Whim ruled.

The first whim you had was the white cowboy suit. We

laughed all the way to Neiman-Marcus in the taxi and all the way back. Then we got on lots of planes and flew to Jamaica. The last one had a black stewardess with a British accent. She was so exactly right we made her talk as much as we could. She told us about Blue Mountain Coffee, Appleton Rum, the tiny beaches of Ocho Rios and Dunns River Falls.

Please quit floating!

She was a treasure, that girl. She also told us about the kinky Englishman's restaurant on the way to Ocho Rios. You re-mem-bah him, don't you, the one who tied the cardboard flowers on his almond tree to fool the *National Geographic* photographer. His name was Clive, or Cliff, or Clown. The centers of his flowers were inverted pop-bottle tops sprayed orange. The *National Geographic* man was not fooled; we were, I would have liked a picture of the almond tree in bloom, but we'd sworn off cameras.

At Ocho Rios I wanted to stay in one of those immense, immaculate, secluded hotels, and you insisted I had to see how the other half lives so we had to go to the one with bunny rabbits on the carpet. Miles and miles of ears—someone's idea of how the middle class would like to sin, walking on rabbits' heads. The bathtub was black, seven feet long, three feet deep. It was big enough for copulation, large enough for sleeping, deep enough for drowning if you were drunk and you were not. That bathtub was meet, and fit, and right for the scene, a lovely prop. The couch was all right too, even to its pretend leather cover, but the beds were twins. Very strange. I should have packed up and gone to Florida the minute I laid eyes on those beds.

You said, "That is not how a kept woman behaves."

I said, "Dear Amy Vanderbilt, What are the rules of behavior for a kept woman?"

We couldn't put them together. A light fixture and a table were rooted to the wall between. Do you think the owner of the bunny rabbits believes his guests would cram lights and side tables into their suitcases along with his hotel towels?

"Ring for room service! Call out the housekeeper!"

No. We had a do-it-yourself fit. It wasn't hard to lift the

mattresses off the beds and put them side by side on the floor. I had a practical housewife's fit. "How can anybody make up beds like that?"

You assured me, "Nobody is going to make up this bed."

I thought, "How squalid!" but I kept that to myself. Discretion is the better part of vice. New rules have to be made all the time. I may write that to Ms. V.

I flang myself into the bathtub. You flang yourself right after me. Relaxation was what I craved. You craved fornication, difficult in the bathtub. Too slippery. In bed we fell. You drilled me, your dentistical metaphor, not mine. We are all hung up by the tools of our trade.

"Rum and Coca-Cola."

That's a song my mother used to sing. Now I drink it every afternoon when I come in from school and the oldest child is playing the piano. Yesterday my husband discovered me sitting on the piano bench with drink in hand trying to pick out the tune with one finger. Elusive, that tune. What is the second line? Tomorrow I will give my students ten extra points on a ten-minute quiz if they can tell me the second line. They won't be able to.

Where was I?

What will the Little Flowers of Mercy or the Brothers of St. Poverty do with your skis you left in the men's room of the old Dallas airport at Love Field?

Did love have anything to do with it? I think not. We were two people who had arrived at middle age, that time in life, like adolescence, when we were convinced nothing else was ever going to happen to us. We had to grab fate by the shirt collar. We had to make something happen.

Could you quit floating?

You loved the girls in bikinis with bunny-rabbit tails. It followed that I had to buy the bikini but go tailless into the Caribbean. While you went to ask the manager for a tail for your wife, I went swimming.

> *Rabbits have no tails atall, tails atall,*
> *Rabbits have no tails atall,*

Just a pow-der puff.

Same song, second verse.
Could be better,
But it's gonna be worse.

Rabbits have no tails atall . . .

That's a song my youngest brought home from camp.
The youngest sings, the middle one makes papier-mâché di-
nosaurs, the oldest one plays rock piano. My husband does
gravestone rubbings. I have already ordered mine so he can
rub while waiting. My epitaph is: Here Lies Melissa Hawkins. She Finally Left Texas. Doing myself in? No, not I. Ennui causes tombstones to be ordered ahead of time. To live in
Texas is to live in ennui. I've never liked the landscape here, a
great blah, half of it creeping toward the desert to be dried
out, half of it oozing toward the Gulf to dirty up the continental shelf. Jamaica was most beautiful, a garden rioting
above the sea.

I was in the water floating when you arrived with the
bad news.

"The Bunny Mother is very particular about the tails."

She would not sell one, give one, or trade one to a cowboy in tropic white. We consulted. You bought three powder
puffs which I cleverly pinned together and sewed onto my
black panties. Dear Heloise, I was the one who wrote you
asking for directions for rabbit tail construction. Signed:
Melissa Makedo. The pins clanked together. For some things
there are no substitutes. We had to be content with the ghost
of James Bond playing ping-pong with Malcolm X reincar-
nated in a dashiki. We had to put up with an alloyed steel
band. But you cried out when I pinched you. It was real, as
real as sun in rum and poinciana blooms in hair.

Oh, what's to do?

Everything would have been all right if you hadn't insisted on the expeditions. A small run-away vacation is simple
if you keep it to bed, beach, and bar. Not for you though. You
had to see things, to be instructed. We went to Kingston to

find Harry Belafonte. He wasn't there. It was hot. There were no ships in the harbor. Port Royal was still mostly under water. The guide kept saying, "Whiskey!" and I kept telling him we didn't have a camera. His disappointment followed us to Bremmer Hall. Did he put a hex on us? You noticed he had beautiful teeth. Nobody else did. Bananas grow up; they point their baby fingers to the sky. That's what I learned at Bremmer Hall. The overseer waited to hear the camera click. Everything was going wrong.

"The other half lives with cameras," I said.

"Never mind," you said.

So, I neverminded awhile.

An interlude, a lull.

"We'll learn to scuba dive."

"OK." But I didn't like the look of the weights they hang around a diver's waist.

> *Full fathom five thy father lies*
> *With lead weights about his waist.*

Literature is instructive.
I took up the snorkel.

> *I must down to the seas again,*
> *To the lonely sea and the sky.*

We went down in an elevator, the only time we used it.

"Is this how the other half lives?"

You said indeed it was.

The elevator opened on the beach. We walked to the pier carrying our flippers, looking quite pro. Out into the blue we rocked in a glass-bottomed boat. You swam under the boat and broke off the piece of coral. I watched. Our instructor went in after you. Wilson was his name. You remem-bah Wilson, don't you? He was the one who forgot to warn you sea urchins sting. Yeah, Wilson. Skinny. Wore a red nylon bathing suit. His teeth were filed to sharp points. Wilson. Vampire Man we called him after you came up bloody with sea urchin spines. You were a trifle hysterical then, babbling about sea horses and underwater rodeos. Wilson wanted to hit you. I shook my head. Years of pedagogy were behind that head shake. He held his hand.

The interlude was over. Back to the expeditions, to the last expedition. Dunns River Falls falls hundreds of feet to the sea. The thing to do is to walk up it with a native guide— Tarzan climbing up the boulders through the spray. We approached the sea. Wilson sailed us within the reef all the way.

I said, "Must we?"

"Yes," you said.

Fatal, that yes. Are you floating on your own whim? Where does the truth lie? It lies, and lies, and lies.

On the beach below Dunns River Falls there was a gang of tourists. A black man danced in the midst of them balancing a tray full of rum drinks covered with hibiscus blossoms. Another black man wove green bamboo fronds into hats. Another black man made violins from hollow bamboo canes. He rosined the bow with sea water. Very industrious people, those Jamaicans. What is the Salvation Army going to do with a bamboo hat gone brown and a dried-up bamboo violin? My souvenirs. We danced the limbo with the tourists. Dear Arthur Murray, Do you need a limbo teacher? Inspired by mass frivolity, I played "The Blue Danube Waltz" on my new violin.

That's when we got separated.

A student is standing by my desk. He wants to know why he's failing the course.

I tell him we are all failing the course.

How did we get separated? Some spirit of misadventure lured me. Other people, friendly tourists, took my hands. We formed a human chain. The one who got to hold the guide's hand was the luckiest. I saw you far below holding hands with two strangers. I could not shout. The guides did all the shouting, ha-lo-o-ing over booming water, screeching like mad parrots. We climbed. I watched where I was going. The water was icy; slippery rocks spewed jets of spray. All around the jungle hung. At a turn you saw me and lifted your hand to wave, wrenching yourself loose from the human chain. You were miles below, but I saw you fall. Your body slithered toward the sea. Everyone in your chain stopped while the guide pulled everyone in mine on up. You floated top side down, the deadman's float. I knew it. I passed my Red Cross beginner's test. Our guide was busy imitating the mating call of mynah birds. He saw nothing but the boulders in front of him. The chain of hands pulled me over the boulders. I looked again and saw you floating. Still. People were staring at your back.

I took the coward's choice. Because your life was over, should mine be ruined? Before we had whims. Now decisions were to be made. In my bikini shielded by a see-through shirt, intensely vulnerable and thoroughly shocked, I stepped out of the jungle to the car park and hailed a cab. Back at the rabbit warren I collected my things and dressed myself with lively trembling fingers. Oh, so carefully I printed your name in large, block, childish letters on an envelope. Inside I folded one piece of paper with the following message: Go home to your wife and children. That's all you ever talk about anyway. Signed: Suzy Floozie. Your wife was going to have to pay your double-room hotel bill. It was the most I could do for her. I stomped up to the hotel clerk, simulating our first and only lover's quarrel, pretending great anger which was not hard. Anger is near to fear, neighbor to grief.

"Put this in Dr. Grodall's box." I shoved the envelope over the black marble counter. Funereal. Dear Mr. Rabbit, Down at your hotel in Jamaica sex and death clasp hands and hold on for dear life. Something needs to be done about the ambiance. Love and kisses, Slutina Mae Harlot.

I didn't say please. Tears dribbled down my cheeks. Most undignified.

Slamming out of the hotel was easy. So many doors. Bang! Bang! Bang! July 4th exit. Cab again. Airport again. Only plane there was flying to England. I flew.

"You didn't!" That's what you'd say, your right eyebrow a lofty arch. You used to practice raising your eyebrows in the bathroom mirror.

I did. I must have. There's a ten-pence piece in my coin purse. I bite it now and then to remind myself I went.

London. January. Raining. Cold. Not much money. I couldn't stay inside the bed and breakfast all day. Wallpaper roses swagged and bunched and swagged. Dizzifying. Dear Dorothy Draper, London needs you. All night I circled the walls with the roses while you floated face down.

Roses are red.
My toes are blue.
I will quit floating
If you will too.

Dear Witch of the West, Could you send me the spell for laying a ghost? Ten pence remuneration enclosed.

I rented a raccoon fur coat (unendangered species) from a costume shop, highly reputed, costumers to H. M. the Queen. MARKS AND SPENCER HAVE GALOSHES CHEAP. An Italian maitre d' at a restaurant in Soho gave me an umbrella left behind by an Englishman emigrating to Australia.

I went to the National Gallery, looked at Venus, Cupid, Folly, and Time and decided it's time I went home.

Art is instructive if you're ready to be instructed.

Three students are standing at my desk. They want to know if they have to take the final examination. I tell them, no. They are going to take it anyway. The course I teach is English 60002.Q. The 19th Century Romantic Novel. The real title is The Will to Fail. Those three will pass, which means they have learned nothing.

Planes again. Airports, Home. Austin Public Library. Newspaper files.

AUSTIN DENTIST DROWNS IN JAMAICA

If we hadn't had two hours between planes a month ago— If you hadn't started talking to me— If I could have gotten to New York without going through Dallas— If we hadn't sat next to each other on the plane from Austin to Dallas, I could still be a not-too-sheltered academic intellectual and you could be back in your office with a sprained ankle complaining about the ski patrol at Sun Valley. Maybe.

Why do you keep on floating?

If I had slipped, I would not haunt you.

Dear Carroll Righter, I was born under the sign of Aries, the Ram, at 3 A.M. on the morning of April 7th. Is tomorrow a good day for sending messages?

I'm putting this in an empty rum bottle, one I emptied while I wrote. Tomorrow the bottle will be dropped into the Colorado River, which flows to the Gulf, which mingles with many seas. The final message is: SINK, PLEASE.

Catherine Petroski

Beautiful my Mane in the Wind

I am a horse, perhaps the last mustang.

Walking

I hate you, I said. I hate you I hate you I hate you I hate you. The grass is green. This is my yard, this is my pasture. And I told her I hate her. My dam-mother. She does not understand horses. She doesn't even try. There are many things she doesn't notice about me.

Horses move their feet like this.

Horses throw their heads like this, when they are impatient, about to dash away to some shady tree. See how beautiful my mane in the wind.

Horses snort.

Horses whinny.

Horses hate her.

There is something in my hoof.

A rock. I must take off my shoe and try to get it out.

Siree, siree, yes-siree. Get-up horse.

My dam-mother.

Resting her hoof, at home

I am a girlhorse. I am building a house under the loquat tree. It is taking me a long time.

The blossoms are gone, fortunately, and the bees and the asps.

My house is made of logs, logs that daddy doesn't want. That is because our fireplace goes nowhere. It is just a little cave in the wall. There is no chimney on our house because there is neither a real fireplace nor a furnace because this is Texas and it is mostly hot here. Our fireplace has a permanent log. I am six.

I will be six next month.

The log has a little tube that connects it to the gas. I am told constantly that it is dangerous. The gas you can turn on and light with a stiff wooden match, then the log looks like it's burning, but it doesn't *really* look like it's burning. It *is* all very dangerous. After a while the log begins to glow orange and red fire colors and soon it begins to look like it is growing grey ashes on it. But not really. And it is so dangerous some of us or all of us could die from a mistake. The log gets hot.

And that is why I got the logs when our weeping willow died and mama pushed it over one Sunday afternoon. I called it my fountain tree, leaves instead of water. The bottom of the trunk was rotten and the tree just fell over and mama laughed and the baby laughed and I didn't laugh. We found some ugly grubs in the stump, sleeping. I hate her.

I hate also the baby who is a botherboy.

Daddy cut the willow tree into pieces I could carry and gave them to me and now I am building a horsehouse under the loquat and waiting for a manhorse to come along, which is the way it is supposed to happen.

I saw a picture of one and its name was centaur.

Of a Sunday afternoon, in her stable

My room I also hate. Bother loves it best and squeals when he gets to its door, because he thinks it's nicer than his own room, nicer than the bigroom, nicer than anyplace at all. Maybe because it has four windows and is on the corner of the house and it's easy to see why he might not like it. But the windows aren't the real reason, I don't think. He likes best all the blocks and the toy people. I build temples and bridges sometimes but then he comes along. He just throws blocks when he plays because he's just a baby. And a boy. And not a horse. Maybe a dog.

What I hate most about this room is picking up pieces of

the lotto game when he throws it all over, picking up pieces of jigsaw puzzles that he has thrown all over. Picking up the spilled water, the blocks, the people. I hate his messes. I know that horses are not this messy. Mama says it is our fate to be left with the mess, but I don't think she likes it any more than I do. She doesn't clean up many.

I will just throw everything into the toy chest, a quick way to clean up. Maybe she won't look in there and see how I got the room so clean so fast. Half the time she doesn't pay any attention to how I do things anyway. Just so they're done.

She pays very little attention to me actually. She thinks I just read and I'm pretty sure she doesn't realize about the change. To a horse. She acts as though I'm still a girl. She doesn't observe closely. She is stupid.

This is a dumb room, and bother is even dumber. And lotto is a dumb stupid game and it's easy to see why a horse would hate it. It's supposed to make you sit still and be quiet. It's easy to see why a horse would not like a dumb brother. A horse has better things to do.

Administering herself first aid

The fact is there is a fossil in my hoof.

At school we have a hill that is called Fossilhill because there are a lot of fossils to be found there. She doesn't like it when I bring lots of fossils home in my pockets, but I always find more fossils than anybody else and you can't just throw them back. Actually the fossils are very easy to find. You just pick up a handful of dirt and you come up with fossils. The trick is to find big fossils. I can always find the biggest fossils of anybody, snails and funny sea snakes and shells of all kinds.

The boys run up and down Fossilhill and don't look where they're going. It's no wonder they don't find many fossils. They come and pull Horse's mane. They scuff through where Horse is digging with her hoof. They sometimes try to capture Horse, since she is perhaps the last mustang and of great value. But mostly they are silly, these boys. They don't make much sense, just a mess.

I dream sometimes I will find the fossil of an entire eohippus. The first horse, my ancestor. We learned that in Study.

Today I was trotting on the side of the hill and found the biggest fossil I have ever found in my life, which in horse is I think twelve or maybe twenty-four. Mrs. B didn't think it was all that nice and big, I guess, but she said she *thought* it was nice and said, That's nice, and then I found more and more fossils and other children came to the hill, even the girlygirls who never look for fossils because they always play games I don't know how to play, House and Shopping and Bad Baby. But they tried to find fossils today and asked me if this was a fossil or that and they found many, many fossils. And we all had a good time and got caliche all over ourselves and ground all into our knees, even the girls. And when we had found all the fossils we had time to find, Mrs. B. said, Put them in your pockets, children, and if you don't have pockets put them in your socks. And we did, and that's why there is a fossil in my hoof.

Girlygirls vs. Boyannoys vs. Horse

In my kindergarten there is a girl whose name is Larch. It is a funny name for a girl. It might not be such a funny name for a horse, but Larch isn't a horse because she knows the girlgames and is in fact the girl leader because she decides what games are going to be played and will let the boys tie her up. And the other girls too. When they tie people up they don't use real rope because Mrs. B wouldn't allow that. If they tie me up with their pretend rope it doesn't work. They think I just don't want to play, but the truth is I'm a horse and stronger than a girl and can break their girlygirl rope.

Larch's name is not just Larch. It is really Mary Larch but her mother calls her Larchy and my mother says it sounds like she has designs on smith. Whatever that means. I don't really care. My mother says so much I don't understand that I don't try much any more. It's more fun being a horse. More fun than being a girl too, because they just play Housekeeping Area and none of them really knows yet how to read even though they pretend to. I can tell because they can't get the hard words. So they don't let me play with them, especially Larch, and she can get the rest to do it too. My mother says it's all right because they wish they could enjoy stories themselves and next year they will all read and everything will be all right, but there are a lot of stories you can't really enjoy because they make you cry like the death of Charlotte. I don't know. Maybe Larch wouldn't cry.

The reading is the real problem between the horse and the girls. I guess. But sometimes they do let me play with them, if they need a victim or a hostage or an offering.

The girls talk out of their noses funny.

They wouldn't understand about being a horse, even though they know sometimes I am one. It wouldn't make sense to them. It wouldn't be possible to explain.

Cantering, loping, and hand galloping—What's the difference

After dinner, which wasn't anything good again tonight, I sat and banged my hooves on the chair rungs until they took me to the stock show in the City Colosseum and we sat in the bleachers with cowboys and ladies who had mated and old men with broken legs and poodle puppies wearing holsters. I had to go to the bathroom. They asked me before we left the stable but I told them no, no for sure, because I was anxious to get there. Then we walked through the stock barn part and saw the hungry pigs bend the buckets flat and squeal and knock the sides of their pen. So it was hard to sit still and the men in the arena took forever to clear away the fences and bridges and everything from the trail ride, which was just finishing when we got there. The man behind me had pretty cowboy boots, the fanciest ones ever. Finally they did it though and the next class began. And the announcer is telling the riders. Walk your horses, please, walk. And they all walk. Then the announcer tells them, Trot please, trot your horses. And they all trot. And then the announcer tells them, Canter your horses, canter, please. And they canter, but some of them gallop, some lope, and the announcer has to tell them again, Canter, please. Then they walk again. Then they lope. Then they hand-gallop. Then when they are all through, with the reverses and everything thrown in to confuse them, they line up facing the side of the arena, all in a row down the middle. And I have to go to the bathroom. A horse out there being judged goes teetee.

Herself among the others

Horses are I think lucky. They do not seem to have friends, such as people, you know, for they do not seem to need friends. They have enemies—the snakes, the potholes, the cougars, the fancy booted cowboys who don't know the difference between a canter and a hand gallop. What friends they have are on a very practical basis. Other horses with the same problems, any mustangs that might be left. There may not be any.

The wind.

A talk with herself

If I tell her what I am she will not believe me.

But what does it matter? I hate her.

If I tell the others what I am they may rope me and tell me to pull their wagon.

But what does it matter? They are stupid and could probably not get their wagon anywhere otherwise.

If I tell a boy what I am he will invade my loquat house, and maybe it will be good and maybe it will be bad.

But what does it matter? He will finally run away.

If I tell daddy what I am he will act interested for a minute then drink some beer and start reading again.

But what does it matter, what does it matter?

And if I tell bother he will not understand even the words but will grab my mane and pull it until he has pulled some of it out.

What does it matter? I will whinny and run away.

Who could blame me? Horses should not be abused, ignored, or made fun of. After all they have done for man.

Discussing the weather or nothing at all

Just a little while ago, when I needed to go out to race a bit and throw my head in the wind, she stopped me and asked me who I thought I was. A girl? A horse? My name? I know what she's thinking. The others at school ask me the same question. So I said, A girl because I know that's what I'm supposed to think. One thing I know, not a girlygirl, which would be stupid playing games talking teasing being tied to the jungle gym. I won't. Sometimes it's hard not telling her what I really think, what I know. That sometimes I'm a girl, sometime I'm a horse. When there are girlthings to do, like read, which a horse never does, or go in the car to the stockshow or for ice cream or any of those things, I have to be a girl, but when there are hillsides of grass and forests with low hanging boughs and secret stables in loquat trees, I am a horse. Maybe someday there will be no changing back and forth and I will be stuck a horse. Which will be all right with me. Because horses think good easy things, smooth green and windy things, without large people or bothers or other kids or school, and they have enough grass to trot in forever and wind to throw their manes in high to the sky and cool sweet stream water to drink, and clover.

Roland E. Sodowsky

Landlady

The ceiling fans on the screened veranda had not always been silent. For months, the housing on one had clacked around lazily as the blades whirled; the other had just two speeds, one too fast, the other too slow, and the regulators for both had buzzed steadily, irritatingly. So, armed with tools and coils of insulated wire, the *mbakara* had come home from the Project and dismantled the regulators and re-wired them. Then he had the stepladder brought from the storage room, climbed up, and in ten minutes the housing was more securely fastened than when it came from the factory. The white-jacketed steward had watched him casually, without curiosity: for who can say what a *mbakara* will do? When he was finished, he had turned the fans on and watched and listened, nodding; the buzzing was gone, the housing stable, each fan had five graduated speeds.

"Bring me a drink, Ezekiel," he had said, and sat in a large wicker chair under the silent fans with a tight smile on his face. For he was a technical man, a technical man first; what, they all agreed at the club, even the Indigenous Director, the Continent would never have of its own: a technical man who was not afraid to step from the *Big Oga* seat of his Mercedes, elbow through the gawking, idled workers, and get his hands dirty; who could glance over a warehouse inventory sheet or a drainage layout and have fifty backs bending to in minutes, looking into the guts of a diesel engine and restore power to a city by saying do this or do that; who,

when a hard decision was necessary, would not remember
some urgent business back in his home village and disappear,
but would make it, make it and stand by it and not squirm
and lie and accuse a subordinate of misunderstanding him.

A technical man first: generations of grim men who
could make derricks suck oil out of the ocean, transform silt-
filled rivers into deep-water harbors and rain forests into endless miles of rubber trees set in geometric patterns.

Or repair a noisy fan. He had sat in the silent breeze, and
then it was that he had heard the mad woman for the first
time, somewhere beyond the bare, clean-swept strip of
ground behind the house, somewhere in the bush back there,
scolding in that odd, cadenced voice, not angry but cross, *patiently* cross, he thought: like someone explaining and explaining what has been explained before and has to be explained again. He listened and peered, and saw nothing, but
it grew dark and the voice still came from the bush, somewhere in there among the mud huts and gleams of light from
candles and kerosene lanterns and cooking fires. On and on.
The steward called him to dinner, and afterwards he took his
whisky on the veranda and listened again.

And again the next evening. He asked the steward,
"What is that? Who's that talking?"

"Sah?"

"Who's that talking? That voice?"

"Sah?"

It was to the steward, he realized, as if he had asked,
"What is that air?" As indistinguishable as one long banana
leaf from another, as children's cries in a schoolyard.

When he understood, the steward explained without
even a shrug, as though he were speaking of rain in the rainy
season.

"She mad, sah. Mad woman."

"What's she saying?"

"Sah?"

"The mad woman. What does she say?"

He listened. "She say dey don take her land. Dis land her land."

"Who took it?"

He shrugged then. "Dey, sah. She say all dis land her land. Dey don take ahm."

A few evenings later he saw her. The gardener next door was breaking out a plot of land for planting, swinging a heavy-bladed, short-handled hoe, when the voice began, cross, insistent—*reasonable*, somehow, he thought, knowing she was in the right, assuming the gardener would eventually understand, would do what she wanted. Would leave. The *mbakara* listened, the fans rotating softly, the glass with the clear ice and the fresh slice of lime cold in his hand, and then she was there, directly across the bare strip of ground, scolding the gardener, gesturing in cadence with her voice. The gardener glanced at her, went on with his digging. Her skin was the color of the freshly turned soil. She held a matchet in her right hand, the long blade thin from many sharpenings. She wore a sleeveless, collarless knit shirt, or undershirt perhaps it was, a lusterless maroon color, with a large tear on one side, and her lappa was the color of dead banana leaves. She was barefoot. Her headcloth was green, brighter than the palm fronds behind her, and tied in a stiff, slanting, high-crowned way that reminded him of those pictures of that Egyptian queen—what was her name? Her breasts swung gently as she shook her finger at the gardener.

The ice in the glass tinkled, and the steward said as he set down a fresh one, "She distahb you, sah?"

"Why should she disturb me?" Then he saw that she had moved a step closer to the veranda and was looking at him, talking to him, in that same steady, impatient voice.

"No, she is not disturbing me," he said.

The message was clear enough, he thought, even though he could not understand the words: *You have wronged me. In this way. And this. And also in this. Do you understand now? Why do you persist in not understanding?* Occasionally she broke off to turn and jab the end of the matchet into the ground, as if to resume the work, the life they, *he*, had interrupted. Then she straightened and began again.

He did not see her for a few days, and then she returned, standing in the same place next to the rotting stump of a matcheted pawpaw tree, the stump and the twig-like beginnings of a sapling beside it, just leafing, barely reaching her hip. She seemed more disturbed than before, and as she talked she edged closer to the veranda, jabbing the matchet hard into the cleanswept ground, until she was a few feet from the screen. He saw that she had the delicate features of the riverine peoples, those who centuries ago had floated in their black canoes down the river that curved southward out of the Bambuto Mountains, down to where the webbed delta area of mangrove swamps began, had settled and spread slowly inland and back up the river and become the land-owners, the landlords to the tribes that followed. A small-seeming face, unlined, crisply symmetrical.

As she grew more agitated her voice rose a pitch higher, although her face remained calm, her lips did not contort in anger. She waved the matchet, not threateningly, he thought, but to punctuate, like a lecturer's pointer; her breasts lifted and fell, and once when her headcloth slipped he saw that her hair, like the market women's, was short and tied in half a dozen black twists. Her eyes never left his face.

"Ezekiel," he called. When the steward came, he said, "Tell her to go away."

The steward went out the side door of the veranda and spoke to her, gesturing toward the bush. She took a step backwards, but her eyes were still on the *mbakara* and her voice rose higher.

"Go!" the steward shouted in English, and again she stepped back, still talking. She retreated stubbornly, her voice rising steadily. At the far edge of the bare ground the steward suddenly picked up a palm branch and, before the *mbakara* realized what he intended, stripped its leaves and slashed at her twice, once across her arm and chest and again across her back as she turned.

"Ezekiel! Stop that." The *mbakara* swore. "That's enough. Finish. Get back in here."

Even then the woman continued to scold, not the steward but the *mbakara*, rubbing the welt on her arm, her face calm, the rhythms of her complaint undisturbed, irrefutable.

The hot months of the dry season passed, the rains began; now as they returned from the Project the driver, squinting over the wheel to avoid the potholes and the treacherous taxis, would sometimes plunge the gray Mercedes into a dark wall of water, a torrent, and just as suddenly come out to the dry road again; or in the night, a single deafening crack of thunder, and then the rain would roar on the corrugated metal roof for hours. Soon, the *mbakara* knew, the hours would be days; the bills of lading, letters, even manila folders in the office would be limp with humidity; the steward would have to iron his clothes dry, and still they would smell of dampness and rot, like the decaying undergrowth in the bush.

I will tell you once more of my wronging, and of the cause of this wronging.

She was there. She had not come close again since the steward had struck her, but kept by the pawpaw stump and the new tree beside it, fully leafed now and shoulder-high to her. She scolded him as he drank slowly, dully listening; he had gotten used to her and her voice, like the women along the highway with their staggering headloads of firewood or the small ragged men pushing their black bicycles loaded with cassava roots up the long hills.

He thought of other things, the threatened strike at the Project, the exasperating disappearance of copper tubing, the letter—letters—he had not written to his wife. He frowned; tonight he would write. Or this weekend.

It is you who are to blame.

"Sssst!"

What?—the *mbakara* started, then scowled; that voiceless call, irritating to all foreigners; he had trained himself to ignore it. If a man wanted to talk to him, let him speak, not hiss like a snake.

"Sssst!"

The mad woman stopped her scolding and turned. It was, the *mbakara* saw, the gardener next door, standing among the yam hills he had shaped on the plot of freshly broken land, his narrow face alert, mobile, smiling broadly as he beckoned to her. She watched him without moving. He was barefoot and shirtless, his tight black trousers rolled above his knees. The evening sun glinted on his biceps and the smooth muscles of his chest. He motioned to her to come closer, pointing to something in his other hand, something hidden by the green yam foliage. She stepped toward him, then stopped. He grinned, white teeth glistening, glanced admiringly at the thing concealed by the leaves, beckoned. When she did not move, he held up a brassiere—black, gauzy, light as a spider's web, not at all like the bulky things the market women wore. The *mbakara* chuckled softly: almost certainly, the gardener had pilfered it from the young wife of his master, the engineer who lived next door and who had gone home on leave.

As the mad woman started toward the gardener, he backed away, matching her step for step, grinning, waving the bit of cloth. He backed out of the yam hills and moved slowly toward the doorway of his quarters, a little one-room house of concrete blocks with a single screenless window, stopping when she stopped and holding the prize out invitingly to her. Reaching the doorway, he stepped inside, never taking his eyes from her; he held the bra out with both hands, beamed, shook his head in wonder, fitted it against his chest. She came steadily toward him, and as she passed through the doorway he kept the bra just out of her grasp. The door closed, the *mbakara* heard the wooden bar being dropped, and then the gardener closed the shutter of the window also.

After dinner the *mbakara* returned to sit with his whisky on the dark veranda. The security lights had been turned on around the house, illuminating the yam mounds, the young pawpaw tree and the stump, the door of the gardener's quarters. The *mbakara* thought of the mad woman, grown silent as she succumbed to the gardener's strategy. The smoothly functioning mechanics of the transaction, the gardener's perception of the barter value of the stolen or perhaps discarded garment, of what he could do—distract with a wisp of foreign nonsense a mad woman from her madness, trick her vanity or petty acquisitiveness into overruling her obsession, into closing her mouth and opening her thighs—pleased, appealed to the *mbakara*. Sweating in the heavy night air, he watched the gardener's door, even strained to listen; he recalled the workers' quarters he had inspected at the Project, houses like the gardener's: a bench, a wooden chair and small square table, a bed without mattress or springs, or a mat on the floor, a piece of coarse cloth for cover. Her eyes, he wondered . . . lappa tossed over the chair, headcloth tumbled away by the grinning, eager gardener . . . would her eyes be fixed on the prize, the bit of cloth?

He drank his whisky and called the steward to bring another, and later still another before he sent him home. The night watchmen, armed with slinghots and stout *iroko* clubs, said "Good evening, sah" to his silhouette on the veranda, and returned to the front porch to sleep on their mats. The breeze from the silently turning fans kept away the mosquitoes that slipped through the mesh. He finished his drink and stretched, settling back in the chair, and was just dozing off when he heard the voice of the mad woman, muted but scolding as usual, and the gardener's grunting reply as the door opened.

There was a flicker of a candle from inside. The woman stood in the doorway: *Here is how you have wronged me. In this way, and this.* She jabbed her matchet against the door. *And also in this. Do you understand? Why—*

"Ennhh! Finish! Go now!" the man said. His hand flashed into the light of the doorway and she stumbled backwards, but did not fall, barely interrupted the rhythm of her complaint. The door slammed, but she stood her ground: *And in this. And this also. Must I explain it to you again?*

The *mbakara* lifted his glass, found it empty. He went in to the bar, refilled it, and returned to drink and listen and watch the woman. At last she turned from the door and walked along the edge of the bush, scolding, occasionally slashing at the ground with the matchet.

When the rainy season came in earnest, the *mbakara* began to think of his annual leave. Eleven weeks, ten weeks it was now. He thought of the things he would do: repairs to be made on the house, investments to be made from the account fattened each month by his stateside paychecks, possibly a vacation trip somewhere. And he thought of his wife, vaguely, irritably; he could not associate the attractive woman in the large framed photograph on his bedroom dresser with the fragments of remembrances, images in his mind: filtered sunlight on her as she opened the drapes in the den; the jangle of the telephone and her assured warmth as she accepted an invitation to someone's house; their immaculate bedroom and her somewhere in it doing something, always something that was somehow done without disturbing, displacing anything; Sunday mornings, coffee with her on the patio, talk of—what? The poodle racing wildly about the fenced yard, the yellow-tinged patch of grass which was never quite green? Something. The poodle brushing against the hem of her gray robe.

Home leave. It irritated him that he felt no compelling need to go home such as one could hear in the voice or read in the eyes of the men, especially the younger ones, at the club. He had only a vague desire not to stay: the lushness of this place sometimes oppressed him, disturbed, like his oversized house, its walls bristling with air conditioners, his sense of function. Wet vegetation crept over the swept ground around the house; he could feel mold, smoothly alive, on his shoes as he tied them in the morning; the new pawpaw tree now stood eight, nine feet high, clusters of fruit already forming.

The mad woman had discarded her torn knit top and replaced it with the gardener's barter. When she appeared to scold the *mbakara* in the morning, protected by a large piece of green banana leaf if it was raining, she wore her lappa tucked at her waist and stood by the new pawpaw tree in her odd combination of native cloth and the product of western

engineering and chemistry and notions of displaying the female body, jabbing the wet soil and berating the *mbakara* for
his part in her disenfranchisement. Later, when the sun
burned overhead and the steam rose from the bush, she
wrapped the lappa tightly over her breasts.

On a Saturday afternoon, the rain falling steadily, the
mbakara left his papers scattered the length of the dining
table and went to the veranda. By the chair was a letter from
his wife, opened but unread since the day before. He read it
slowly, stopping to watch a fat-bodied bird with a long beak
dart from the new pawpaw tree to snatch food from the
clouds of insects above the strip of bare ground; he read of
bridge afternoons, a plumber's bill, children's grade reports, a
brunch, a luncheon while a lizard scampered noisily on the
metal roof of the veranda and the rain whispered, and then
the mad woman, a battered porcelain basin balanced on her
head, appeared at the edge of the bush, talking to him.

With her matchet she cut two banana leaves and wedged
them in the branches to keep the rain off; she tugged at another banana leaf and braced up its flappy sides with sticks
so that it curved in a long vee down to her feet; a rivulet of
clear water soon ran from its tip, and she set the basin to
catch the water. She began to wash a small pile of clothing,
using a piece of the yellow soap which the women sold
in long unwrapped bars in the market. She stood as she
washed, bending from the waist, but now and then she
straightened to look at him as she talked: *this land, you see, is
mine; it is not your land; you are here wrongfully on this land, for
first some mbakara like you took it from me and then they gave it to
black men and now the black men have given it to you, so it is not
right that you are here.* The word *mbakara* he could clearly
understand as she talked, for it was shouted at him by the
children along the crowded streets every day as he was driven
to and from the Project; everything else he felt he understood: the logic, the . . . balance? . . . yes, like lifters in an engine, the balance of her arguments, *what is* against *what is not*,
as he heard it in the rise and fall of her voice.

When she had finished she cut another banana leaf

to broaden her shelter and draped the clothing on the dead limbs beneath it. Then she took off the bra and unwrapped her headcloth, washed them, and hung them to dry, carefully smoothing out the creases in the headcloth. Her heavy breasts lifting and swaying, lighter in color than the sodden earth, she adjusted the vee-shaped leaf so that the rivulet was shoulder-high. As she talked to the *mbakara* in her measured, impatient rhythms, she opened her lappa and removed it, folded it neatly, and then stepped beneath the trickle of water, flinching as it struck her, shifting her shoulders and arching, then bending, turning to wet her chest and stomach; she interrupted herself only when the water struck her face. She stepped back under the shelter to soap herself, using the piece of soap frugally, making a small triangle of lather in her pubic hair, replacing the soap on its scrap of paper, working the lather with her fingers, now her knuckles, over her stomach and breasts to her underarms. Her intent scrubbing somehow reminded the *mbakara* of the way she jabbed the matchet into the soil. He watched the mad woman, the full rounds of her belly and buttocks, her sturdy thighs and arms, and thought again of his wife—of shimmering emerald or silver or ruby liquids in gracefully curved bottles in her bathroom, of the shrill hum of her hair dryer, the mingled odor of scents and heat from electric coils as she opened the bathroom door and came out in her gray robe. He remembered their utility room—the intricate array of lights and switches on the washer, the low roar of the dryer, the thick discs of glass in the doors of the machines.

When she had rinsed away the soap, the mad woman patted herself dry with a scrap of cloth, shook out the lappa vigorously, and wrapped herself in it again, tucking the loose end tightly under her left arm. With a quick stroke she slashed the vee-shaped banana leaf and, holding the severed piece over her head, came to stand by the new pawpaw tree and scold the *mbakara*. As he studied the smoothness of her face, the fineness of detail of cheekbones and brow, her heavy lips and large, wide-set eyes, he wondered what she saw of him through the mesh in the darker shadow of the veranda—

khaki shorts, the whiteness of his legs perhaps and of his face and neck above his chest, matted, unlike the gardener's, with thick brown hair, beginning to gray? Always her eyes seemed fastened on his as she spoke: *since you do not belong here, it is only right that you leave; I have explained this to you before; you must leave, for I must plant yams here, and cassava and pumpkins.*

She dropped the leaf and pierced it with the matchet, without anger, the *mbakara* thought, but simply to show that she was ready to begin her work. The rain, he realized, had stopped; the gray overcast was breaking up, the sun glinting through. He called the steward to rouse the dozing driver to take him to the club.

Late that night he awoke and could not sleep again. He lay on the broad bed under the sheet listening to the air-conditioner, watching the thin gleams from the security lights outside. He switched on the bedside lamp and then turned it off to shut out the starkness of the large room, the bare walls, the dresser with the single framed photograph on it. Irritated by the whine of the air conditioner, he got up and made his way to the veranda, clad only in his briefs, and when he opened the veranda door, he heard her: *There is no question about this. You know I have been wronged, you are part of this wronging. You must make it right. It is far too long now that you have not made it right. Where are my yams that should be leafing from this soil, in this season of new rains? Where is the water leaf? Tell me where.*

Her eyes, her teeth flashed white in the glare of the security lights. She loosened her lappa, adjusted it, tucked in the edge as she talked. Standing close to the screen, he glanced at the gardener's dark little house, at the bush where no lights shone, heard a single heavy drum far off, somewhere beyond the hills of oil palm trees. He listened to the woman, remembering her bathing under the clear rivulet of rain water, and then he went into the house, took from the storage room three—no, he thought, four—large bars of soap packaged in gold foil, returned to the veranda, and opened the screen door.

"Sssst! Come," he said. She watched him silently.

"Come. Come here." He held out one of the glittering bars. "These are for you. Come here."

As she came slowly closer, he realized in surprise how short she was; no more than five feet, he thought, or even less. She shifted the matchet to her left hand and took the gold bar, turned it this way and that, then looked at him, waiting.

"Soap," he said. "Good soap." Taking the bar from her and opening the foil, he held it for her to smell, then made lathering motions over his chest and stomach. He pressed it into her hand and held out the other bars.

"All for you," he said, and motioned toward the door. "Come." He put his hand on her shoulder and pushed her inside.

In the bedroom she stood dumbly, blinking in the sudden bright light. He took the soap from her and put it with the other bars on the dresser, gesturing and saying again, "for you," while she watched him. A white man, he thought, taking the matchet from her and laying it on the floor: a *mbakara*, sweat, hairy chest and all; her first good look. He pulled the tuck of the lappa and opened it, drew it away and tossed it over a chair. But when he pushed her toward the bed, she resisted, turning from him and picking up the lappa to fold it as she had done that afternoon. He kept his hands on her, and, when she had finished, urged her toward the bed, pushing her onto it. As he switched the light out, he saw that she was fearfully testing the strange resilience of the bed, putting her weight on one knee, then the other, watching the mattress sink and rise. He smiled then, thinking: and your first real bed. A pulsing exaltation surged through him, a need to master, and he found her quickly in the darkness and covered her.

He awoke with a start. Morning? No, the security light still glinted on the ceiling over the top of the heavy drape. She was sleeping, curled close to him for warmth, the sheet and blanket pulled in tight against her. He found her breast and lifted it, felt the thick nipple, then thought: No. They'll be up, all over . . . the gardener, houseboys out. He switched on the light and shook her shoulder, and when she sat up sleepily, handed her the lappa, motioning that she put it on. When she had finished, her eyes dumbly inspecting him, he put the bars of soap and the matchet in her arms, turned off the light, led her to the veranda, urged her down the steps, saying "Go. Go now," and locked the door behind her.

As he recrossed the veranda, she began once more. *Mbakara, I ask you, where are the yams that should be leafing here? Where are—*

The *mbakara* bought a parasol in mid-week, returning with it wrapped in a sheet of newspaper to where the driver waited in the Mercedes. And on Friday, coming home from the Project, he again plunged into the muddy, reeking labyrinth of the market and came out with bags containing a large bath towel printed with pink and purple and yellow flowers, a pair of green plastic sandals, underclothing in iridescent colors, a filmy American-made blouse, pink with red buttons and an enormous flounce, and a headcloth of some heavy synthetic material, brilliantly orange. He locked the bags carefully in his steamer trunk, having no desire for the flapping tongues of the steward and night watchmen and driver to carry the story of his purchases back to the Project.

He now took his evening drink in the living room, slumped in one of the blocky overstuffed chairs where he could not see or hear the mad woman. Only after the steward had left, the faint lights had gone out in the bush, the night watchmen had made their sleepy circuit, did he appear on the veranda.

He began to write to his wife regularly. Sitting nearly every evening in the living room with a yellow legal pad on his lap, he described for the first time the trees along the narrow, crowded streets loaded with enormous calabash fruits, avocados, mangos, and green oranges; the women who squatted along the road selling cigarettes one at a time from goldfoiled Benson and Hedges packets, selling curled and blackened smoked fish impaled on long sticks, selling *ogusi* seeds and peanuts ("ground-nuts they call them here; makes more sense, doesn't it?") measured out in little milk glass jars and wrapped in cones of paper torn from used cement bags, selling strings of snails each larger than a child's head and mounds of wet black periwinkles shaped like thimble-sized Christmas trees, tiny piles of dried crayfish and slices of cooked goatmeat cut skin and all from a fly-covered haunch while buyer and seller haggled over the size. He even told her of the leper who had pressed his face, like melted plastic, against the window of the car one day, and of the thing, the head and trunk of a man, a madman, he had seen half a year earlier rotting in the marketplace.

He described the problems at the Project, his frustration at having to hire "brothers" from the huge extended family of the Indigenous Director, typists who couldn't type, file clerks who stole reams of photocopying paper and re-sold them in the market, laborers who made cement blocks by day and stole them by night. He wrote about the break-downs that allowed dozens of workers to chat or snooze in the shade until he and his grim, swearing, sweating crew of technical people found a solution—had a replacement for a burnt-out bearing flown in from Lagos or Frankfurt or Liverpool, welded a brace under a tottering storage tank, sorted out the crackling wires at a sub-station struck by a fool, killed of course, driving a bulldozer.

Sometimes, when the steward's clatter of dishes annoyed him, he went to the veranda. The mad woman was almost always there these days, waiting to begin her lecture, he thought, or maybe rehearsing it. He listened to her with contentment; he might call her in later, might not. He had taken to setting his alarm clock to go off well before daylight, before the night watchmen stirred and the driver and steward came from their quarters, chewsticks in their mouths, to urinate at the edge of the bush. It amused him that the alarm never awakened the woman; it was to her, he thought, an alien, meaningless sound, indistinguishable from the air-conditioners. On Saturday nights, when he knew the steward would not appear the next day until time to prepare lunch, he was tempted not to set the alarm; he liked the woman's warmth against him, liked to stroke the strong smoothness of her thigh when he half-awakened in the darkness and dozed off again. But he thought better of it.

It is wrong that these strange houses of yours are here, with their metal roofs and machines which make strange noises; remove them. My father and his wives, my mother among them, and their fathers before them, built good houses here; they built houses of poles stripped of their bark and set in the ground with pliant branches woven skillfully among them, wove them together and then dug a hole here—do you see where I show you—dug a hole here and found the proper clay and the women packed it carefully around the woven branches and the poles to form strong cool walls, and the boys cut the mats, many hundreds of mats, from the proper trees to make a strong cool roof, and now you have destroyed all of this. The women put a leafy green twig in the wet clay of the new walls and when the twig died the walls were dry and the house was ready for life, and now you have destroyed all of this.

It amused him to take the lappa away and find her wearing the lavender or mint-green or bright yellow wisps of underclothing he had doled out to her. He began showing her things in the house, not to satisfy her curiosity, for she seemed to have none, seemed only to stare dumbly at him, at the thick graying hair of his chest, the whiteness of his upper thighs, the brown hair of his arms and legs. In the bathroom, he put her hand against the stubble of his face, then switched on the small black machine in his hand, shaved the place she had touched, and made her touch it again. He made her hold one end of the shaver's coiled cord, then pulled it out straight and released it. He put her hand under the tap, watching her incomprehension as the water became warm, chuckling as she jerked away when it was hot. He took her to the kitchen, being sure that the curtains were tightly drawn before he turned on the lights, and showed her the cookstove, pointing to a burner where blue flames suddenly appeared, disappeared. He opened the freezer and made her touch the frost-coated side, smiling again as she flinched and shivered; he made her hold a frozen chicken, smell the stone-hard flesh. In the living room, she muttered some low sound of fear and clutched at him as she felt the thick carpet yield under her feet. He forced her to feel it, touch it with her hands, and then, aroused by her fear and uncertainty, he powerfully pushed her struggling down on the strange synthetic fur.

He thought of his leave more often—eight weeks, seven, six—and discussed plans, projects in his letters to his wife: a new sprinkler system for the lawn, a gas line to the outdoor grill; a trip to—where? Somewhere, anywhere. His son had taken an unexpected interest in computers, his wife had written, and this pleased him; he wrote of systems, of applications, the limitless possibilities.

The Project, he wrote, would be the first of such magnitude ever completed on schedule in the country, without requiring additional money at a critical point; the Company was sure to be offered new contracts, and he would be in an enviable position, for the Government would insist that he have a hand in all new projects. He could name his own terms; he might even quit and become a consultant, spend a few days here, a few there for staggering fees, return home. The Indigenous Director was a powerful man and, with a little encouragement, would see to it that he was called often. . . .

When he went into the market now to buy earrings with bits of colored glass in them, gold-colored bangles, and small boxes of talcum for the mad woman, he also bought gifts for his wife—lengths of heavy cotton splashed in tie-dye patterns, woven raffia mats, carved ebony figures, batiks, bronze heads of ancient rulers from Benin, grotesque little carved stools, huge ceremonial masks.

The mad woman now came to the veranda door quickly when he opened it. Sometimes, when he awoke in the night but had no wish to bring her in, he quietly opened the jalousies to the veranda and, hidden by the curtains, listened to her: *It is long past the time when you should have left; take away these machines which make strange noises in the night; the night should be silent; take away these machines which carry you quickly from place to place and make the dust to fill the air in the dry season; a man has feet, a man should walk slowly when he must go to some other place, and not fill the air with dust in the dry season.*

Mbakara, go now. Why do you not go now? He listened, and felt a certain contentment, and it did not occur to him to wonder why he felt this way, just as he did not wonder that to the rise and fall of her voice he now supplied meaning, or that, though he supplied it, it did not touch him; less than a woman's fluttering, ineffectually arresting hand was her constant injunction to him to go. He listened, and returned to bed, and occasionally he would think of his wife in the soft directed flow of her bedside lamp, adjusting as she turned the pages of her novel, her reading glasses, moving the ivory bookmark he had brought from somewhere. But more often he thought of the woman standing outside by the new pawpaw tree, of the whiteness of her strong even teeth, the brown heat of her breasts and their darker centers, the warmth as while she slept he traced the straight path of her spine and the sudden sweep of her buttocks. Sometimes when he thought of her in this way he rose again and brought her in.

One night, when less than a month remained before his home leave, he walked through the darkened house and opened the jalousies to hear her, but there was no sound, no movement along the strip of bare ground or in the edge of the bush beyond it. The *mbakara* peered at the shadows where he imagined there might be openings into the bush, but saw nothing. He unlocked the door to the veranda, walked to the screen, and waited expectantly, for on the rare occasions when she had not been there already, talking, the sound of the lock, or the appearance of his silhouette on the veranda, he was not sure which, had produced her quickly. But she did not come. From somewhere toward the center of the city he heard music, not the intricate patterns of native drums but the steady amplified beat of electronic instruments. It began to rain, although lower in the sky over the oil palms he could see a handful of stars.

He waited, but saw nothing, heard only the rain falling. He waited, his eyes searching the bush for flickers of light, but there was nothing. He went back to the bedroom and took a pair of earrings from his steamer trunk, ignoring the unreasonableness of the idea that, if his presence had not lured the mad woman forth, the earrings would. At the outside veranda door, turning the earrings so that they flashed in the light, he said "Come" once, and then again, before the absurdity of it—a *mbakara* in his briefs holding out a pair of earrings and calling to the rain, apparently, in the middle of the night—silenced him.

The rain's tempo increased and then abruptly stopped. He listened once more, squinting at the shadows in the bush, and turned to go in.

Then he heard her.

And in this way also have I been wronged; I will tell you—
"Ennhh! Go! Go now!"

The gardener's hand flashing in the light of his doorway, the mad woman stumbling backwards—the *mbakara* had seen it all before, but had felt nothing, nothing like the coldness gathering inside him. She stumbled, but this time, encumbered by the matchet in her right hand, the parasol and something else in her left, some small thing, she fell heavily in the wet grass as the gardener's door slammed, her flame-orange headcloth tilting, her voice rising sharply. She got up quickly, shouting *Yes! I will tell you of this wronging!* She raised the matchet and brought it down hard against the door, embedding the end of the blade, wrenched it out and struck again, leaving the knife quivering in the door while she adjusted her headcloth.

Tell you of it very simply—
She opened the parasol, although the rain had stopped, raised it, and then worked the matchet loose from the door. *When the first mbakara came to this place, my land, they brought machines—*

Cold he felt momentarily in the hot wet night, and then the hot anger flashing through him like the flash of the matchet, of the flame-colored headcloth.

In that concrete shack, he thought; that grinning little bastard.

—brought machines and the machines of the mbakara pushed the trees and the yam plots from this place—

Something in his hand, like dried peas: he looked at the earrings, grimaced, and opened the veranda door to fling them out, then stopped. She was moving toward the veranda.

—pushed me and the trees and the yam plots from it.

She stood by the new pawpaw tree, her bangles flashing on her wrists, headcloth towering and glinting in the security lights, holding her parasol over her. Something, what looked like wadded brown paper, was stuffed under the edge of her lappa, between her breasts.

The mbakara built these strange houses—

As she talked she bent and struck the ground with her matchet from this, then that angle, cutting wedges from the wet soil.

—these houses which are not of stripped branches—

He glanced at the gardener's quarters, saw that it was dark, then held out the earrings in the palm of his hand.

"Come," he said. Birdseed, he thought as he shook the earrings in his hand. Crumbs. As she moved from the pawpaw tree to him, he felt the pure heat of his increasing anger and smiled.

—are not of stripped branches and the clay of this earth—

"Come," he said, taking the parasol from her and closing it, putting it back in her hand and pushing her up the veranda steps. Her plastic sandals flapped as she walked ahead of him to the bedroom.

—are not roofed with the proper mats, which should not be built here.

After he had shut the bedroom door behind her and turned on the light, she opened the parasol again and held it up, as if to shield herself from the bright bulbs.

Then the new black men came, and the mbakara gave these strange houses which should not be here to the new—

The *mbakara* held out the earrings. "Look. For you." he twisted the matchet from her hand, laid it on the floor, and placed the earrings in her palm, but when her fingers did not close upon them and she continued talking, he took them again and held them to her ears. "For you. Take them now."

He smiled again. "Bonus night. Take them." He pressed their sharp edge against her ears, watching her face, but she turned her head away without changing expression.

—gave them to the new black men, and those mbakara went away. And the new black men lived in these strange houses which were wrongfully built on my land.

"All right, all right now," the *mbakara* said. When he turned to put the earrings on the dresser, she stooped and retrieved the matchet. He pulled at the tuck of her lappa and as it came away the wad of brown paper fell from her breasts to the floor, opened, and peanuts rolled and scattered around their feet.

They lived in the houses and would not return my land to me, although they were black men.

For a moment, he could not comprehend the meaning of them; the shelled peanuts rolled away in every direction while he stood holding the corner of the lappa, and then he understood. He dropped the lappa.

They lived in the houses for a few seasons—

"Peanuts," he said. "Peanuts he gave you." He slapped her, the sound sharp even over the air conditioner, bending her over and turning her sideways to him, the headcloth tumbling away. "Ten kobo worth of peanuts, God damn you!" He brought the open palm of his other hand up and caught her full in the face, knocking her back against the wall, and stepped forward to hit her again, the wetness of her saliva and the impact of her flesh rich and sweet in his hands, but she swung blindly with the matchet and he barely dodged out of the way.

—for a few seasons, and there were no yam plots for me, no frames of bent sticks for the long pumpkins to grow large on. Her voice high and wavering, she stood erect again, blood dribbling from her nose and over her mouth and chin.

"Shut up, shut up now. No more talk." Remembering the night watchmen asleep on their mats on the front porch and fearing that she might be heard even over the noise of the air conditioners, the *mbakara* tried to put his hand over her mouth, but she backed away, gripping the rough wooden handle of the matchet and raising the blade. Setting the open parasol on the floor, she stooped to retrieve her headcloth without taking her eyes from him, settled it on her head, and then took up the parasol again.

No place for the waterleaf, and the bitterleaf, and the small peppers to grow—

The impatience and crossness in her voice increased, its pitch, the *mbakara* thought, going ever higher. He could not, for the moment, make out what to do, what to do quickly; the feel of her, skin and soft flesh beneath the skin, and bone and teeth, was still in his hands, and he felt, remembered, an exultation, a . . . freedom in the hitting of her, and he wanted to do it again; the peanuts crunched under his feet and he remembered the gardener, stared at the iridescent bit of cloth tapering down to her crotch, its wetness, and thought, *from him*, and anger shot through him again, his hands raised, tightened into fists. But he thought of the night watchmen and dropped his hands to his sides.

The black men would not give my land back to me, and then the new mbakara came, the new mbakara, you among them—

She kept the parasol over the regal folds of her headcloth. She regained her composure, except that her voice quavered higher. Her eyes held his as she talked, and as always the reasonableness, the balance of what she had to to say touched him, appealed to him. He listened to her, let his anger drain away as her brown African eyes held him. He thought of other nights, and he regretted the swelling of her lip, the blood not yet dried under her nostrils. He remembered with a sudden rush of tenderness the acquiescence of her in their silent threshing on the bed, the comfort of her sleeping close to him; and a warmth as pure as his earlier anger flowed through him; he smiled and moved quickly to her, opening his arms to pull her to him, but she twisted away and simultaneously he saw the effortless movement of her wrist, the flat blurred arc of the matchet, and a long straight colorless line across his thigh, thin as a hair, an instant later red as blood, and then he felt the pain.

"Damn you!" He leaped back, stumbling against the bed,

then regained his footing. Her voice was high now, strong in her anger: *the black men would not give my land back to me, and then the new mbakara came, the new mbakara, you among them, and the black men gave the new mbakara this land, my land, with the strange houses which should not be built here, gave it to the new mbakara—*

"All right, damn you!" The blood was pouring from the cut, already spotting the floor. He grabbed the lappa and flung it in her face. "All right, go! Go now!" He pointed at the door, but the lappa dropped and she stepped over it, the parasol still poised, and stood in the center of the room. *And now they are here, you are here as wrongfully as the other mbakara and the black men who came after them. Why do you persist in remaining here when I tell you of these things?*

"Go now!" he hissed, mindful of the night watchmen. He stepped toward her but stopped when he saw the matchet blade draw back. "God damn you," he whispered, nearly sobbing, "Go! Get out!" But her voice rose steadily, and she did not move. The wetness down his leg frightened and infuriated him, and his hands began to shake.

You understand now the wrong which has been done to me; you understand now what must be done to undo this wrong; you must leave.

He went into the bathroom, pulled the coiled cord from the shaver, and stretched it, testing it, his hands quivering. Then he went back into the bedroom and began moving around her, taking a step, stopping, another step, the black cord doubled and concealed in his fists at his waist.

You must leave now, with your machines which go too quickly from place to place, which disturb the night. You must leave, and the other mbakara with you, and you must not send other mbakara or other black men to this place, for this is not their place.

She turned slowly as he moved, but he circled to her right so that the arc of the matchet would be away from him, gradually closing on her, and when he was within arm's reach he stepped forward quickly and put the cord over her head and jerked, snapping her neck back and knocking the head-cloth away. He drove his knee into her lower back, and as she dropped the parasol and fell he spun and fell with her, pinning her beneath him, driving his forehead into the black twists of her hair and grinding her face into the metal braces of the parasol. The matchet blade struck weakly over his leg, but he kept the cord taut and buried in the softness of her throat and shifted so that both knees were on her back, his leg beyond the matchet's reach, and soon the matchet clattered on the floor and her writhing ceased.

He watched the clock by the bed: two minutes, three. Four. Five. He pulled the cord from her, stood up, and went into the bathroom. There were new, shallower cuts on his lower leg, and blood seeped steadily from his thigh. He bathed the cuts, dried them, and poured on antiseptic, groaning as he opened the long cut.

When he had stopped the bleeding and dressed the deeper wound, he took a basin of soapy water and retraced his steps, washing up the trail of drying blood as best he could. With his foot he turned the woman over on her back, noting the angular marks the parasol braces had left on her face. He closed the parasol and laid it by her side, refolded the lappa, and stood with it in his hands, thinking of new contracts, consultancies, of what to do with the body at his feet. He remembered the thing he had seen at the crossroads in the marketplace, the madman, his legs and arms gnawed and torn away by dogs and God knows what else in the night. A madman. She was mad: no one, not her family, not the other squatters there in the bush, not the police, not even a beggar, would touch her. He opened the lappa and rolled the matchet, the parasol, and her sandals in it, then went to the living room and looked cautiously through the curtains: the watchmen were asleep, curled tightly in their thin blankets. The rain was falling again. He opened the door to the veranda and unlocked the outside veranda door, then returned to the bedroom and took a flashlight from a dresser drawer. Kneeling, he hoisted her over his shoulder, grunting at the unexpected weight; he snugged the rolled lappa under his arm and carried her to the veranda, where he stopped and peered about intently; there was no light, no sound but the drumming of the rain on the metal roof. He walked quickly over the bare wet ground past the new pawpaw tree, and after several false starts found the opening into the bush. Flinching away from the wet branches, he went in carefully a few steps before switching on the light, keeping the beam down on the narrow path. Mindful of things he had heard about but not seen—cobras, even more deadly green mambas dangling from the tree limbs—he followed the erratic path for twenty-five, perhaps fifty yards, shivering in the rain, and then he dropped the rolled lappa in a clump of tall green grass by the path and laid her awkwardly over it, face up. He held the light briefly on her face, already wet from the rain, the eyes wide and staring, her lips drawn back from her white, even teeth; then he hurried back along the path and across the cleared ground into the house.

By the next evening, as he sat on the veranda, the brown vultures were circling thickly over the bush.

"Dis mad woman dead, sah," the steward said as he set the *mbakara's* drink down.

"What?" A squeak, barely discernible, was beginning in one of the overhead fans. He frowned. A bit of oil there.

"Mad woman, sah." He pointed toward the bush, the vultures. "In dah. She dead."

"How did she die?" Like all wounds in the tropics, his had become infected quickly, but the doctor at the Project had opened it and cleansed it thoroughly and given him antibiotics and a booster shot for tetanus, and now he rested his bandaged leg stiffly on a footstool.

The steward looked at him, perplexed. Who can tell what question a *mbakara* will ask? "She *mad*, sah. She dead." He padded back to the kitchen.

Home leave. Less than four weeks now. The *mbakara* thought of his wife's dry floral arrangements in asymmetrical, imperfectly brown glass vases, found in an antique shop somewhere . . . Vermont? New Hampshire, maybe. He smiled as he imagined her vaguely irritated, vaguely amused protestations when they unpacked the crate, the huge, grinning, triple-faced masks topped with white crocodiles and pink-spotted snakes, the reliefs of toad-shaped men squatting with club-like erections, of women with swollen bellies and navels like bananas and breasts like pawpaws. . . .

"But what . . . what do you expect me to *do* with these monstrosities?" she would say.

He smiled and sipped his drink, shook the quarter of fresh lime down into the ice. The new pawpaw tree was as high, no, higher now than the metal gable of the house, and a second tier of fruit was forming below the first, yellowing to ripeness. He stretched, grimaced at the pain in his thigh, and thought of the mad woman bathing her brown body with the yellow soap under the broad green banana leaf, bedecking herself with the gold-colored bangles and pink blouse and wisps of underclothing, thought of the rhythmic, patient reasonableness of her complaint as she stood under the rainbow-tinted parasol, remembered with a stab of regret the quiet close warmth of her sleeping and the quiet close struggling of her dying, and then the *mbakara*, master through and through, frowned and put her from his mind.

Marshall Terry

The Antichrist

CARL WOLFGANG WENDLAND.

It was a name that brought me pleasure, and then suddenly seemed the most sinister that I had ever known.

Now it seems to me more sad than sinister, but terrible still.

The year I am recalling is 1952. I was a new graduate student then, doing Master's work in English in the university here, a Teaching Fellow, taking three courses and teaching two freshman classes, teaching in the mornings, boot grammar by negative example, often reading from the textbook in desperation when hung up on the use of the gerund as an abverb or some such thing, pacing the classroom, staring out the window at the still campus, then in the afternoons trying to sell pharmaceuticals about which I knew nothing but the Latin names I memorized to doctors I never got to see (my biggest, perhaps my only, sale was of a large order of testosterone to a lady doctor), and in the evenings throwing a paper route, being yelled at because the paper was delivered late, or cursed because often it was not folded correctly and would open as I threw it and sail in several flapping sections into the waiting yards.

It was a confused and crucial, and beautiful young year, when I was poor and idealistic and just married, and I was living under several influences.

One was Eich. One was Milo. The other was Karl Wendland.

Milo was the one whose spell I was most under, because I truly loved him.

Milo was a teacher. No advanced degrees, weary peripatetic who had taught freshman courses here or there for many years, a ruined, defeated old teacher, Milo was, for all his satiric shield and timeworn oblique edges of personality, yet sweetly spirited. Who loved to teach those damn kids, to read and mark and form their ragged themes. (*Old*. My God, who was then about the age that I am now.)

Milo, who had, who never had any more than, the rank of instructor was my office mate in the basement of the old building. Sometimes he would suffer me, and we would talk.

And Eich. He was critical, cynical, objective, a brilliant mind, a scholar. His study was of the structure and history of the language, but sometimes he would relax and teach Shakespeare, making of the plays a pattern of neologisms and syntax, a scholar's code, relieving them of their humanness, their glory. I despised Eich, and feared him. I thought that he was almost evil, that he stood for the dead hand upon life and literature, in comparison to Milo, who loved the merest essay that he taught, if it had any worth at all, and made you love it too.

And Wendland. How shall I describe Wendland and what he meant to me, and then came to mean to me?

Eich wished for me, for all of us who were the department's slaves, its Fellows, to go on and take the Ph.D., a good Ph.D. somewhere reputable, and never to return to his university, but to bring honor to the department. His family had been killed in Germany.

Wendland gave a piece of silver to my wife and me when we married. He had us, with other students, out to his farm in the evening to roast franks and drink cider around a fire, when he sang to us Middle English ballads.

He was in his sixties. Tall, white-haired, ruddy, a splendid-looking man, but somewhat shambling in his gait. He carried a stick and wore a pith helmet as he walked to and from his house nearby to the campus, and his little dog accompanied him. For forty years Karl Wendland had taught in the university. It was legend that he was, early, one of the best and most popular teachers. It was said that he'd taught *Beowulf* to standing-room classes of sixty or seventy students. I knew that he had written books. You could find him in *Who's Who* and in the *Dictionary of International Scholars*. He had done definitive work on the *Finnsburg Fragment*, and then had turned to a series of pleasant little works for children on the tribes who held England in the days of Alfred. His was a distinguished name in Anglo-Saxon.

And he was Ph.D., Johns Hopkins, and B.A., Oxon., and of an old family of southern aristocracy.

All of which, I am sure, contributed.

I remember so well the pleasure of my first class in Old English with him.

Together we chanted the Lord's Prayer in Anglo-Saxon.

Then: "How do you pronounce this word?" he said, writing O-h-t-h-e-r-e on the blackboard.

I raised my hand, having studied in advance alone the old language, relishing it.

"Oht-here," I said.

His blue eyes, the yellow-white moustache crinkled with pleasure over the rich red lips. "Only one other student has ever got that right," he said. "Most are not aware, and pronounce it with the *th* sound. You will do well, my boy, you will do well."

After class he called me up, and congratulated me again, and asked my name, and if I was Jewish, which I thought a little strange.

And I did do well, and enjoyed him and his class thoroughly, though others seemed somewhat cowed in there. I told some other students that Karl Wendland was the best teacher I'd ever had, much more alive and spirited than Eich, under whom I was reducing the history of the language to formulae. They seemed to think that I was crazy, but not many people liked Old English, its difficulty, much.

Milo it was who told what I should have found out, should have known. He had taken to coffee once or twice a beautiful young senior student named Sally Cohn. I came into our office when she was there and saw that she had been crying, and she looked at me and left.

"The old bastard," Milo said. "The damnable old bastard. Made her stand up in class, in the middle of his Renaissance class, and admit that she was Jewish."

I sat down, dumping my load of unmarked themes.

"Oh, she admitted it all right," Milo said, smoking his cigarette savagely. "She made public confession of the fact. It would not be a bad idea for me to get up from here and go up into that evil stinking office of his and kill him. That, I suppose, is the only remedy for him."

Milo, the old seeming-apathetic stoic.

"What?" I said. "Wendland? What?"

"Go read that book he inscribed for you so beautifully," Milo said. "You stupid little horse's ass."

Karl Wendland had presented me with a copy of his latest book a few days before. Its odd title was *The Wall Around America*. With a plain cover, privately printed, it had seemed to be something out of his field, perhaps even political, but I had been busy and had not gone into it, not taken it beyond the title page. There he'd written, in his elegant script *To a brilliant young linguist. Ad astra!*

And I went and read the book then, read through it in one searing night of reading.

At first I could not believe what I was reading; but then I came to believe it all too well.

Essentially Professor Wendland held the idea, presented in the book, that all Jews were Communists and all Communists were Jews.

It was a very neat idea, and it framed all his view of history, and of the present situation in our nation and the world.

Jews were identified with the Eastern hordes. The greatest moment in history came with the halting of the advance of these hordes at the Elbe by the Teutonic Knights. But their insidious inroads had perverted the cross of Christ and the destiny of Western Christian man ever since. For Jews, you see, were in secret control of all the nations of the world, and ever had been, since that early noble, courageous time. Secretly, using a veil of anti-Semitism over the minds of the peasant mass, Jews in the Comintern ran Russia. Oriental Jews were in control in China. As for America, Wilson's advisor, Colonel House, whom Wendland once had met, was a Jew, and in control throughout Wilson's term, through his sickness and his phony internationalism and his leading us on the secret course to war. It was no secret that F. D. Roosevelt was a Jew, and an ally of the Reds. Now, Eisenhower was a Jew.

Thus, with Jews in control of all the nations, and all wealth, and all power of the world, all wars were waged for their profit, nations rose and fell to their benefit. America was completely surrounded, and rotten at the core. But there were still good Christians in America, still some who could and would rise to fight the Red Jewish menace and save America.

These, I supposed, comprised those who had already taken Dr. Wendland's book into its seventh printing.

"And do you see that the bastard has dedicated this last edition, the one you have, so proudly signed, to the B'nai B'rith," Milo said, "without whose interest, as he says, its success would not have been possible? Jesus God!"

"That's it exactly," Milo said as we talked of it again, when my dismay had begun to turn into the coldest kind of anger. "The worst thing about it— Oh hell, boy, bigots abound, always will, I reckon, skunks smelling their own odor and callin' it bad— But what this man has done: lent his name as a scholar, his reputation, to this fabrication of genius: genius because there is just enough truth in it, enough facts—an actual battle here, a historically valid judgment here—to make the straw into the phony brick to make the construct, and to give credence to it in the eyes of the stupid and the ignorant. That's a sin, boy," Milo said. "For a teacher, a scholar, that is a terrible sin. To say nothing of the basic hatefulness of it, the sickness of the man."

And that is what I did: say nothing.

But I went to class sparingly, only just as much as I calculated could let me keep my A. He knew, of course, I could tell it from his smile at me, which in a darting, nearly maniac way if you began so to interpret it, was really very merry. And I begrudged and berated myself the times when he taught well, moved me and the class to an appreciation of the old language—the saga of the slaying of the monsters. And hated myself when something in me could not help but respond to the magnetism of the man, his vitality, his zest. My God, what vital force is it that evil has, that we pale before it?

I began to join those who knew who slunk down the hall to the classrooms by his large office lined with books and dusty portraits of Jespersen and God knows who else where his secretary—the only private secretary in the department—sat like a blackiron stove sorting, filing, never smiling, a Mrs. Woodcipher, and where he would be, laughing jollily, with men in dark shirts and brown ties with floppy hats they did not remove. I remember so clearly the seamed set faces of those men as they sat in there, as if drawn into some sort of absurd cartoon.

And the semester went on. Wendland wrote, and distributed, to us, to the town, and beyond, a pamphlet pointing out how our university was in the hands of the communist Jewish conspiracy and quite out of the hands of the church from whose womb it had not too long before tottered.

Everyone knew, then.

"He is the Antichrist, the very Antichrist!" said on campus to me our president, a handsome, athletic young man. "Do you know what he said to me? He *smiled* at me and said—he smiled at me— 'Who's going to bell that cat?'"

"Well, I'm glad we're smart enough not to do it," Milo said. "I'm glad we ain't going to grant him martyrdom."

"Shit," Milo said, "that would take it into twenty printings."

And in November, late, young MacDowell, of History, petitioned for a called meeting of the General Faculty, and got enough votes to call it, declaring he would offer a motion of faculty censure of Dr. Karl Wolfgang Wendland.

I was talking about my term paper in linguistics with Eich, and abruptly asked him what he thought of this.

For a moment I did not think that he would answer me,

wondered if I had disappeared for my presumption. His cold eyes stared away from me, his icelike face held in one bony hand; then he answered, spitting as he spoke, speaking to me a speech.

"I have hated every fascist thing he has ever done, said or written. For thirty years.

"And yet, much as I favor, emotionally, Dr. MacDowell's notion as odious as he is to me, I refuse to vote to censure him.

"I have fought him—and finally just avoided him—in this department. He has made my life hell. He has severely damaged the reputation of this department which I—and I must say this, which he too—labored to build over the years.

"But strictly speaking, and no matter what—no matter what in *hell*—they are, he has the right to hold to his opinions.

"Have you found that he presents these opinions to you in his class?"

"No. But he—"

"What?"

"Never mind," I said. His cold eyes looked at me, and I could have read more mercy or humanity in a snake's. Were these the eyes of justice? I could not feel so . . .

Yet, my own eyes said into them, they killed your people, man!

Do not presume to say another word to me, they glittered. *I have relish in this: My only pleasure is to hold the ark in my hands and smell of it, that it stinks.*

So I went away from him, my idea of writing my paper on international languages having been rejected.

And in early December the faculty held its meeting.

MacDowell moved his resolution of censure.

Milo got up and left the meeting.

The vote was 351-1 to censure Wendland. I voted against him. Eich cast the only dissenting vote to the resolution. That evening I stayed late in my basement office (Milo off somewhere, I imagined drunk), grading themes. Walking home along the edge of campus I encountered Wendland, going along with his little dog, and his hat, and stick. The sky was gray, and the sun had a peculiar orange light to it not common to the prairie. He was going along laughing, talking to himself, shuffling almost into a dance. He grabbed my arm as I nodded, before I could dart by. He looked at me with great good humor and forgiveness. He leaned his ruddy red face into mine and the bright blue eyes caught mine straight on for a moment: "The only thing I fear," he said, "is an assassin's bullet." And caned forward, walking like a bear, following a new route toward home, the little dog sniffing the way before him along the trail, warily, warily.

The censure bothered him about that much. The book had more printings. The university let him teach until retirement.

Eich, I understand, died a few years ago. Milo is still teaching somewhere. Soon after all this I left graduate school and went into advertising.

In retirement Wendland wrote a very pleasant novel of his childhood and had it printed. Wendland died finally, neither admired nor feared nor much remembered by anyone. Which was in my mind just now as I took from the shelf and balanced in my hands my inscribed copy of his book.

Allen Wier

Campbell Oakley's Gospel Sun Shines on Roy Singing Grass

Framed in the windshield, the country looked like a color snapshot. The engine was still running thickly, tight with last night's freeze. Roy's fingers were pink and stung where he'd nicked them on the hood when he re-filled the truck's radiator. He scrunched his shoulders up to his ears, trying to recall the warmth of his sleeping bag.

I'm getting too old, he thought, to run all over hell and half of Georgia. This is the last year for me. I'll send the boys next year. Roy smiled at himself. He had made the same resolution every year for the last four. Next year, next year I'll send my work and let Bill Tom and Jimmy do the hawking. I reckon they can have a rodeo without me. One Indian's good as another, and Bill Tom and Jimmy are good boys. I can stay home and work my loom.

Roy had gone to the Indian reservation to find out how to construct the loom. He had spent months creating his most important work, a beaded tapestry of intricate detail and difficult patterns. It was his life's history told in Indian picture writing designs. He was getting old and he wanted to finish the tapestry before his death. Now, as he rocked and bounced down an Arkansas highway, he was anxious to get home and return to the loom. In the regular, fast flashings of stripes on the highway Roy saw the loom moving, bright stripes of wool working lines of color into shapes.

Hungry, Roy began to look for a truck stop along the highway. In the distance something reflected the morning sun, and he slowed the truck. He could not make out a sign, but a wood building began to fill in between the trees. The shed was the gray of a newspaper photograph, the boards were loose and warped, showing dark cracks of the interior. Nailed in rows on the side wall were scores of shiny automobile hubcaps, like Viking shields on the side of an old ship; the heraldry blazoned on their chrome fronts was the reflected color and form of the sun and trees and junk strewn before the shed. Unfurled above the hubcaps was a white tin sign bearing the familiar Coca-Cola, and the words, ODESSA'S ODDS N ENDS. Hanging from the sign was a figure made of old tires wired together in a crude effigy. All manner of harness, strap, bridle, and blinder hung off a nail on a lopsided plywood door leaning off its hinges under an enormous horseshoe. To the side of the shed a once red '39 Pontiac knelt forward on broken axles like a camel kneeling for a rider, its rear end hiked up on cinder blocks. A heap of rusted mufflers rose up around a telephone pole like logs piled around a stake. Sitting on a porcelain commode, astride a heavy saddle thrown over the commode seat, one foot in a dangling stirrup, the other leg missing from just above the knee, was an immense old man.

As Roy got closer he slowed the truck to a crawl. Beside the man was a short clothesline with several quilts and a string of license plates hanging from it. Roy pulled off the highway onto the gravel shoulder and stopped short of the rust-gutted Pontiac.

The man did not even look up.

In front of him sat a gray granite tombstone, and on the flat crown of the stone marker an ancient radio blared through the spittle of static. Badly cracked bands of black electrician's tape holding it together, the radio had a huge dial on its front with a red pointer like the speedometer on Roy's truck. From behind the dial two wires ran to a black box on the ground. Walking around a quilt of red heart-shaped designs and blue flowers, Roy saw that the radio was connected to an automobile battery. One post of the battery was covered with white dirtlike grains of corrosion; a copper penny stuck crookedly out of the soft, tarry battery by the dull silver post.

"Howdy, old man. What've you got there. Old radio?"

The man looked up slowly, his mouth leaking chocolate colored juice. He spat, but said nothing.

"Mind if I look around? I like junk shops. Like to see what I can find I might make something out of."

Roy pointed to the red letters painted on the side of his truck, "My name's Roy Singing Grass. I've got a crafts plant down near Shreveport."

The man spat again and took a plug out of his shirt pocket, cut a thick slice of the tobacco, and pushed it into his cheek.

Roy continued, "I've been coming up this highway eight, nine years now. Never saw this place before."

The man took his foot out of the stirrup and pulled himself up on his one leg. Leaning over the tombstone and radio he pulled a wooden crate over.

"Sit a spell, Indian."

Roy straddled the box, "You Odessa?"

The man looked puzzled.

"Well, sign says Odessa's—"

"Oh, no—no, not me. My wife. That's Odessa. Second wife, that is, Her name's Odessa. I'm Prute."

"Been here long?"

"Yep, been here since Cambell Oakley started his show."

The old man rotated his neck, stretching; the wrinkled skin making loose diamond patterns on the back of his neck, his stubble of white beard crinkling like dry, crisp grass.

"Never missed Cambell Oakley's show. Had him to dedicate a gospel song in my name once. Wrote him myself. That was four years ago. Had a bad snow that winter. Sixteen inches, more in drifts."

"Sixteen inches? Not around here."

The old man looked deep into Roy's face. Barely moving his lips, as if he were revealing a dark, terrible secret, "Des Moines, Des Moines in Iowa."

Roy was fascinated. "You get Des Moines, Iowa, way down here?"

Prute grinned and nodded, chuckling, almost giggling.

Roy hunched over, elbows on knees to hear. "Can I turn it up?"

"That's as high as she goes. See for yourself. Here, use these, ain't got knobs."

Roy took the pliers and twisted the rod sticking out where the knob was missing. He turned it both ways, but the volume remained low and treble. He used the pliers on the rod marked Tuner. The red needle moved back and forth across the face of the instrument like a loose windshield wiper, but the station did not waver or change.

> *Will the circle be unbroken*
> *By and by, Lord, by and by*
> *There's a better home a waiting*
> *In the sky, Lord, in the sky . . .*

Prute's foot was tapping out the tune in the stirrup. "That there was one of Odessa's favorites."

"Was? She's dead?"

"Oh, yeah. She passed on not long after I got the radio. Been twelve years now. We was in Murfreesboro then. Took her all the way to Arkadelphia to the funeral home. She always admired that funeral home in Arkadelphia."

Roy said nothing, but the faraway singing coming through the radio filled the silence. When the singing ended, Roy stood. "Guess I better be getting on down the road." He stuck out his hand to Prute, and, just then, his stomach growled.

Chuckling again, Prute poked Roy in the belly. "Come on Indian, you better eat with me first."

Roy glanced at his truck and thought about the miles ahead of him.

"Oh, come on, Indian. I don't usually get nobody to eat with. We'll get the noon weather report in a little bit. You shouldn't go on until you know what weather to expect."

Roy grinned. "Yeah, in Iowa. But I might as well grub with you as some greasy spoon on down the road."

"Good. Help me with the bat'ry, I've got the radio." Prute was up on his leg, the radio cradled in one arm, a heavy walking cane in the other hand holding himself up.

Roy leaned down and picked the battery up. "You live in the shed?" he asked.

"Out back. We can go through, though."

They stepped through the loose plywood door into the cool dark of the shed. The floor was hard earth. Inside, the smell was of dirt and cobwebs. Dirt dobbers' nests lined the ceiling where it met the walls. Several iron beds were stacked up on one side, shipping tags wired to each, prices marked on them. A wringer washer sat crookedly in the corner, surrounded by empty mason jars on the ground. Nailed to the wall were more hubcaps and a scythe with a broken blade. Rows of old straight-backed wooden chairs were stacked along the front wall, their legs sticking stiffly up toward the ceiling.

"What do you do with all this junk, Prute?"

"Oh, you'd be surprised what some folks'll pay for this stuff. Lots of them chairs are antique. Lady from Memphis paid me fifty dollars for one of them brass beds, just last Tuesday. I don't have to have many sales like that to keep me in grub. Besides, I've got my leg money." Prute slapped his thigh where the leg was missing, "Government." He paused a moment to spit. "Lost it in the war. Got run over by a damned truck. Right here in the U.S. Whole friggin war I never left the country, and lost my goddamn leg." He laughed. "Been worth more to me since I lost it."

They went out a narrow back door across a strip of dead grass into Prute's little shack. He had two small rooms and a toilet stuck on back with a board fence tacked around it. A blue bedspread divided the makeshift bathroom from the sitting and sleeping room. In the kitchen was a huge wood stove and a small refrigerator. A hotplate sat on a cardtable.

"Set'er down there." Prute indicated an apple crate under the table, and Roy gingerly set the battery down. Prute put the radio on his cot beside the table. "I've been sleepin in here lately. It's warmer."

Roy sat on the cot and listened to the radio:

. . . and for Des Moines and Central Iowa we'll have partly cloudy to cloudy today, with a chance of rain come this evening, maybe turning to freezing rain mixed with snow by tomorrow morning. Here at our studios we have a humidity reading of 67—or maybe it's 76—I can't read old Country Red's scribbling. Anyhow, friends and neighbors, it's cold out today. We have 33 degrees here on the Cambell Oakley get together, so you stay right where you're at, and we'll do our part to bring some good old gospel sunshine into your house.

Prute heated up a can of soup and put some cold fried chicken on the table. "That old wood burner's too much trouble. I usually just use the hot coils."

They ate in silence, listening to the radio.

After Prute stacked the plates in the sink, Roy helped him carry the radio back to his seat in front of the shed.

"I like to sit here. I can watch people pass. See a good piece down the highway in either direction. I saw three wrecks since I've been here. Saw just one when we was in Murfreesboro, but that wasn't no highway to talk about. Course, only one killed in all four I saw. Little girl died in her daddy's arms right there beside that litter barrel. Likely I'll see one or two more killed before I pass on to glory. Just sitting here and the whole world comes to me. Know what I mean, Indian?"

"Yeah, sure, but don't you ever want to go someplace? I mean just move about a little?"

"Not me. I been to Chicago and New Orleans. I lived in Murfreesboro, Caddo Gap, and Stamps. I lost my leg smack in the middle of Kansas. Moving is just meddling. I suspect I'll make that last trip back to Murfreesboro and be laid out beside Odessa. Got me a plot, it's all arranged. Meanwhile I can tramp around here and keep an eye on the road. You know, Indian, you're about the first person I've spoke with, since the parson, same one spoke Odessa's burying, come by and got him some hubs for his boy's jalopy. I tell you, I don't think I like talking so much anymore. You just seem better than most. Because you're an Indian, I guess. You've got knowing eyes, and you don't come in here trying to overpay me for no brass bed. I'm glad you come, Singing Grass, but you better get on if you plan on makin Louisiana tonight."

"You know, Prute, most all this junk you've got I wouldn't want, but I sure do like your radio. I remember one kinda like that when I was a kid living with my Momma in a trailer. Course it couldn't pick up Iowa programs. That radio, I sure would buy that from you."

"This ain't no ordinary radio, that's for sure. Course, I can't sell'er, and you know it. You know, I've got the weather in Des Moines every day for over twelve years. I'm the only man in Arkansas can tell you if its fixing to snow in Des Moines. I got Cambell Oakley, and I got gospel sunshine coming in from Iowa, off the snow, off the cold wind, beaming in from farms and trees and brick buildings in Des Moines, from Iowa; I got names of stores selling at special prices in Des Moines, I know robbers and killings and elections and sports scores from Iowa."

Prute shook his head from side to side, coughing up little laughs from deep in his chest, "I been knowing the weather in Des Moines for over twelve years now."

Roy laughed and, thanking the old man for the food, climbed back into his truck.

He caught the litter barrel in the corner of his eye as he pulled onto the highway and he thought about the little girl for a moment. Then he saw the gleam of the hubcaps in his rearview, as the shed and junk and Prute disappeared behind him.

As the truck hummed down the road the afternoon sun flickered bright and soft shadows through dense pines. Roy was warm and comfortable. He thought of his loom and of his life he was weaving into the tapestry.

His mother was Navaho Indian. His father, a cajun from

Belle Chasse, Louisiana, had been an occasional jockey at New Orleans. Edgar Bertrand Larousse was his name, and he was a transient, following the horses. They led him through Santa Fe one sticky, moonless night where he spent his last six dollars on a pint of gin and a young Indian girl at a bawdy house known as Moma Luz's. The girl was seventeen and pretty. Larousse told her he would take her to New Orleans to live on his daddy's plantation if she could get them some money. She took extra customers without telling Moma Luz, and that money, with forty dollars she stole from Moma, got them back to Belle Chasse.

There was no plantation, only a rundown trailer house that a man named Faciane had given Larousse for riding Faciane's horse to a second place finish at the fairgrounds in New Orleans. Larousse promised to save enough to send Roy's mother back to her family in Albuquerque, but long before he got any money, he got her pregnant. Nearly ten months later, Roy Singing Grass Larousse was born.

"I took that extra month trying to decide whether I wanted to be born," he used to tell people. "And now I see what a big mistake that was," he'd laugh. "My momma," he told them, "named me Singing Grass because it's an Indian custom to name the firstborn after the first things the mother hears and sees after her delivery."

"Hah," someone would laugh, "that'd of made you named Cussing Jockey." Roy laughed too and managed to get along in a white man's world.

Roy's father may have cursed Roy's birth, but he continued to follow the races and send enough money to keep his new son and common-law wife alive. When Larousse was in New Orleans he slept at the fairgrounds, but sometimes he staggered into the trailer in Belle Chasse, and Roy buried his face in his pillow trying not to listen to his father's loud demands.

When Roy was eight, his father left New Orleans, as was his custom, to find other races. He sent them ten dollars from Hot Springs, and they never heard from him again.

The sun was down and lights coming on as Roy slowed to pass through Prescott. As it got full dark and cars became pairs of red or white lights, he could not shake the words of the song he'd heard on Prute's radio:

Will the circle be unbroken
By and by, Lord, by and by
There's a better home a waiting
In the sky, Lord, in the sky . . .

He imagined the radio station in Des Moines. There was a room, so black dark that, at first, it seemed to have no floor or ceiling, just endless blackness. Then, as his eyes adjusted to the darkness, he saw a dull yellow light near the back of the room. There was a glass partition between him and the light, illuminating a shadowy figure hunched lazily over the turntable, the record arm a skinny, dark, Indian child's arm, the cartridge and needle a clenched hand dragging one long, thin fingernail over the records; or now he saw it as a snake curved over the records, flicking his tongue into the grooves and hissing out the dusty songs. The stacks of records were plates stacked in Prute's sink, pancakes in Mother's trailer, the leaning stacks of old tires at the junkyard, the skyline of a monstrous black metropolis. The disc jockey's cigarette glowed one red dot, suspended in air, growing out of his black chest, trailing red streaks in the darkness—like taillights in front of Roy's speeding truck, like the red-tipped wand of the conductor or the magician at the Strand when Roy was a boy, like the trail of the sparklers he wrote his name in the air with the Fourth of July before his daddy went away for good. The cigarette wrote the words in the air, easily, slowly; the turntable revolved insolently; the words floated out of the black outline of earphones on the figure's head:

I was standing by the window
One dark and cloudy day
When I saw that hearse come rolling
For to carry my mother away . . .

From behind the disc jockey a clock peered out at the scene, its minute hand revolving effortlessly, monotonously. It whined, softly, electrically, with the tune:

Will the circle be unbroken
By and by, Lord, by and by;
There's a better home a waiting
In the sky, Lord, in the sky . . .

The disc jockey raised his head, the light cast dusky shadows on his features. He stifled a yawn and glanced over his shoulder at the clock. Leaning back to stretch, he shuffled his feet to wake them. They were cold; it was down to 30 degrees in Des Moines. Only 7:30. He was working Country Red's shift tonight, as well as his own. Country Red's wife was in the hospital with pneumonia. What the hell, he thought, I'll get some overtime. But I'd rather get some sleep. He listened as the song was ending and wondered how many times he'd have to listen to this hick country gospel music between now and six o'clock the next morning.

Roy grinned, the fantasy was funny, but at the same time sad in a way he did not understand.

The image of the disc jockey spoke gaily into the microphone: "Let the gospel music warm your hearts this cold, dark night. Wherever you are friends and neighbors, this is Cambell Oakley bringing you the good news and glad tidings in recorded sound. Stick around, we'll be here all night. Our good buddy Country Red had to be with his wife who's laid up with pneumonia. Turn up your sets and let the good gospel sounds ring for Red and his wife. We hope Red'll be back here in his usual slot tomorrow. Now here's the weekend sports report . . ."

Roy imagined a huge map of the United States encased in a glass-topped box with red lines crisscrossing all across the map; red lines running up and down, back and forth, across the land. On these lines tiny black cars moved slowly and steadily along. From beneath the glass top of the map, tiny colored lights blinked along the lines with the cars. A black transformer sat beside the map, beaming Cambell

Oakley's voice to each car. His words and gospel sounds droned into each car, powering it across the country. Roy envisioned the black representation of his truck, moving relentlessly southward. He felt certain that if Cambell Oakley left the air, transportation would come to a standstill.

Paying for a hamburger at a truck stop just outside of Lewisville, Roy remembered how long he and his mother had managed to live on the amount of money he was spending on one supper. After Roy's father deserted them, Roy did what odd jobs a half-breed eight-year-old Indian could get. His mother took in wash, and she made leather goods whenever Roy could get skins. Soon she was teaching him to tan and cut and stitch the hides. She taught him to polish the rocks and shells he found along the river.

As he got older, he made crude traps and caught more varmints, and the leather and hide articles he made sold quickly to tourists in New Orleans. Soon he had enough money to buy steel traps, and, sometimes, he could buy very fine leather from a crafts shop near the French Quarter. He and his mother set up a roadside stand and sold their goods to travelers, and he went in to New Orleans nearly every weekend, catching a ride with Larry Jackson, a black man who drove a beer truck.

Roy went to school off and on, and he learned to read and write and do simple math. He was seventeen when his mother died, and he decided to go to New Mexico and find some of his mother's family; he got only three hundred miles north of New Orleans when he ran out of money and ended up at the Faith Rescue Mission in Shreveport. There a Methodist preacher, the Reverend Don McCall, brought him some tools and some fine cowhide and Roy made the preacher a tooled billfold. Reverend McCall told Roy that he was an artist and asked him to come live at his house with him and his family. They gave Roy a room they fixed in a tool shed beside the house. Roy kept the church cleaned and the grass cut in return for his room and board and a place to work.

Roy had never cared much for religion—his mother's mixed-breed Navaho-Catholicism, nor the fervent Methodism he observed in Reverend McCall. Apparently the people who lived near the small country church didn't have much more interest in Methodism than Roy, or they went in to Shreveport to the red brick church buildings that were air conditioned. Eventually, Reverend McCall was told to sell the land and wooden buildings and was sent to another church. He persuaded the church leaders that the property should go to Roy, provided he recruit other Indians, to begin a crafts factory.

So Roy Singing Grass became the proprietor of an empty church building, a four-room house, and a large toolshed. He hired two young Indian boys, Bill Tom Bond and Jimmy Slater, and the preacher's house became Singing Grass's Indian Craft Shop. Roy kept his converted shed room and the boys had a room in the house. They had a small mail-order department, but the main business was dependent upon fairs, rodeos, and horse shows.

Roy spent most of his time at the shop, either working with the boys, training them, or in his room at the tapestry of his life. He had learned to avoid spending time in the city, weary of worn Indian jokes, curious children, and crowded streets.

When Roy swung the truck off the gravel road into the side yard of the shop it was late, and the lights were all out. He unloaded the truck and put his things away quietly. He didn't want to wake Bill Tom and Jimmy. He knew they'd keep him up another two hours telling them all about the rodeo and show.

Too tired to bathe, though he smelled of the trip, he stripped, dropped his clothes in a pile in a corner of his room and, after looking quickly over his tapestry to make sure it was as he had left it, crawled under the clean sheets Bill Tom must have put on the big iron bed.

Mopping up the last taste of syrup on his plate with the corner flap of a big pancake, Roy finished his recitation of the rodeo and horse show.

"You know, Bill Tom, I may send you and Jimmy next

time. I'm tired of doing all that traveling. I'll let you boys get some experience hawking. I may just devote myself to my tapestry."

Bill Tom grinned, spreading his milk moustache across his face, "You say that every year. You've been calling us boys for years, too. You know we're not all that young."

"No, I know you're not. And I'm going to prove it next year come that Arkansas show, going to stay right here."

Bill Tom laughed, "I'll believe you when I'm in the truck, waving goodbye."

"Okay, okay, we'll worry about it when it comes round again. Now let me tell you the best part of the trip. It was purely by accident. Coming back I stopped at one of those junk sheds along the highway, just outside Malvern, Arkansas. Run by a one-legged man. Must of been damn near eighty, white haired and wrinkled. That old man was more Indianlike than any white man I ever knew, and some Indians," he chuckled. "He was sitting on this saddle rigged on an old commode. Damndest sight. And he had this radio sitting there on a gravestone running off a big twelve-volt truck battery. That radio picked up Iowa. No other stations, just Des Moines, Iowa."

The boys laughed.

"It really was something to see. Funny, but it seemed to attract, like watching a fire never gets tiresome cause you keep seeing different things in the flames. Anyway, I sat there and kept seeing and hearing different things in that old beat up radio. Guess partly because it looked like the old set my momma had when I was a kid."

He paused, gulping coffee.

"It was just like me and him was old friends. We didn't say much, just listened to some gospel music on the radio. Then he up and invited me to lunch."

"You ate with him?"

"Yeah, yeah I did. Just soup and cold chicken in his shed there, but a lot better than eating alone. He carried the radio in to eat and then back out again. Listens to it all the time."

"Sounds loco."

"I guess there's nothing wrong with it. He was all alone so I guess he liked having someone to listen to. He always listened to that same station."

Jimmy got up and began clearing the table, "Takes all kinds, doesn't it? We got work to do. Besides," he winked at Bill Tom, "I want to get through early and run into town."

"You keep going to the Club Hi-Lo and messing you're going to pick up a fine crop of the clap."

Laughing, Jimmy flung a wet dishrag in Bill Tom's face, "I always did thrive on penicillin."

Leaving the dishes to the boys, Roy went out to walk around and see if anything had changed in the six days he had been gone. The day was cool, the sun, a bright spot behind the clouds, trying to break through the gauze. He wondered if clouds covered the sun at Prute's place, or in Des Moines.

The winter was unusually long for Louisiana, but Roy used the time to work on his life tapestry. He was beginning to get arthritis in his hands, making it painful to work the loom. The doctor gave him salve to rub heat into the stiff joints. When it grew warmer his hands hurt less, and he worked more.

All winter the boys made vests and moccasins and belts and purses, and when spring came they sold them to travelers from a stand on the highway. Roy's loom stood idle during much of summer, their busiest season.

Near the end of summer some men from Pennsylvania came and talked to Roy about buying the rights to run a gift shop called Wampum Wigwam in an authentic Indian village they wanted to build in the state park, if they could get a lease on the land. He listened and told them to let him hear from them when they had the land and were ready to start operating. He never heard from them again.

In September he got his usual letter informing him of the dates of the Arkansas horse show and rodeo, and he began to make plans for the week in late October. About three weeks before he had planned to leave for the show, a Railway Express truck pulled up in front of the shop.

Roy watched the man go around and unload a crate from the truck and pull it up on a dolly.

"Jimmy, go see what he's got. We didn't order anything, did we?"

Jimmy shook his head and went to the door.

"Railway Express—got a parcel for Roy Singing Grass."

"I didn't order anything."

"This one's prepaid, so if you'll just sign for it it's all yours."

Roy signed the invoice and told the man to roll it into the shop.

After the man left, Roy got a hammer and knocked the boards loose. The contents were wrapped in heavy canvas padded with burlap. When he peeled the wrapping away, there sat the radio, still playing, the heavy battery strapped to the bottom of the crate.

". . . ever notice how the gals pay all the attention to the guy who's dressed in step with the fashions? Well, yessir, that man's probably wearing fine apparel from Fashion Mart, the store for men and young men with discriminating taste. Men who know where they're going go with fashions from Fashion Mart, corner of third . . ."

Taped to the top of the radio was a brown envelope containing a letter which explained that Pruitt Early died September 30, and that a letter was found which said that he wanted Roy Singing Grass of Shreveport to have the radio when he was dead. He left instructions that the radio was to be shipped with battery intact, still playing.

Funny, Roy thought, his last name was Early. That doesn't seem to fit, but I can't think of any last name that would. He ought to be just Prute.

Roy would not let Jimmy or Bill Tom help him carry the radio into his room. He did it alone. That night he sat up in his room and listened to the Cambell Oakley Program while he wrote a letter.

He listened all the next day, and every day thereafter. The radio was never off. If he woke during the night, it was speaking softly in the dark room.

Jimmy and Bill Tom were worried about him, and when he sent them to the Arkansas show in his place they decided to have the doctor come to see him.

The doctor told them Roy was just getting old.

"The arthritis is a little worse, but that's not going to get any better at his age. He has high blood pressure, but not unusually so for a man pressing seventy."

"But, Doctor, what about the radio? And the show and rodeo? He's always gone by himself, and now all he does is listen to that country music."

"Maybe his age is catching up with him. You know sometimes a man realizes he's too old to do just like he used to. And I don't see anything wrong with listening to the radio. He may be a little eccentric, but that's no illness. If you're really concerned, and if you can talk him into it, which I doubt, I'd be happy to run some psychological tests on him, or recommend another doctor for advice on his emotional state, but I don't really think that's necessary."

The boys gave in to the doctor and went to Little Rock for the show. They looked for Prute's junk shop along the highway but it had disappeared.

When they returned, Roy had not done any work on his tapestry. He spent his days sitting in his room looking out the window and listening to the radio.

One evening just before sundown, he called excitedly for them to come listen.

"Here it is," he said.

"Here's what?"

"Shh," he cut them off with a sweep of his arm. Holding a finger to his lip he beckoned them into the room, and he pointed to the radio.

They listened.

"From way down south in Dixie comes a special request to the gospel hour. Roy Singing Grass, a real Ameri-

*can Indian, wants to hear this next number and dedicates
it to, simply, 'my brother Prute.' Roy also asks that we give
the Des Moines temperature with the dedication. What
about that Roy, you a weather watcher? Well, it's clear and
cold in Des Moines, 12 degrees. And here's an old gospel
favorite for Roy's brother Prute."*

There was a loud sneeze of static as an airplane
passed over the room. Then they heard the music, clear and
mournful:

> *Well I told the undertaker*
> *Undertaker please drive slow,*
> *For this body you are hauling*
> *Lord I hate to see her go.*
>
> *Will the circle be unbroken*
> *By and by, Lord, by and by;*
> *There's a better home a waiting*
> *In the sky, Lord, in the sky . . .*

Roy had his hands on the radio like he was a faith healer
about to cure a cripple. He was looking out at the darkening
sky, and his lip quivered in a smile.

Jimmy and Bill Tom left him alone.

In the months that followed Roy seemed to age years.
He stayed beside the radio and refused again and again to see
the doctor, who told Jimmy and Bill Tom that, since Roy was
peaceful and seemed happy, they might just as well leave
him alone, as long as they kept an eye on him.

"Even if we diagnosed some emotional disorder, all we
could do to treat him would be some form of institutional-
ization. At his age I think it's just as well to let him be. You let
me know if there are any significant changes in his health,
mental or physical."

So time was allowed to pass Roy by. He still ate and
slept well. He talked less, but did not ignore the boys. He
signed papers and checks whenever they asked him to. He
refused to discuss the radio, however, and no longer did any

of the work in the shop. He complained of the arthritis, especially on cold days.

For the last year of his life he listened to the radio. Two days after Christmas, the year after the radio arrived, North Louisiana had one of its rare snows, and Roy stood in his open window catching stray flakes whipped in by the wind. The next night he ran a fever and developed pneumonia.

He lay in the middle of the big bed, swallowed in the heavy quilts and soft mattress, listening to the radio and breathing loudly. He called Jimmy and Bill Tom into the room and asked them to get his stationery box. They called the doctor and then went to Roy, with his stationery.

He pulled a long envelope from the tooled leather box, "It's all in here, all legal and certified. I know it's no surprise to you two that I'm leaving the shop and truck and what we have in the bank to be divided equally between you. I'm worried about Prute's radio, though. There is no proper person. So I want you to crate it and send it to Cambell Oakley in Des Moines." He looked long at the loom and unfinished tapestry. "You know, I think Prute was right. Traveling is just meddling. There's a whole world wove into that loom, but I just couldn't finish it. It isn't alive. Just like Prute saw that little girl die on the highway and couldn't do a thing about it."

They heard the doctor at the door and Jimmy went and let him in. He took a quick glance at Roy and called the ambulance.

Roy shook a little, speaking to the doctor, "I just couldn't finish, Doc. I wanted those dangling strands. I needed that undone, open corner."

They stayed until he ordered them out.

"Okay, Roy, but just till the ambulance gets here. You won't get us out of that hospital room as easily." Roy shook a little more and grinned as they backed out of his room.

When they came back, a few moments later, he was dead. His eyes were closed, his arms folded across his chest, and he lay perfectly straight on his back.

Before they buried him, they finished the tapestry. The

unfinished part covered three panels, but they used the entire space for one large pattern, three times as large as any other woven image in the long tapestry. Spelling each other through the night, they wove Prute's radio into the end of Roy's life.

They laid the fine woven cloth over Roy in his coffin, folding it from his feet back up to his chest, his hand resting on the image of the radio.

After the funeral, Jimmy and Bill Tom cleared out Roy's room to make space for an addition to the leather works. The radio sat beside the iron bed, still playing.

Thomas Zigal

Curios

After baseball season in the summer of his thirteenth year, Eddie Korenik's parents put him on a Greyhound Bus for Memorial Hill to spend the remaining weeks before school with his cousin Snookum Pospisil and his family. Snookum was a year older and had a summer job pumping gas at Old Man Cervenak's Sinclair Station on the main strip that routed Houston-Austin traffic through town, a derelict shack of a station as extinct as the peeling dinosaur creaking back and forth above the advertising pole out front. Two pumps, a garage no one patronized except the trashy Cervenak family and an occasional nigger farmer in town for a Saturday haircut, and a cracker-box office stocking a few rusty cans of oil, some corroded anti-freeze, and a half-dozen varieties of rubbers.

As they lay awake at night, sticking to the sweaty sheets in the same bed like blades of grass on tarpaper, Eddie listened through the fan's hum and the friction of a million cricket legs and the rustling of cottonwood leaves in the moonlight while Snookum spilled his dreams about pressed blue uniform shirts with his name embroidered in a perfect white oval over one pocket, a crisp orange Gulf decal over the other. A matching blue cap and fresh red rag for his hip pocket every morning like the Wessel boys working in Buck Tiedt's station up the strip. "Now *there's* a service station," Snookum sighed, sitting up to place a comic book under the fan to stop its walking—two weights of oil and that new STP stuff, brake fluid, car wax, jumper cables, anti-freeze, batteries, bicycle pumps, funnels, oil spouts, transmission fluid, assorted wrenches and screwdrivers, reflectors, fuzzy dice, ice chests, cold cups, personalized key chains, Texas ashtrays, plastic litter bags, bottle openers, Dixie license plates, suction-cup Jesuses, miniature Memorial Hill monuments, car fresheners shaped like household pets, floor mats, decals of flames and tiny checkered flags and Bardahl cans and Woody Woodpecker smoking a cigar—everything arranged in neat clusters in a bin behind the office's plate glass like items in the vegetable section of a grocery store. Someday Snookum would have a gas station of his own, he assured Eddie, where he'd cherry out every chopped-down heap in town with glass packs and Twin Smitties and even Hollywood Straights.

For working in an eyesore that more resembled a nigger beer joint than a gas station, Snookum Pospisil might have been the pitied object of sidewalk whispers in the courthouse square or the butt of classmate abuse hurled from passing cars, but instead he was revered as a kind of Olympian messenger, an annointed savant of the one mystery in town nobody could decipher, a riddle so perplexing it left the noblest of citizens scratching their heads—Why, of all the brand-new sparkling four-pump stations along the strip, with green stamps and free vacuum service and giveaway dinner plates, did the girls from the Chicken Ranch choose to fill up their Cadillac at Old Man Cervenak's ramshackle Sinclair Station every time they left town for their monthly health inspection in Austin. It was an enigma as insoluble as a three-headed calf in a traveling show and a source of annoyance to every decent, hard-working station owner and businessman in Memorial Hill. Yet there was no lack of curiosity.

When Snookum and Eddie took their lunch breaks to shoot pool in the dark, latrine-smelling corners of the Passtime Club on the square, smoke drifting upward around metal lampcovers as though the muted light was sucking in the tobacco fumes of decades, the domino shufflers and nine ballers and even the bartenders would wander over one at a time, like bootleggers on the sly, to where Eddie practiced his English and Snookum rolled his eyes and shook his head at the awkward plink of cue tip slicing cue ball wrongly, and ask How's it goin, Pospisil? Who's the kid here? Say, if you see that little gal Rosalie from the Ranch, you know, the short little Meskin girl with the big knockers an' the teased-up hair, would you give 'er a message for me? . . . Hey, Pospisil, I heard your brother's gittin his Stingray painted candy-apple red. Tell 'm it's still a hunk o' junk. Say, you still working at Cervenak's? You think you could find out if any o' the girls from the Chicken Ranch would like t' go to a dance? . . . Howdy, Snookum, this your little brother? Say, how old do ya think that one chippy at the Ranch is—that blond girl the spittin image o' Sandra Dee? To Eddie's amazement Snookum always gave definitive answers as though he knew the girls like sisters: You got it chief, I'll tell 'er. . . . Naw, they're not allowed t' socialize—it ain't a high school, Forest Lee. . . . Twenty-three in September. . . . Twenty bucks for half 'n' half.

What Eddie realized after a few weeks in town was that the men of Memorial Hill—a snuff-dipping brood of field hands, meat packers, store sweepers, grease monkeys— couldn't afford the luxuries of the Ranch for the most part, and those who could were often restrained by the conventions of religion and family. So they required Snookum Pospisil to create a reliquary of venerable whores for their worship, based sometimes on hot midnight memories of the one trip there on a furlough fifteen years before, sometimes on only a fleeting glimpse of the girls in their Cadillac as they purled through two stoplights on their way out of town, sometimes on less. And Snookum took great pride in his chosen office as if the souls of all the town's living depended on his mercy to save them from the everlasting flames of the day in and day out.

For years Eddie had witnessed his uncles and his father nudge one another and wink, when the womenfolk were off in the kitchen, and make passing jokes about the Chicken Ranch: Har, har, Red, there was this ol' bohunk shows up at the Chicken Ranch with six bits in his pocket and asks what can he git. Grease up the cat's ass, hollers Miss Molly. . . . But he had a hunch that this Chicken Ranch was just another straight-faced yarn the people in these parts had conjured up to make fools of Yankees and traveling salesmen. After all, hadn't Uncle Rudolph pulled his leg with that jackalope story and those tiny antlers on a jackrabbit's head mounted above the mirror in his beer joint? He'd told Eddie the little critters spawned by the thousands out in the prairie lands, and the boy had believed him for years. But not this time. The Chicken Ranch demanded more proof.

The morning it happened was no different than any other, perhaps hotter. Old Man Cervenak sat by his cluttered desk in the musty office examining pictures in a magazine called *Nugget* and absorbing most of the one-speed fan's meager breeze. He rarely budged from his chair all day except to visit the restroom, only six feet away, which he did with surprising regularity. He was a hulking beast of a man with deep fleshy crevices in his face like creekbeds trailing downward to his jowls; cracks in the corners of his mouth were permanently plugged with sticky brown tobacco juice and his khaki shirt and lap were constantly speckled with dry chaw. With a cocky grin he had just given Eddie a copy of *Sunshine and Health* to peruse—"Now don'tcha think you'd like t' live in a place like this?"—and Eddie had found some space on the floor near the door and had begun to study the shapes and sags and muffs of hair of the men, women, and children living on some farm in California while he listened to Snookum's radio blare the bouncy rhythms of a colored man singing *Sittin in lala, waitin for my yaya, uh-umm.* He was searching for cotton-haired boys his own age to see if they too lacked body hair when the old man coughed and spit into the coffee can by his foot—"Well, well, here are my girls," he said. "Git off your butt, kid, an' go tell Snookum t' roll out the red carpet." A spotless white Cadillac had arrowed through the dusty heat toward the shade of their pumps, clanging the station bell twice as it idled to a rest.

Wiping his hands on a scrap of old sheet, Snookum emerged from the garage, where he was lubing Son Pospisil's candy-apple Stingray, only the second car Eddie had seen up on the rack in two weeks, and motioned for Eddie to get the windshield, his usual assignment. Eddie dragged his feet and waited for Snookum to approach the driver's window, his face glowing with sweat and thrill—"Yes, ma'am. Can I help you, ma'am?"

The window lowered with a mechanical whine, and Eddie could hear the soft cadences of a woman's voice, a voice that raced spidery chills into the base of his skull before disappearing again into the air-conditioned vacuum. Snookum pulled down the license plate, fumbled with the car's gas cap, inserted the pump's nozzle with a nervous clamor; and Eddie slowly squeezed soap from the sponge floating in the water bucket, slapped a damp chamois over one shoulder, and applied a steady back-and-forth thrusting to the grasshopper entrails caked on the windshield. He managed to smear dirt and yellow insect guts across the glass like a wax finish, forcing himself to scrub even harder, the soapy water dripping from his fingers, down his elbow, and onto the gritty surface of the white hood. When at last he squirted the windshield with the hose, the suds and muck slid like rancid cream from the glass and he could see three exotic faces smiling at him from the front seat. The driver was his mother's age, her hair resting stiffly like a nest, her skin a soap-powder white. The other two were not much older than his high school cousin Julie, and like her hid their blemishes with a goopy face plaster that only marginally suggested real flesh in color. A blond with pixie hair giggled at him from the silent world of unreal air like a guppy staring through aquarium glass, her pointed fake sideburns rigidly perfect and unmoving as she swung her head to whisper to her friend. They both began to laugh, their long black lashes fluttering above eyes trained on him, and even the older woman's calcified features splintered into wide mirth.

"Ain't you finished here yet?" asked Snookum, "I gotta check the hood. Git the back winder."

Relieved, Eddie grabbed chamois and sponge and darted

for the Cadillac's rear glass, where the work was easier. He was slowly pulling the chamois across squeaky glass, observing the waves and side tilts of silky hair falling to the shoulders of the three women in the back seat, when the rear door popped open and a long slender leg as smooth and white as a bleached cow's skull touched a black patent-leather pump to the cement. His stomach tipped and his toes and the soles of his feet flooded with sweat: the girl unraveled from the car, shifting and straightening her navy blue dress sashed narrowly at the waist with a patent-leather belt, her neckline cut to the deep fold of skin between her starchly housed breasts, and without a question she could have passed for a lookalike twin of Annette Funicello. "Is the girls' room still around the corner?" she pointed to the side of the building, regarding Eddie through owl-eye sunglasses like Annette wore in every Beach Party movie ever made.

He nodded and watched her clip-clop away, her derriere sliding to and fro as if a couch cushion were stuffed underneath her dress. He was trying to imagine which of the young women she resembled in *Sunshine and Health*—the size and color of her nipples, the thickness below her belly—when Snookum sidled up to him: "Their battery's nearly dry an' we don't have no pure-fied water," he said quietly. "Git some dough from the register an' make tracks over t' Buck Tiedt's real quick an' buy a jug."

Eddie hustled into the office of the Gulf Station, refrigerated air freezing the sweat trailing down his back and shooting a sharp throbbing pain behind his eyes. He asked for distilled water, and a Wessel boy sucking a toothpick, his legs propped up on the desk, said "Sure, squirrel, we got battery water. You old enough t' buy it?"

His brother was rearranging rear-window poodle-dog blinkers in the accessory display. He gave a goofy chortle: "That Ol' Man Cervenak don't know a gas station from a gypsy's armpit."

"I'm in kind of a hurry," Eddie explained. "The girls' battery is nearly dry and they need to get on the road to Austin."

"The girls?" The boy dropped his feet to the floor and extracted the toothpick from his mouth. "The girls are there?"

The brother didn't question; he bolted outside and leaned against the Coke machine, his arms folded, watching the sleek Cadillac, its hood raised high in the shade of Cervenak's carport shelter. By the time Eddie paid for the water and dashed out, two mechanics from the garage were standing in the open sun like heatstruck sodbusters gawking at a desert mirage. "Say, bubba," said the Wessel boy against the Coke machine, "what's the name o' the girl that jus' come out o' the toilet?"

Eddie stopped and watched the tall dark-haired beauty spike her way back to the car in patent-leather high heels, her legs like wooden stilts. "Annette," he said without regarding the boy. "She's only nineteen," he said, and began to run with the jug of water.

It was Friday, and like every Friday Snookum had to stay late to turn off the pumps and lock up. Even after Son Pospisil picked up his candy-apple red Stingray and delivered some fried chicken from Eddie's Aunt Sophie, even after Old Man Cervenak gathered his magazines and shuffled on home, the two boys remained in the soft still haze of twilight, watching high schoolers squeal by in their fuel-injected Barracudas and moon-cap Chevys, drinking and howling and laying rubber in reverence for the coming dark. At nine sharp, just as Snookum shut off the lights, a metallic blue Impala with silver mudflaps over the rear tires screeched into the station. "Hey, Snookum," yelled the driver, "how 'bout some suds, good buddy?"

Eddie wouldn't have recognized Buster Wessel without his Gulf cap and uniform except that the toothpick was wedged in his mouth at exactly the same angle. His oily black hair glinted light like a rain puddle on a dark night; a perfect widow's peak curl clung to his forehead, and his slicked-back wings met precisely at a single ridge behind his head.

"You buyin?" grinned Snookum.

Buster held up a Lone Star by the tip of its neck as if it were a dead fish. "Come on in, sugarfoot triggerleg," he smiled through clenched teeth and toothpick, "the water's fine!"

Snookum and Eddie tumbled into the back seat, and Buster scratched rubber for thirty feet fishtailing out of the station, nearly spilling Eddie from the unclosed door. Emil Wessel, the boy so enamored of the dark-haired whore, rode shotgun in the front seat and fetched beer from an ice chest. Eddie was parched and guzzled long and hard till his eyes teared. "T' true love," Emil Wessel raised his bottle in toast, and the others copied with laughter. Emil was the younger brother, a high school junior, rawboned, his poor eyes like flint-gray ballbearings behind horn-rim glasses; a bald spot the size of a sand dollar cratered the top of his Chicago box-car haircut as though the last barber had gone too far.

"Whatta ya say we drag the square t' see if there's any action," suggested Buster Wessel, "an' then head on out t' the fairgrounds. The Deltones are playin tonight."

"Wicked!" said Snookum.

Ol' woman, ol' woman, don'tcha treat me this way, sang raspy Ray Charles on the car radio. . . . *But I guess if you say so—* blast of sax—*I'll have t' pack m' things an' go.* Emil Wessel turned it up so everyone could sing *Hit the road, Jack, an' don'tcha come back no more no more no more no more!* Eddie could already feel the beer dizzying his brain. His father had never allowed him a whole can before.

They cruised the south end of the square past the old high-ceilinged grocery store with loose wooden planks you creaked over on your way to the rear, where sweating colored men turned brisket and sizzling sausage links over a smoky pit and neatly wrapped up barbecue in slick white butcher's paper, past the tiny picture show with cedar-wood benches and roaches in the popcorn now showing *Ma and Pa Kettle Go to Hawaii*—"Y'all see that un yet?" laughed Emil, "where Ma 'n' Pa take a vacation t' Honolulu an' end up on a pineapple farm with these crooks"—past the five'n'dime where Eddie and Snookum's great Aunt Vlasta had sold perfume and licorice for decades, past the fat trunk of a dead live oak now stripped of its limbs, a marker imbedded in its bark explaining that Sam Houston had once slept in its shade.

"There's Mary Patek an' her crowd," said Snookum of an approaching heap, a rusting '52 Mercury.

"Is Trish Davis with 'em? She got knocked up by David Gene Krause an' had t' drop out o' school," said Emil Wessel.

"Don't wave," instructed Buster Wessel.

The girls waved and honked, but the boys only nodded with cool regard.

The Impala shrieked rubber cornering the square where an iron deer poised on the courthouse lawn under spotlighting diffused through the leaves of towering cottonwood trees. They passed the kolache bakery, the domino parlor where feeble old veterans with canes and wheelchairs played out their days, the Western Auto store, the bank with its new clock high above. A pickup truck roared up to the passenger side of the Impala and crawled along at their pace. "Howdy," grinned the driver, a farmboy wearing a baseball cap. "Any action up on the Hill road?"

"Beats me," said Emil Wessel.

"How 'bout we go make some," suggested the farmboy. "Let's see whatcha got under that perty hood."

"No thanks," Buster Wessel was quick to reply.

"Aw c'mon," said the farmboy. "Mus' be you can take this ol' piece o' shit truck in a quarter."

"Some other time," said Buster Wessel.

The farmboy reached into his shirt pocket and extracted a five-dollar bill, waving it loosely. "What if I make it worth your time?"

Emil Wessel snapped his head toward his brother. "Five bucks!" he whispered with a child's excitement.

"Not tonight," Buster Wessel lowered his neck to look up into the pickup's cab.

The farmboy's face hardened into sudden contempt, "Chicken shits!" he sneered, jamming into another gear and darting ahead with uncanny agility and speed, his taillights gleaming an eerie blue-green hue like stars from another galaxy.

"God damn!" Emil Wessel's jaw unhinged.

"You idjit" said his brother. "That sombitch is Danny Blaha from Moravan. He's got a torque 413 under that baby. Nobody but a yo-yo'd run against him."

"Wowww," Emil Wessel drew out the word with the greatest respect. "Tough enough," he said.

The Passtime Club, the barber shop where they dabbed hot lather around your ears and scratched your scalp with a straight razor, the newspaper office, the Manhattan Store where the only Jews in town sold the skirt-and-jacket suits and dapper men's hats that New Yorkers wore. Emil Wessel popped another cap for Buster and Snookum, but Eddie was slowing rapidly over the inch or two of beer left in his bottle, his stomach as bloated as the inside of a basketball. "S'matter, li'l brother," Emil Wessel's words were beginning to slur, "you short hittin on us?"

"Chugalug!" Buster Wessel said, his dark pencil-thin brows arching at Eddie from the rear-view mirror.

"Here's mud in your eye," Snookum saluted with his full bottle.

Eddie had no choice but to down the remaining beer in one long swallow. Again his eyes burned; he belched quietly and dropped the bottle onto the floorboard, where it clinked against Snookum's empty.

"So her name is Annette," Emil Wessel said as he offered Eddie another icy bottle. "Where's she from?" he asked.

Eddie had a feeling this would happen; he suspected from the beginning that the Wessel boys' curiosity had brought about this sudden friendship. He hesitated, sipping beer as any excuse for more consideration. "California," he said finally. Snookum's long horsey face drew up with confusion.

"How'd she end up down here?" Emil Wessel persisted. He'd twisted his body to rest his chin on the smooth leather upholstery.

"She had it made in the shade with some Hollywood

star," said Eddie. "They lived in a great big glass house on a cliff overlooking Muscle Beach," he explained, "but one day out o' the blue the guy turned queer and wouldn't touch her."

"Are you shittin me?" Emil Wessel's chin raised in outrage.

Snookum's forehead wrinkled in three perfect lines. "What'd she do?" he asked.

Emil jerked erect in the seat. "Don't you know?"

"She's new," Eddie said. "I don't think Snookum's met her yet."

"Naw, naw," Snookum said, "I ain't met that one yet." He stuck the bottle in his mouth and slouched against the door.

"Zat when she come down here?" Buster Wessel craned his neck to ask.

"Yep," said Eddie. "She took the first bus out o' California."

"Heard there wadn't a limp dick in Texas," slurred Emil Wessel.

"God damn California queers!" said Buster Wessel.

Roy Orbison crooned *Cry-i-yi-i-in, o-ver you . . . cry-i-yi-i-in, o-ver you . . .* on the radio, and the four of them falsettoed his note like shrill-throated girls in Sunday choir. As they burned rubber around another corner of the square, Snookum jolted upright suddenly and said, "What the hell is 'at?" He pointed his bottle toward a vacant lot next to the abandoned creamery. A silver bullet-shaped trailer squatted there in darkness, and Buster Wessel flipped on his brights to illuminate the crudely colorful sign that stretched the length of the trailer's roof. CURIOS, the lettering said.

"Ain't you been t' see that yet?" said Buster Wessel, swerving the Impala to idle at the curb. "Some ol' boy travelin through with this weird freak show."

"They got Siamese-twin chickens an' these little maremaids that washed up in Hawa-ya the size o' trout," added Emil Wessel.

"But the best part of all is the perfick peserved lady o' the Great Salt Lake," said Buster. He tempered his voice to a spooky half-whisper. "Her ol' man kilt her 'cause he thought she was runnin around on m' an' wrapped these chains all over her body an' dumped her in the Great Salt Lake. But he was such a moron he didn't know salt water'll peserve a body forever." Buster pulled a pack of Luckys from his shirt pocket and fed one into his mouth, then shook one loose for his brother. "Ten years later," he said, "the chains rusted off an' the body floated up. 'Cept the skin'd turned black as a nigger, she coulda been asleep. Sheriff sent the husband up the river for ninety-nine big ones."

The tip of Emil Wessel's cigarette glowed red, and he filled the chilly silence with a long draft of smoke. "You oughta see 'er," he said, his voice hushed and somber. "They got 'er laid out in this coffin, see, wearin this white weddin dress. Her perty red hair an' fingernails never stopped growin the whole time she was in the Great Salt Lake, so they're out to' here," he demonstrated with his own fingers. "You gotta see it t' believe it."

Eddie stared at the little trailer, his spine crawling with a creepy respect for the dead at rest inside. In his lightheadedness he saw the dull silver coach as a moon-washed gravestone marking the entombment of all the misbegotten flaws of God's mysterious creation. To him there were no sounds on earth tonight, at this very moment, except Snookum's shallow breathing and the soft mufflering of the Impala. Emil Wessel was saying something with a quiet restraint as though praying, and Eddie leaned forward to catch his words: "The really weird thing, man"—his voice mellowing even more— "I mean, the really crazy-ass myst'ry about the lady is she had on a gold weddin ring when they found 'er. . . . But the husband swore he never bought her one," Emil's voice trailed off. He dragged his cigarette deeply, pensively, hesitating, poised in thought. "So you know who I think stuck it on 'er?" His words thinned out to a faint murmur. "You know who I think stuck it on 'er?" he said, and Eddie strained closer for the answer. "YOU DID!" Emil Wessel screamed, grabbing Eddie's arm, the boy's bladder almost collapsing.

Buster Wessel floorboarded the Impala, jerking Eddie against the seat in an explosion of tires and laughter, and they shot down the street and through a blinking light for the road to the fairgrounds while Del Shannon and the Wessel brothers howled *wishin you were here by me, to end this mi-se-ry, and I wonder—I wah-wah-wah-wah-wah-on-der. . . .*

Soon the headlights were reflecting the tiny pink eyes of furry animals hiding in the dusty green Johnson grass bushed along the country road. A rotting armadilla carcass, some fool's bag of empty beer cans tossed carelessly ahead, a jack-rabbit dodging in a dozen angles at once. Emil Wessel flung an empty bottle at a curve sign riddled with bulletholes but missed wildly, the bottle swallowed into darkness without a sound like a missile disappearing into the void of space. "Know what I dig about the girls at the Chicken Ranch?" he turned to breathe liquor on Snookum and Eddie. "What I dig is they don't tool you around like most girls—ol' Jo Ann Psencik an' Linda Hofner an' their type, ya know. You gotta buy those broads corsages 'n' initial rings 'n' shit like 'at an' take 'em shoppin in Austin an' buddy up with their ol' man an' give 'em the deed to your fuckin soul before they'll let you git your finger wet." He retrieved his comb and swerved back ducktails mussed by the wind. "You don't have t' play the part with those girls at the Ranch," he said. "They know what it's all about."

Eddie wondered how he'd arrived at such certain knowledge. He knew that to take your pleasure at the Chicken Ranch you had to be eighteen, or pass for eighteen, and Emil Wessel had a boy's freckled face that required a razor only twice a week.

"You guys'r lucky," said Buster Wessel into the rear-view mirror, his words measured and final as if he was bestowing upon Snookum and Eddie the respect due to town elders or war heroes. It was the first time he'd spoken since the Curios trailer.

Emil Wessel popped another cap and stared at Eddie in the dark. "Damn lucky," he said.

In time the Impala rutted up the incline to the fair-grounds, a swath of road carved into a hillside, ancient tuburous roots of live oaks exposed like giant veins along the eroded walls of the gulley. They rumbled along past the dark baseball stadium, home of the Memorial Hill Monuments in the Texas League, the undersides of the car pelted with thousands of stones churned up by their rocking motion. The weathered old dance pavilion was ringed by exposed lightbulbs like Christmas ornaments, and as they approached, Eddie could hear the saxophone soloing some sad lovesick two-step while the band waltzed time. They crept through narrow lanes between parked cars jammed together like wrecks in an old junkyard, heads bobbing up here and there, radios blasting the Shirelles, smokerings coiling through open windows. The taillights of an empty racing-striped Mustang flashed mysteriously, and as they passed, a shoeless, clean-shaven leg crooked upward into sight, the heel coming to rest on the dash. Buster whistled lowly through his teeth, Emil bit his knuckle and grunted, and all four began to groan.

The large gaping entrance of the pavilion seemed to Eddie like a forboding dark tunnel into which an occasional explorer would penetrate. On one side of the entranceway a group of boys lounged on their hoods, laughing and scuffling and combing their hair butch-waxed into place or molded stiffly with a Brylcreme sheen. They gossiped loudly about the girls huddled several yards away, across the cleared entranceway, and now and then taunted them with shouted remarks. As the Impala lolled by, several boys hooted and joshed. "Hey Buster," one said, "you got us some beer?"

"That's for me t' know an' you t' find out," Buster Wessel mumbled through the cigarette glued to his lip.

"I jus' saw Mary Ellen Koenig dancin with some nigger from Post Oak," said a husky boy wearing a bowling shirt.

"Eat me raw, Crawford," Buster Wessel said, lazily giving him the finger.

The crowd of boys oohed, "Put down!" oohed "Drop!" "You grew it, you chew it!" someone called.

The Impala puttered to a standstill next to the party of

girls bunched in threes and fours, gabbling absently without gesture or movement as though pegged in the sandy earth like fenceposts, ignoring the boys, oblivious even to the rock 'n' roll rhythms now rattling the rotting old wallboards of the pavilion. The Impala's passengers studied them in silence—prim knee-length summer dresses from the Manhattan Store wasted on such skimpy frames, shoulders knobby, legs like sparrows', hair uniformly drab and as dated as grandma's bun. Group by group the girls began to notice the onlookers hunkered down in the car, and silence swept over their conversations. They stared back with uneasy reticence, mute as scolded infants; and in this awkward moment Eddie thought of his shy country cousins Julie and Emily, homely girls who spent all their time looking at clothes in catalogs and drawing fancy floorplans of the dreamhouses they'd some day live in with a strong husband and many children. It occurred to him that Snookum and the Wessel brothers might do no better than match up with these doe-eyed, moon-faced farmgirls, and for the first time in weeks he was happy he'd be returning home to the Gulf Coast, where all the girls had televisions to teach them about style.

"Whatta ya say?" Buster Wessel muttered vacantly, breaking the hypnotic silence in the car.

Emil Wessel spoke without turning his gaze from the girls: "The Chicken Ranch," he said.

Buster Wessel stomped the gas and scudded away in a billowing plume of loose dirt that chased the girls in all directions as if a poisonous fog. Snookum disdained with a puzzled shake of the head; the Wessels cackled wickedly, Emil scraping through ice in search of more beer, Buster turning up Ricky Nelson singing about the beautiful foreign girls waiting for him in every port and town, wherever on earth he wandered sadly in search of fame.

Snookum didn't appear to take them seriously until Buster Wessel toured the glassy blue Impala onto the DeVaca Highway and sailed past the Monument Motel and Club 71, where the grownups were drinking and dancing away their Friday night in the bubbling electric rainbow colors of a country jukebox. "You really headin for the Chicken Ranch?" he asked sheepishly.

"Damn straight," said Buster Wessel.

Snookum's goiterlike Adam's apple dipped as he swallowed more beer. "You gotta be eighteen t' git in," he reminded them.

"That's what we got you along for," slushed Emil Wessel. "We figure you could git us in safer'n a tick in a dog's ear."

"Rules is rules," Snookum said, sitting up suddenly. "You don't think they let *me* in, do ya?"

Buster Wessel's eyes left the road and wandered to the back seat: "Forest Lee Johnson said you know the girls so well they give you a free ride whenever you want," he said defiantly, as though defending Snookum's honor.

"Uh, well, uh," Snookum stammered, nervously peeling the label off the Lone Star bottle, "uh, they don't ever let me in at night, when there's lots o' business," he said. "I have t' come around in the daytime."

"Aw, you're jus' bein modest," said Emil. "But we got faith in ya. Don't we, Buster?"

"Fuckin A," said Buster.

"Betcha can pull some strings with these gals if you give it the ol' college try," said Emil. "Tell 'em you're doin a favor for a couple o' pals goin in the service tomorrow morning."

They swerved off the highway onto a feeder road and bumped across the cattle guard at the entrance to the Chicken Ranch property. A wide caliche road, in better condition than any farm-to-market in the county, flattened smoothly through the dark woods and dead-ended in a pool of automobiles' rowed evenly in front of a two-story white farmhouse with the appearance of a stately old sharp-roofed mansion only a cotton baron could afford. Several windows glowed with the dim yellow hue of a kerosene lamp; others were dark, their shutters open to the soothing dry breeze of a summer's night.

"Looky here," Buster Wessel said, wheeling into an empty space between a Lincoln Continental and an Army Jeep, "they saved a spot for us." They were so close to the house that after the engine shut off, Eddie could hear a rocker creaking back and forth on the dark screened-in front porch.

"Dubs on that girl Annette," said Emil Wessel.

"You guys are out o' your gourd," Snookum said. "Let's make like horse shit an' hit the trail."

"Relax," said Buster Wessel, cracking open his door with a noise that seemed to echo a mile away in the deep quiet woods. "We gotcha covered on the moola. Our treat," he said. "Least we can do."

"Come on, you guys, I ain't cleaned up or nothin. Let's make like a tree an' leave," Snookum said, panic creeping into his voice.

Emil Wessel opened Snookum's door, and Buster bent his thick shoulders and head in close enough to kiss Snookum on the mouth. "Now look," Buster said with the patient, serene manner of a father having a serious talk with his son, "We been real nice t' you tonight, Pospisil. Let you ride around in the cherriest coup in town. Give you all the beer you could swill. Now you ain't tryin t' be rude t' Buster an' Emil Wessel, are ya?"

"No," Snookum said timidly.

"Then you'll wanna git out 'n' come in with us 'n' talk t' your friends, won'tcha, Pospisil? For ol' time sake."

Snookum glanced at Eddie but quickly dropped his eyes, realizing the boy was no help. He sucked in a breath like a weightlifter readying to jerk iron, then forced it out sharply. "I never been here before," he said, tapping the beer bottle slowly up and down on his thigh. "I don't know these folks."

Emil Wessel peered through the open window of the door he held ajar like a hotel doorman: "We ain't fallin for that one, Pospisil. Jerry Svoboda said you brought 'm here once an' interduced 'm t' the sweetest li'l chippy in Texas. Now if you can do that for Jerry Svoboda, what the hell's wrong with the by-god Wessel brothers?"

With his hips Buster Wessel scooted Snookum closer to Eddie and sat down, draping his long bristly arm around Snookum's shoulder and squeezing him affectionately till Snookum's head bobbed like the dog's in the back window of

Son Pospisil's candy-apple red Stingray. "You don't think we ain't *good* enough t' meet your friends, do ya, ol' buddy?"

"Course not," Snookum's words vibrated in his throat.

"Then what say we go git us some smelly poontang," he squeezed and shook Snookum again.

Snookum exhaled tiredly and handed Eddie the beer bottle. "You're in for a big surprise," he said. But Buster slapped him on the back—" 'At's m' boy," he crowed.

As the two of them struggled awkwardly from the car, Eddie realized he had no part in their plans, that the Wessels had never considered even for a moment that a skinny thirteen-year-old kid with a sweaty pompadour could join them in this escapade. The trio circled behind the car, and almost out of spite, just to remind them that he was more than a car cushion discarded after a vacation drive, Eddie stuck his head out the window and said "What am I sup-posed to do?"

Emil Wessel wobbled over and dropped his head limply, breathing beer fumes into the Impala. "Suffer!" he said, then laughed loudly and stumbled off to join the other two.

Eddie could see that the Wessels had invited Snookum to go first, and his cousin slowly ascended the steps, hesitat-ing at the screen door; but with a slight shove from Buster Wessel he opened the croaky door and disappeared inside. Buster followed stealthily, then Emil combing his hair. Sud-denly the invisible rocking ceased and a big man's bassy voice rolled out of the porch's darkness as if it belonged to some forest giant possessing the eyes of a nocturnal predator: "You boys know better than t' come messin aroun' out here," the voice growled deep clear notes in the hollow chamber of eve-ning. It came to Eddie who the man was as instinctively as a child knows fire and water, and though he had never heard the sound of Boots Prause's tongue, he had seen the old stoop-shouldered sheriff lurking about the courthouse square many times and had imagined him talking this gravely, blowing snot from his nose with a finger pressed against a nostril, crushing the skulls of ornery jailbirds with delicate precision between those enormous, calloused hands.

"Looks t' me like two Wessel boys an' a Pospisil," he said

with the accuracy of an all-knowing God, even in the porch's gloom and with eyes that had always appeared to Eddie like the yellowing dead things his science teacher pickled in formaldehyde jars. "Git your butts out o' here 'fore I make up my mind t' remember this nex' time I run into your daddys," he said.

"Yes, sir, thank you, sir," one of the boys said.

"An' don't ever let me see you out here again till you git out o' high school," he said.

"Yes sir, thank you, sir."

The door sprang open and the three of them bounded clumsily down the stairs and made straightaway for the car. Eddie's head was reeling from the beer; his skin tingled a rubbery good feeling, and he didn't much care what he said: "Real swift idea," he deadpanned.

"Another word an' you die, squirt," said Emil Wessel as the Impala arced backward, shushed gravel, and spun noisily away, its glass packs popping like gunshots between second and third gears. Headlights approached, and Snookum slid low in the seat, grabbing Eddie's arm and forcing him to do the same. Eddie glimpsed the spotless waxen gloss of candy-apple red glowing in the Impala's beams, and as the car passed and tooted, Buster Wessel giggled "Looks like at least one Pospisil's gonna bust a nut tonight."

On the dark highway back into town Emil Wessel began to moan "Oh Annette, Annette, my sweet pet Annette," raising a bottle to his mouth with the automatic regularity of a pull-string doll, his head wagging slackly from side to side atop the leather seat. Once he asked his brother to pull over so he could puke on his hands and knees in the dry grass while Johnny Horton sang *I'd build for my Jenny her ho-neymoon home.* Eddie was looser than he'd ever been in his life, happy and grinning like a kid in a hobby shop, and he couldn't resist saying "Hey, Emil, taste as good comin back up as it did goin down?" Even Buster found this amusing, but Emil dragged himself back in the car, wiped his mouth with the side of his hand, and blinked sleepily as he struggled to focus on the boy: "Wanna make somethin of it, mullet?" he scowled.

He tried to stare Eddie down for several minutes, but the

glaring lacked any hard edge or the possibility of sharp cold reflex. It was clear that Emil Wessel was brewing punishment for such audacity, that his muddled brain was turning over hideous schemes. When he finally spoke, his high cheek-bones shifted into a demented smile that smothered his eyes into puffy slits: "I think this kid here's ready t' meet Big Ivy Nell, don't you, Buster?"

Buster Wessel laughed dumbly.

"Aw c'mon," said Snookum, "it's perty late. Why don't y'all take us on home? My ol' man's gonna be pissed off as it is."

"Mind your own business, Pospisil," Emil Wessel slurred. "You already let us down real bad once tonight. We cain't all go home on a Friday night without a little fun, now can we?"

"You gonna like Ivy Nell," Buster Wessel yukked into the rear-view mirror at Eddie. "She takes real good care o' li'l white boys like you," he said.

"She's three hunerd pounds o'nigger guts," leered Emil Wessel, sweat gathering on his top lip and trickling from his sideburns. "She'll do anything for five bucks," he said, "but if ya suck the sores on her big fat thighs she'll do the trick for nothin."

Buster turned to his brother. "Think she'd let us watch the kid suck her pus?"

"I don't see why not," Emil Wessel grinned.

"That's *your* speed," Eddie interjected. "Sounds like you two are her best customers."

Snookum signaled for him to keep quiet. "I think y'all oughta drop us on home," he said quickly, "or we'll end up grounded for a month o' Sundays."

As if he hadn't heard either Eddie or Snookum, Buster Wessel glanced at his brother. "I got a better idea," he chuckled.

Eddie didn't care what happened next. He perched his head out the window and let the car's wake tousle his hair, now gobbed with sweat and Wild Root Cream Oil, and sang Johnny Horton's "North to Alaska" with all his heart though the song had ended and the station was now advertising some all-purpose ointment. They banged over the railroad tracks into town, Eddie drinking it all in—the meat-packing building where Snookum's father worked, the cedar-clogged cemetery, the Dairy Dream, the high school where Uncle Tony serviced buses, the strip of gas stations. Before Snookum could formulate another complaint, the Impala had veered into unlighted back streets and circled to a halt within opaque shadows of the abandoned creamery, just off the square. The darkness here was deep and silent and cool like a murky lagoon, and Eddie shuddered slightly, rolling up his window without a sound, smothering the click of the door's lock with a fake cough. The four boys sat speechlessly for some time as if awed by the inert presence of the bullet-shaped trailer in the adjacent lot. A match crackled and Buster Wessel touched it to his cigarette. "We're gonna steal the body," he said flatly.

"Whut?" said Emil Wessel.

"The peserved lady," he said, blowing smoke through his nostrils. "You three're gonna steal 'er an' I'm gonna drive the gitaway."

Snookum groaned painfully and put his hand on his forehead as though checking for fever.

"What the hell're we gonna do with a stinking stiff?" Emil Wessel said. "Jesus!" he gagged, and Eddie thought the boy would vomit again, "You tryin t' make me barf?"

"They're gonna do all the work," Buster Wessel nodded toward the back seat. "You'll jus' supervise."

"Yeah," Emil's shoulders shivered as if he'd been taken by a sudden chill, "but what're we gonna *do* with it when we git it?"

"I dunno," Buster shrugged, coolly inhaling smoke. "Maybe we'll open up our own kind o' Chicken Ranch," he giggled. "Maybe the kid here'll be our first customer."

"Hey, yeah," Emil Wessel bared his teeth at Eddie through a cruel smile. "Bitchin idea."

Snookum groaned again. "You guys need t' be put in a straightjacket an' sent directly t' Rusk," he said.

"Listen here, you squirrelly peckerwood," Emil Wessel spewed a light spray of saliva, "you done lied to us about the girls out at the Ranch. How'd you like word t' git around town that you got no pull what-so-ever out there, buddy boy?"

"I ain't never said—"

"I'd hate for your ol' lady t' git a phone call from the sheriff's office sayin they'd seen you 'n' the kid here an' your big brother out at the Chicken Ranch," Buster Wessel said with calm, studied deliberation. He stretched his arm along the top of the seat and rolled his head lazily to wink at Snookum: "I think you git my drift," he said.

With a flashlight and screwdriver from the glove compartment, Emil Wessel led the expedition across the grassy lot in a stumbling jog. Trotting side by side, Eddie whispered to Snookum "You wanna run for it?"

"Naw," Snookum whispered back, "they'd end up doin us dirty somehow."

"We could beat the shit out of Emil real easy."

"Same problem," Snookum huffed. "But don't sweat it none, I'll git us out o' this."

With the screwdriver Emil Wessel pried open a window on the narrow end of the trailer. "Okay, boys," he pointed with the flashlight, "up 'n' at 'm."

Snookum balked. "Cain't we talk this over?" he asked.

Emil Wessel nudged him with the flashlight. "Git your butt in there," he said.

The insides of the trailer smelled close and musty like an attic, dirt-wet like raindrops on a bare yard, yet faintly traced with some peculiar petroleum substance you might notice in a service station garage. From the window Emil Wessel leveled the flashlight across the turbid enclosure, hazing the shell of curiosities in soft gray silhouettes. They made slow, halting steps down the center aisle as though fighting the force of a denser atmosphere. The soles of Eddie's feet pinpricked with each footfall and fluttery numbness rushed up his legs and spine. He was a graverobber, a marauder in some sacred mausoleum, a ghoul with fiendish, unholy intentions, and in his mind he turned over the wording he would use to confess this sin. To his right a pair of fishlike creatures were suspended in an aquarium, and as he looked closer—the ashen light quivering long, angular shadows around him—he marveled that the small mermaid heads resembled the rubber African shrunken heads you could order from comic books—shriveled black skulls with mops of hair, eyes squinted shut, lips stitched tightly with jagged string. Across the aisle two chickens were stuffed and mounted on a pedestal, their twin heads were spurred legs sharing the same feathery bulk of organs. The walls were framed with unexplained photographs of famous gunfighters and crumbling newspaper clippings of troops in World War I trenches, and up ahead a glass case produced an array of old Colt pistols.

"Hurry it up!" Emil Wessel whispered.

Snookum approached the coffin first, an antiquated black casket with ornate carving, its lid opened back against the wall, the lining an ancient gauzy white lace that in daylight would show a frayed yellowing. Reluctantly Eddie came up next to his cousin and forced himself to peer down into the coffin as one would flinchingly observe the bloody victim of a highway wreck. The grotesque figure shook him; he could feel the blood drain from his face. There was enough light to make out the gnarled frame of a woman, her face and arms like black petrified wood, her light hair combed out in delicate curls past her shoulders and down her arms as though she were some tragic Sleeping Beauty who'd been denied the magic kiss and had atrophied where she lay. A pearly white wedding dress covered her from bare ankles to the flatness of her chest, where wisps of hair tucked inward across the board-hard surface between neck and bustline. Snookum extended his finger and poked her exposed flesh where in life cleavage might have dipped. He snapped his hand back as if he'd been burned. "Jesus, that's disgustin!" he said.

Eddie was certain of one thing—he would not touch her flinty bones, would not let that wooly, brittle hair rub against him; and if the Wessel boys had other ideas, they could crawl in here and try them out. He lowered his face cautiously to see if he could discover the wedding band or the long fingernails the Wessels had described, but the weak flickering light permitted no disclosure, only patches of undecipherable darkness. But his eyes were growing stronger now, and after staring at her face for some time he realized that someone had stretched her lips back in a ghastly smile to demonstrate the unspoiled evenness of her clean ivory teeth. The wicked smile terrified him and he stepped back from the coffin, his legs beginning to tremble.

"Hustle up, you dickheads!" Emil Wessel said from the window.

Snookum turned to Eddie with a finger to his lips: "We just about got 'er up," he said loudly.

"No shit?" said Emil. "You guys're really *touchin* that nasty thing?"

They weren't, though Snookum was fingering the frilly dress like a mother buying linen, and it suggested to Eddie something both horrible and richly tempting. After all, they had been chasing skirts all evening; indeed, for a couple of years now he'd been aware that beneath every dress lurked something soft and curving and beautiful, some delectable prize every boy pursued with slavering intensity. It occurred to Eddie that the Wessels would prefer a woman with little resistance and no idle chatter, and that this fragile figure before him might be the perfect partner they'd always dreamed of. She would require no money or proof of age, and nobody would raise hell if she was out past eleven. But Eddie knew there was something awesomely real and inescapable here: in the end all flesh would solidify and smell of stale ashtrays like this poor creature, and the mystery that boys craved so hungrily and girls protected so preciously would become little more than meat for worms. Then what was all the fuss about?

"Got it out o' the box yet?" Emil Wessel asked, his voice on the edge of drunken hysteria.

Snookum faked physical strain. "Yeah," he grunted, "here she comes!"

"You do? You sick goddamn bohunk bastards're really holdin a dead body?" his words broke with frenzied laughter. "I hope the smelly rot soaks in your skin an' you can't ever git it off again!" He clicked off the flashlight. "So long, suckers!" He slammed down the window and ran away with wild cackling laughter.

By the time Snookum and Eddie felt their way to the window and forced it open, the Impala's glass packs were popping far off in the starry stillness of evening. "Assholes," Snookum muttered to himself.

On their way home they stopped by Cervenak's service station for a package of gum they shared to clean their breath of beer. Uncle Ernest waited for them on the porch swing in dark brooding silence and quizzed them for several minutes with sober deliberation, then sent them to bed with a perfunctory scolding. That night Eddie dreamed he tried to remove the dress from the perfectly preserved lady and she seized him violently, her eyes flaring open with ancient lust, and pressed him to her cold hard mouth in a kiss of death. He jolted awake in an imprint of sweat, his breathing deep and ragged. Snookum was sitting on the edge of the bed, his elbows propped on the window sill, his face wedged between fists, staring out into the night where every cricket in the universe chimed in perfect unison like bells jangling on a Christmas sleigh. He lowered one arm and swiveled his head on a knotted fist, looking at Eddie. "I know how it is," he said in a voice wide awake.

Days rambled into the hottest time of summer at Old Man Cervenak's Sinclair Station. Eddie scoured the growing library of adult magazines, washed layered dirt and splattered mosquito hawks off an occasional college-boy's windshield passing through to Austin. Snookum's garage work slackened even more, though business was thriving up at Buck Tiedt's Gulf Station, where the Wessel boys strung up wire after wire of party-colored triangles that ran from the station's roof in all directions like clotheslines full of rainbow diapers. (It seemed to entice traffic; their station bell rang with the steadiness of a church clock.) On their lunch breaks at the Passtime Club the patrons disturbed Snookum and Eddie's pool game less and less with questions and messages for the girls at the Chicken Ranch, and Eddie suspected that the Wessels had something to do with the lack of attention. And one day without ceremony, the silver bullet-shaped trailer slipped away with its bag of curios for the next small town, and an entire weekend went by before Eddie and Snookum noticed that the lot was empty.

On the morning Eddie announced to Old Man Cervenak that he would be leaving for home in two days, the old man raised his cataract eyes from *Men Only*, and the jowls and deep ruts of his face pinched in what Eddie at first took as a painful gas attack. But the old man's features finally settled into a jaded smile that restructured pitted wrinkles like the shifting of the earth's plates. "You're a good kid," he said, "but don't think I'm gonna pay you."

It was perhaps the tenth time he'd reminded Eddie that the boy was not a real employee. "I don't expect anything," Eddie assured him.

The old man worked his mouth and spit tobacco into the coffee can at his feet, leaving a string of dark juice on his chin. "You're all right," he smiled crookedly with half his face like a stroke victim. "Yes sir, Pospisil," he said without regarding Snookum, who sat in the doorway to the garage soaking sparkplugs in a gasoline can, "I reckon the kid passed the test with flyin colors, don't you?"

"Yeah, unh-hunh," Snookum said absently.

"I figure he earned the right t' learn the secret handshake o' the mighty brotherhood o' pump jockeys," the old man chuckled. "Feast his eyes on golden treasures never before observed by simpleminded grease monkeys an' cedar choppers."

"Amen," Snookum mumbled.

"The boy deserves some kind o' reward for his noble labor, don't you agree, Pospisil?"

Snookum looked up, his attention suddenly sharpened into a fine point. His thin lips peeled back around oversized horsey teeth in a wide smile. "You gonna show 'm?"

"Least we can do," the old man grunted, putting both hands on the office desk and forcing his colossal bulk upward until he was on his feet, though still stooped over the desk, his arms like support pins, "You prob'ly been wonderin—like a couple thousand others in this shithook town—why the girls from the Ranch only do biness with me," he wheezed, his face a contorted mask of sweat. Then some unseen spasm passed and he straightened his back, released his arms, and lifted his baseball cap to wipe perspiration from his scalp with a tobacco-stained handkerchief. He trained an eye on Eddie and said "Come'ere."

Eddie glanced quickly at Snookum, and his cousin grinned approval.

The old man stepped to the men's room door a few feet away and gave it a light shove. "Sit down," he pointed to the commode.

Eddie again looked to Snookum for some explanation, and the boy nodded assurance. "Go on, sit down," Cervenak said.

Eddie would have preferred to wipe off the yellow-dribbled seat with toilet paper, as he always did, but he didn't want to appear prissy so he plopped down brusquely.

"See that little plug in the wall there," the old man extended his stubby finger, "right there by the roll? Pull on it."

Eddie looked twice before he noticed the rough end of a circular knob of mortar between bricks. Short nails made it difficult to grasp, but he finally manipulated the knob between thumb and two fingers and slid out a long tubular plug of mortar. Old Man Cervenak whinnied like an old witch. "Go ahead 'n' peek," he said.

Eddie looked through the hole into the adjacent women's restroom, which was entered by a door on the outside of the building. The peephole framed the toilet seat at precisely lap level. Eddie's face charged with embarrassment as he smiled and looked up at the old man. Now he realized why Cervenak spent so much time in the john and why he could rarely be found when customers pulled into the station.

"I'm too goddamn old an' broke t' be trottin up t' the Ranch ever' Satidy night," the old man winked. "The girls know it don't take much t' please an ol' fart like me—they know I'll give em' a free fill-up for a quick look-see ever' month."

Snookum was beside him now, wiping his hands with a rag and displaying long slender teeth in a shameful grin. "College girls ain't a bad show neither," his cousin said. "What they don't know won't hurt 'm."

"Since your time ain't long aroun' here, you can have free run o' the house," the old man said. "Jus' don't make no noise pullin the plug an' keep the door locked behind you."

"Yeah," said Snookum. "You don't wanna git us all in Dutch."

August discouraged travel: the brutal sun melted asphalt into smooth viscous taffy, boiled radiators, glued drivers to their upholstery in rings of sweat. The strip was so still, the town so quiet in this paralyzing heat that Eddie could hear an automobile slowing for the railroad tracks a half mile away. It annoyed him that in five hours of waiting for a female customer—eight to eighty, crippled or crazy—only a half dozen cars had wandered through, and all but some college egghead in his mother's Oldsmobile had decided to search farther for bright flags and giveaway dishtowels. Eddie knew that this was his rare chance to witness in the flesh what he'd been staring at for a month on the glossy pages of Cervenak's magazines, and the prospect seemed even more exciting and reckless than the one time he'd made out with Cheryl Wagner on the dark patio after Ramona Menotti's sixth-grade Coke party. But the day was wearing on and showed no promise of that secret rendezvous. The opportunity of a lifetime was burning away in the glaring mirage of summer.

About 4:30 a two-tone Pontiac lurched into the station and sounded the hose bell. The driver slowly unfurled from the car to stretch his legs—a gangly broad-backed man wearing a short-brimmed Panama hat, his armpits stained in wet circles. He smiled handsomely at Snookum and Eddie and asked for a fill-up. After a short wait his wife said something softly to him through the window and slid gracefully from the car. "Is there a little girl's room?" she asked Eddie, his hand a wad of soap rubbing the windshield. She was not an attractive woman and not young, perhaps the same age as Eddie's mother. Her hair was thin and mousy brown and cropped evenly around her head like a shower cap; a loose flowery dress with straps diminished any sign of shapely womanhood. As he directed her toward the restroom, Eddie's insides willowed and tiny sparks flared in his eyes as if the heat had finally scorched his brain. He signaled to Snookum that his cousin would have to finish the windshield, then darted inside the office. Old Man Cervenak's tobacco-stuffed jaw swole around a ruddy grin and his flabby gut bounced with wheezing laughter, but he didn't raise his eyes from the magazine he flipped through.

Eddie knelt on both knees next to the commode and prudently moved the mortar plug like a surgeon at work. Through the peephole he could see only the woman's flowery dress bunched in her lap and a shank of smooth pale skin. No matter how much he shifted and strained he could decipher little more than dress material and a length of leg, her ringed hand placed flatly near her knee as though she was about to polish her nails. He cursed his luck for not attending her initial unveiling of private undergarments, perhaps his only chance to glimpse something delicious and mysterious. Now he would have to wait for her to stand again to reveal herself. But no matter how wrinkled or venous-blue or disappointingly unlike the enticing pictures in magazines, he intended to fully enjoy this final moment of wondrous, chest-heaving awe, to savor it as one would the first taste of an exotic flavor.

The door creaked behind him, and in a piercing jab of

cold terror, a shard of memory twisting viciously in his head, he realized he had forgotten to lock the door. The man towered above him, his Panama hat chucked back to his hairline, disclosing a band of sunburn on his forehead. Reflexively he half withdrew with an apologetic "Oh sorry," then thought better of it and stepped back into the dank john, his hand still poised on the knob. The man's eyes narrowed and began to blink erratically as he studied Eddie, then the wall ahead as if he could see beyond it, then Eddie again. Finally he spoke: "What are you doing?" he asked.

"Nothing," Eddie replied.

"You're looking at something, aren't you?" His voice was toneless, undisturbed, yet promising rage.

"No," Eddie said. He expected the worst.

"Come on now, son, I saw you looking at something." He closed the door, sealing the two of them into the tiny room together. "There," he pointed to the place on the wall Eddie was trying to conceal with his shoulder, "behind you." He gently tugged the boy aside to show him the hole. "Right there. What's that?" he asked, stooping, his knees cracking through Searsucker stripes.

Eddie struggled to his feet and reluctantly moved as the man doffed his hat, squinted one eye, and peered through the mortar hole at his wife in the next room. He squatted there without motion, jelled for what seemed ages in perfect stillness like a wax figure, his long bony body between Eddie and the door. Eddie dared not breathe; he hoped the man would mete out punishment swiftly—a slap, a head banged against the wall—and be gone. He could not endure the shame of having him drag this indelicate discovery before Old Man Cervenak and Snookum.

Suddenly the man's squinted eye relaxed and a pleased smile split his face. "You know, we've been married for nineteen years and I've never seen her do that," he said. The commode flushed in the next room, a muffled rush of water through pipes. He stood up, his smiling face lost in some distant reverie. "Beat it, kid," he said, placing his hat dapperly on his head and creasing the narrow brim with a salute of the fingers. "I have to take a leak."

Years later, in a city half a continent away, Ed Korenik would remember that man and his wife and the summer at Old Man Cervenak's Sinclair Station, would acknowledge, as he sat alone amid thousands of laughing patrons in an elegant theater playing a musical comedy about the Chicken Ranch and the people of Memorial Hill, that in fifteen years he had gained little wisdom about the curiosities and mysteries that had presented themselves at that lovely age. He had strayed far from the courthouse square and those gentle aquamarine nights cruising through static waves of the radio tunes, had shunned the past often, wrestling with angry rebellion and spiritual escape, and had now settled into a listless comfort and confusion he was quite aware had decayed something deep in him, a laming, torpid rot. He had lost every love along the way, perhaps because someone had once told him that love in its purest form could be preserved perfectly between two people till death and beyond, perhaps because he had once heard that beauty was untouchable and should be viewed at a great distance, as if through a looking glass. But those days were dead.

Now he sat by himself between hand-holding couples, surrounded by strangers whose lives seemed so sure and content and final. They were all secret intruders into the private antics of the people Ed Korenik had once known, peeping toms as he himself had been, and though he knew that those humorous caricatures singing and dancing on stage were only remotely authentic, he felt a twinge of pride that some small part of himself was being legitimized and celebrated so famously. This crowd of starched collars and spangling jewelry and perfect hair was enjoying itself with raucous laughter, the laughter of those who are happily relieved that their lives were never so crude—the distant, joyful satisfaction of anthropologists who have discovered another primitive culture. Naturally they could not see beyond the makeup and costumes and cardboard props into the past as he knew it. The sheriff had ended up in arthritic agony in an old folks home. Old Man Cervenak eventually suffered a stroke and sat immobile in a wheelchair in his station for a year or so, presumably unable to peep through his mortar hole, and after his death the station was torn down as a nuisance and replaced by a cute antique shop. Like so many others, Snookum Pospisil had disappeared into the big city many years ago to find work. Last week Ed Korenik had read in the newspaper that the notorious Chicken Ranch near Memorial Hill, Texas, had been purchased by a chain of discos in Dallas and Houston and that the condemned farmhouse would be disassembled board by board and identically reconstructed in Houston as a bar and discotheque. With a smile he imagined the Wessel brothers, no doubt supporting frumpy wives and skinhead children as aging auto mechanics in the Bayou City, sprucing themselves up some Saturday night and gliding through the humid urban dark in the ghost of a metallic blue Impala, searching neon skyscraper boulevards for the Chicken Ranch Disco of their dreams, trying desperately one last time to make it inside and take some forbidden stranger into their arms and somehow patch their lives that had broken down with four flat tires on a dark, empty backstreet 200 miles from home. Ed Korenik envied them. Someday, he hoped, his dreams would be so beautifully pure again.

Notes on Contributors

Michael Blackman is a native of West Texas who attended Baylor University, where he studied journalism with David McHam. He took his M.S. degree from Ohio State University in 1974. While at Ohio State he was advisor to the student newspaper, the *Lantern*, and was managing editor of the *Ohio Journal*, the university's literary magazine. Since 1967 he has worked as a newsman for the *Baytown Sun*, the *Fort Worth Star-Telegram*, the *Cincinnati Enquirer*, the *Cincinnati Post*, the *New York Times*, and the *Philadelphia Inquirer*, where he is now foreign editor. He has published short stories in the *Ohio Journal, Cincinnati Magazine*, and a sports supplement to the *Baytown Sun*.

J. Y. Bryan was born in Peoria, Illinois, in 1907 and now lives in Riverside, California. He graduated from the University of Chicago in 1927 and subsequently earned the M.A. at the University of Arizona and the Ph.D. from the University of Iowa. There followed a varied career, including positions in research analysis and foreign service, which took him around the world five times and into fifty-six countries. A photographer as well as a writer, his experience is reflected in his forthcoming *Photography for Life Enhancement*. Leaving home to see the world at sixteen "with $5.85 in my pocket and unwarranted confidence under my hat," he rode freights during the Depression, conducting research among hoboes. He has contributed short stories, articles, and photographs to numerous magazines, and his novel *Come to the Bower* won the 1964 Jesse H. Jones Fiction Award of the Texas Institute of Letters.

Pat Carr, who holds the B.A. and M.A. degrees from Rice University and the Ph.D. from Tulane, has published five books, including *The Women in the Mirror* (winner of the Iowa Short Fiction Award for 1977), and has a sixth book in press. Her stories have appeared in such journals and anthologies as the *Southern Review*, the *Yale Review*, and the *Best American Short Stories*. In addition to the TIL Short Story Award and the Iowa award, she has received a South and West Fiction Award, a Library of Congress Marc IV Award, and grants from the National Endowment for the Humanities and the Arkansas Endowment for the Humanities. Currently she lives on a thirty-acre farm at the edge of the Ozarks, is editing a collection of newly discovered Civil War letters, and is writing a series of short stories set in Civil War times.

Doug Crowell teaches at Texas Tech University and has degrees from Rice University, Johns Hopkins University, and the State University of New York at Buffalo. He has published short stories in *New Directions*, the *Mississippi Review*, *Epoch*, *Crazyhorse*, and the *Florida Review*, among others, and has work forthcoming in *Fiction International* and *South by Southwest*. He thinks of his fiction, including his story in this collection, as having to do with "lunacy in high places, and the effect of such lunacy on the populace at large." Besides the TIL Short Story Award, he received a National Endowment for the Arts grant in fiction in 1983. An anthology of short stories including his work is forthcoming in 1986 from the University of Texas Press.

Laura Furman was born in New York in 1945, attended New York public schools, and received a B.A. from Bennington College in 1968. Her short stories have been published, mostly in the *New Yorker*, since 1975, and have been collected in *The Glass House*, which won the Jesse H. Jones Fiction Award of the Texas Institute of Letters in 1980, and in *Watch Time Fly* (1983). She is the author of *The Shadow Line* (1982), a novel that takes place in Houston. She came to Texas in 1978 and has taught at the University of Houston and Southern Methodist University, and now teaches at the University of Texas at Austin. She was a Dobie-Paisano Fellow in 1983-84. She is writing a series of novels about a family in upstate New York, the first of which, *Tuxedo Park*, will be published by Summit Books in the fall of 1986. She lives in a small town near Austin.

David Hall is a thirty-nine-year-old native of McKinney, Texas, now living in Colorado. He sells college textbooks for a living. He has published two short stories in the *Pawn Review* but has devoted most of his time for the past few years to playwriting. He has had several of his plays staged, including *The Quality of Mercy* at Theatre Three in Dallas in 1983. Of his decision to abandon short fiction temporarily he says, "It's been difficult for me to stop writing short stories, but I feel like the squinty-eyed precision watchmaker who would rather put his tools to a different use altogether than resort to turning out what the market seems to demand: battery-powered gadgets that flash numbers at you in case you can't tell time." Still, he has several stories that he feels ought to be written, and applauds "those brave writers and editors who haven't yet given up the good fight."

Beverly Lowry was born in Memphis, grew up in Mississippi, and now lives in San Marcos, Texas. She is the author of three novels, *Come Back Lolly Ray*, *Emma Blue*, and *Daddy's Girl*, the latter winning the Jessie H. Jones Fiction Award of the Texas Institute of Letters in 1984. She has published short stories in *Viva*, the *Texas Humanist*, *Black Warrior Review*, *Penthouse*, *Mississippi Review*, and *Playgirl*. In addition, her essays and book reviews have appeared in the *New York Times*, the *Washington Post*, *Houston City Magazine*, and *FMR*. She has taught at the University of Houston and served as president of the Texas Institute of Letters during 1982–84. She has been a Guggenheim Fellow in Fiction and has held a National Endowment for the Arts grant.

Poet and short story writer Walter McDonald is Director of Creative Writing at Texas Tech University. Born in Lubbock, he served as an air force pilot, taught at the Air Force Academy, and took the Ph.D. from the University of Iowa before returning to West Texas. His stories have appeared in a number of journals, including *Descant*, the *Texas Review*, *Quartet*, and the *South Dakota Review*. "The Track" and another story have won PEN Syndicated Fiction Project awards. His first book of poems, *Caliban in Blue*, won the TIL Voertman Poetry Award in 1976. He has poems forthcoming in *Poetry*, the *Atlantic Monthly*, *American Poetry Review*, *Kenyon Review*, *Missouri Review*, *Poetry Northwest*, and *Triquarterly*. His other books of poems include *Anything, Anything* (1980), *Burning the Fence* (1981), and *Witching on Hardscrabble* (1985). In 1984 he received a National Endowment for the Arts grant.

Carolyn Osborn's short story collections include *A Horse of Another Color* (1977) and *The Fields of Memory* (1984). Her short stories have been widely published in such literary magazines as *Antioch Review*, *Paris Review*, *Georgia Review*, *Texas Quarterly*, and *Cimmarron Review*. A frequent contributor to U.S. anthologies, her stories have also appeared in collections in England, Belgium, and Mexico. Her prize-winning "The Accidental Trip to Jamaica" has been translated into Spanish for *Cuentos de Austin* and has been used as a text at the Universidad de las Americas. She lives in Austin and writes in her office, a room in a small Victorian house near the capitol.

Catherine Petroski lived in Austin between 1968 and 1975, and during this time began to publish reviews, poems, and the stories which led to a scholarship at the Bread Loaf Writers Conference. She has since published the collection *Gravity and Other Stories*, a chapbook, *Lady's Day*, a children's picture book of her prize story *Beautiful My Mane in the Wind*, and a novel for young readers, *The Summer That Lasted Forever*. She has twice held fellowships from the National Endowment for the Arts, twice from Yaddo, and in 1982 was the Alan Collins Fellow at Breadloaf. She has taught at the University of North Carolina, Duke University, and the Duke Writers Conference. She is presently living in Durham, North

Carolina, and is at work on a novel and new stories. She also reviews fiction for newspapers, including the *Dallas Times Herald*.

Roland E. Sodowsky has taught at Oklahoma State University, University of Calabar (Nigeria), the University of Texas at Austin, and is presently teaching at Sul Ross State University in Alpine, Texas. His prize story "Landlady" also won the $5,000 Coordinating Council of Literary Magazines General Electric Foundation national award for fiction in 1983. A poet as well as a fiction writer, he has had recent fiction or poetry in *Sou'wester, Vanderbilt Street Review, Cedar Rock, Poetry Magazine, Cross Timbers Review*, and *Pax*. In 1985 he was a fellow at Yaddo.

Marshall Terry is a former president and secretary-treasurer of the Texas Institute of Letters. He has taught for thirty years at Southern Methodist University, where he has twice chaired the Department of English. He is now Director of Creative Writing in SMU's English department. A native of Ohio, he is the author of the novels *Old Liberty* (1961) and *Tom Northway*, the latter a co-winner of the Jesse H. Jones Fiction Award in 1968. His collection *Dallas Stories* will appear in 1986. He is at work on a projected seven-novel *Northway* series.

Allen Wier was born in San Antonio and grew up in Texas, Mexico, and Louisiana. He has published a collection of stories, *Things about to Disappear*, and two novels, *Blanco* and *Departing As Air*. He has been a Guggenheim Fellow in Fiction and has received a grant from the National Endowment for the Arts. He now lives in Tuscaloosa, Alabama, and is at work on a new novel, *Somewhere at Sea*.

Thomas Zigal was born in Galveston, Texas, and raised in Texas City. He received a B.A. from the University of Texas at Austin and the M.A. in Creative Writing from Stanford University. His short fiction has appeared in *Texas Quarterly, New Letters, Minnesota Review, New Mexico Humanities Review*, and other magazines. He is the author of a collection of short stories, *Western Edge* (1982), and a novel, *Playland* (1982). From 1977 to 1985 he was editor of the *Pawn Review*, a literary magazine which played a lively role in Texas writing during its life. At present he is coeditor of publications for the Harry Ransom Humanities Research Center at the University of Texas at Austin.